LAMENT
FOR A
SILVER-EYED
WOMAN

D1527001

Also by Mary-Ann Tirone Smith
The Book of Phoebe

LAMENT FOR A SILVER-EYED WOMAN

Mary-Ann Tirone Smith

LEE COUNTY LIBRARY
107 HAWKINS AVE.
SANFORD, N. C. 27330

William Morrow and Company, Inc.
New York

Copyright © 1987 by Mary-Ann Tirone Smith

All rights reserved. No part of this book may be
reproduced or utilized in any form or by any means,
electronic or mechanical, including photocopying,
recording or by any information storage and retrieval
system, without permission in writing from the Publisher.
Inquiries should be addressed to Permissions
Department, William Morrow and Company, Inc., 105
Madison Ave., New York, N.Y. 10016.

Library of Congress Cataloging-in-Publication Data

Smith, Mary-Ann Tirone, 1944–
  Lament for a silver-eyed woman.

  I. Title.
PS3569.M537736L3   1987   813'.54   86-33299
ISBN 0-688-06614-3

Printed in the United States of America

First Edition

1 2 3 4 5 6 7 8 9 10

BOOK DESIGN BY SUZANNE BENNETT

To Jere

The rest of us had nothing to do but look at the beautiful city of Beirout, with its bright, new houses nestled among a wilderness of green shrubbery spread abroad over an upland that sloped gently down to the sea; and also at the mountains of Lebanon that environ it; and likewise to bathe in the transparent blue water that rolled its billows about the ship (we did not know there were sharks there).

Mark Twain
The Innocents Abroad

Prologue

I usually don't read the daily *New York Times* so closely, but the *Times* was lying there, open, right where I couldn't miss it. Carefully, I sat down on the edge of the sofa and placed my cup on the coffee table. The headline paralyzed me, broke the early-morning circuits of my brain cranking out the day's schedule of responsibilities.

PERES BEGINS TALKS WITH PALESTINIAN REPS

I shut my eyes. Easy, Mattie, I said to myself, just take it real slow. Maybe it's a joke. Some pitiless prankster has run off a made-to-order copy of *The New York Times* with an article of his own diabolical design meant to torture me. No. It can't be, can it? So maybe I'm still in my bed dreaming those red dreams, the same nightmare always lurking, awaiting me in tiers of progressively worse horror. Will I never be rid of them? Open your eyes. Open them!

I looked down, making sure my line of vision was below the paper, fixed instead on the million little lime-green Laura Ashley sprigs scattered across my bathrobe. I was awake.

Outside the living-room window, the leaves on the birch tree began to tremble, catching my eye, bestowing upon me an excuse to look back up and over the paper. Thank you. No prank, no night terrors, and *The New York Times* doesn't make mistakes either. The breeze died, the leaves settled back into place, and I was forced to read.

The Six-Day War jumped out of the print. I surely knew about the Six-Day War. When I was in my early twenties, about to visit Casablanca on my way to Beirut, where I planned to get Jo, the U.S. State Department revoked all visas for travel to Arab countries. I never thought of Morocco as Arab. I thought it was French or part of Spain, or didn't it have something to do with the Moors? Were the Moors Arabian? Was Othello an Arab? I was one of those students who studied history but forgot all the facts the day after the exam, because whoever wrote history was a fiction writer like me, and I didn't believe any of it. My friend Jo believed every word.

I was asking myself one inane question after another to avoid the *Times* article, obviously planted there by my husband. My coffee was cold. I picked up the paper and immediately, my damp fingertips stuck to the newsprint, turning shiny and black. I've heard if you give newsprint a week to dry, it won't rub off onto your fingers. What was really scaring me was that I knew the inane questions would soon become the unbearable question I had suppressed for such a long time. Would we lose Jo's boy?

Once more, the birch leaves quaked, a reprieve, extra precious seconds. Jo's husband was from a wealthy, educated Palestinian family, and long before the Six-Day War they'd fled—along with all the other wealthy, educated Palestinians—to Paris, or London, or Detroit. And more recently, I discovered, to Puerto Rico. I read it in the *San Juan Star* by the pool of the Caribe Hilton while my three children took scuba lessons. Three children. It seems that several thousand Palestinians live in Río Piedras, a suburb of San Juan. Why not Jo, too? I could have flown down there in a few hours and we could have met for a drink at the Caribe Hilton, where the piña colada was invented. Piña coladas. Damn you, Jo.

She came back to me as I knew she would the minute I

saw that newspaper, and now I found myself unable not to read it. I couldn't restrain the flood of memories. The dam was officially breaking. So I read it, word for word, and when I was through, the paper lay forgotten on my lap and I was looking out the window at the still leaves and the blurred white trunks of the clump birch I'd planted fifteen years before. And I could hear my husband's calculated footsteps coming nearer.

Each autumn, my husband has threatened to cut down the birch tree because the high maples on the lawn block the sun, forcing the birch to stretch up and over the roof in its futile effort to reach the light. And in October all the little birch leaves drop onto the roof and into the gutters, clogging them like wet plaster of Paris. Paul was out there playing under the birch tree, a clump birch growing in Connecticut suburbia. Paul, whose name was once Abdur, before I hastily and desperately changed it to my brother's name in order to get him out of Beirut.

It was his father's name staring up at me from the newspaper. I'd seen the name all along of course, but now I couldn't blot it out any longer. Jo's husband, Paul's father. Ahmad ibn-Burash, one of the Palestinian groups about to talk to Shimon Peres. And to Shcharansky, the refusenik, who had a baby of his own to protect. And with Arafat pushed aside and Begin gone, what need was there to say that Ahmad ibn-Burash and the three others had once been members, indeed founders, of the PLO? It didn't matter now. What mattered was keeping the children alive, Israeli and Palestinian children. The trouble was, there was Ahmad's boy playing out under my birch tree as he had been for the last six years, and Ahmad was supposed to be dead. When I saw him last he was almost dead, gray as ash.

The newspaper slipped to the floor and I was crying for more than my friend Jo, for more than all those Palestinians, for more than the Jews. I was crying mostly for my little Paul. Little? My God, he was twelve years old and that was a baseball he was playing with now, not like before, when all he'd play with was a stick that he told us was a tommy gun. Not very long ago, I had come upon him aiming his ruler, keeping in practice. As soon as I saw Ahmad's name, I knew it would be just a matter of time before we'd lose Paul, too—as soon as his father's cause came to fruition, and I had no right to hope that it wouldn't.

Finally, I got angry. I got mad for the first time since I'd left Beirut with Abdur. I mean, with Paul. Now my anger allowed that tiny door in my brain to creak open. The door opened enough to let me peek into the compartment holding my friend Jo, who had been waiting for me to come to grips with what she'd done. It was time to forgive Jo.

The goddamned *New York Times*! It let Jo out. And she was laughing, so happy to see me again. She said, "Oh, Mattie! Spiro Agnew blamed the liberal Eastern press, too, and look where it got him."

But I couldn't laugh yet. I turned to my husband, standing over me. He didn't know how violent my reaction to the article would be, or to the realization that he'd known all along Ahmad had lived. I said to him, "Get that stupid birch tree cut down. I hate it. I hate it." And I put my arms around his waist while he cradled my head into the front of his soft sweater.

CHAPTER ONE

Jo and I met in elementary school, but it wasn't until the first day of seventh grade at the junior high that we became friends. She was Parsons and I, Price, so I sat directly behind her, the last in the row. In those days we had forty kids to a class, so being in the back, we got to talk a lot, heads bowed, fake scribbling so Mr. Cosker wouldn't catch us. Funny. Just thinking of those clandestine whispers and cloak-and-dagger notes we passed lifts the top layer of pain away—burrows underneath, and there's Jo and there's me, together again. I can't help but smile—smile and enjoy our lives from the time when everything we did was intertwined. It was a good time. I'm glad to be back, Jo.

When we weren't whispering or passing notes, I stared at the back of Jo's head. She had a ponytail. A waving, full, silver ponytail spiraling down from the crown of her head to the middle of the back of her chair. It was held up with a special ponytail barrette they used to have in the fifties; a wide half-circle of colored plastic with the ends joined by a rubber band. I never could work them. The rest of us girls only wore ponytails when our hair was dirty or after gym showers. But Jo's mother couldn't afford the hairdresser, so Jo pulled her beautiful, remarkable long hair up into a ponytail through all of junior high and high school. Much later, after the fifties, Jo was the envy of all of us in college with her heavy curtain of bone-straight silver hair parted in the middle and flowing like a medieval veil down her back. By then, I, too, had a curtain of bone-straight hair, but I had to iron it to get it to look that way. My hair had an unsubstantial wave to it. When curly hair came in, the wave wasn't enough of a wave, and I had to have it permed like everyone else. Curly hair came in during the seventies, when the least important thing in Jo's life was hairstyle. In the seventies, she knotted it in back of her head, managing to look like a ballerina because she was so fine and slim, her features so meticulously wrought.

My hair was brown, not silver. Once we got to Bryn Mawr, all of us with brown hair added reddish-gold highlights, which looked almost as striking as silver. For one week I'd sit with the sun behind me, knowing the effect was almost striking. But we didn't have L'Oreal then. At the end of the week, my glowing hair would fade to dyed-hair orange. One of the initiation rights of going off to college is destroying your hair, since your mother's not around to stop you.

Jo's eyes were silver, too. They were really more like gray-blue, but so big and clear that the way they held the light made them appear silver. She was from the Smoky Mountains, where I decided that the smoke must be silver. Her mother sometimes seemed to have that icy, Nordic quality about her, too, but usually just gray. Smoky. As it turned out, their coloring had nothing to do with the Smoky Mountains. Jo's grandmother, who in 1936 deserted her husband and children purportedly to return home, was from the lakes of northern Italy, deep in one of those alpine valleys where the people, like the white skies, seemed to have the color washed right out of them until their hair was silver and their eyes as translucent as their shining lakes. Jo's American grandfather had been a G.I. in Italy, where he'd found his wife. Those two characteristics— unique coloring and taking the chicken way out—ran in the family but stopped at Jo. Jo's mother deserted her husband, too, as well as Jo's two older brothers, none of whom Jo remembered as she was just an infant when her mother took off with her. Ten years later, when Jo refused to come back to the States, I accused her of taking the chicken way out like the rest of the women in her family, but of course the opposite was true. I was just feeling sorry for myself not having Jo at my fingertips anymore.

Jo was very poor, and the first time I invited myself home with her I noticed that she didn't act the least bit ashamed. She just led me off the bus, around the back of the Brookside Tavern, and up the wooden steps to her door. I'd thought only poverty-stricken blacks lived around there. At twelve, I hadn't known there was even such a thing as poverty-stricken white people. Not in Norwalk, anyway, except for the drunks you'd see sleeping it off in the downtown area. Jo lived in a tenement. All the people walking around were Negroes, as we used to say in my family. I never dreamed that the windows you saw over neighborhood bars had actual people living behind them, even if there were curtains hanging and plants to prove it.

Jo's apartment had four rooms. Her bedroom had two little kids in it waiting for her to get home to take care of them. One kid was that icy-blond color and the littler one had topaz eyes, curly topaz hair, and topaz skin. She was about a year old. Jo looked at me.

"Her father is a black man. He owns the bar downstairs." She looked from me to her shoes. "Your parents won't let you come back here once they find out."

"Ha!" Then I explained to her about my parents.

My parents were liberal. Radical. We always had black people over. My parents "redid" a farmhouse on the highest spot on Jewel Island, connected to the South Norwalk ghetto by a causeway. My parents invented gentrification. Except for our house, all the other houses were ex–summer cottages turned into year-round homes, with the garage doors covered over and the garages made into rec rooms. Blue-collar workers lived there and sent their kids to Catholic school because the elementary school in South Norwalk was seventy-five percent black. We were Catholics, too, but when I was little, my parents only went to mass to set an example for my brother and me. I thought that was very generous of them, because as it turned out, all of us were silently very bored. I envied people who found joy in going to church, although I don't any longer. How I hated having to get dressed for church every Sunday morning and driving through the traffic and listening to the same thing week after week. I measured growing up by the gospels, since the priest had fifty-two for the year. You could measure time by those gospels. Every year, on the second Sunday in March, you'd get the loaves and the fishes. The Sunday around my birthday were the Beatitudes. I liked Jesus because he was a poet. But mass was so boring. My brother and I stopped going to church at almost the same time and my parents were relieved, I felt, and they stopped going, too, having done their duty, duty being a really big thing in the fifties.

Anyway, they wanted me to attend public schools through the elementary grades so that I could "benefit from the mix of cultures and people," etc. And learn Spanish from the horses' mouths. We had a small, but definitely growing community of Puerto Ricans from San Lorenzo, who had lost their farms when Warner's built their bra-and-girdle factory there. Warner's got to pay no taxes, and the United States got to increase the welfare rolls. In elementary school, we'd be assigned to teach things like colors to the Puerto Rican kids in our class, but those kids were so shy and so homesick that they couldn't concentrate. And they were always freezing cold. They came from the tropics, had no heat in their apartments most of the time, and wouldn't take off their coats and hats until ten-thirty or eleven, when they finally began to thaw. After elementary school, I would get to go to Rowayton Junior High, which was the best and the most posh junior high in Norwalk.

Jo got home every day around four, her mother having left for the hospital at two forty-five. The older kid, not the mulatto one, got back from the elementary school in time to take care of the baby until Jo got in. He was only seven, so sometimes he forgot and didn't make it, but Jo said that it was OK because the people down in the bar would check on the baby, who was usually asleep at that time. Jo's mother was a cleaning woman at the hospital, but she was luckier than most, I guess. She didn't actually clean. Her job was to water all the plants, wipe them down, and cut off brown leaves. I told her once that she was just like the doctors there because her job was to see that her little green patients didn't die. She laughed so hard. The difference between her and the real doctors, she pointed out, was that she'd get fired if her patients died.

Anyway, Jo's mother's back was always hurting because she had to carry this stepladder around with her all night, since a lot of the plants were not little; some of them you could classify as trees, easily.

We took Jo's little brother and the baby, who had just learned to walk, to the front lawn of St. Thomas's Episcopal Church where they could play while we sat and did our homework on the front steps. St. Thomas's front lawn was Jo's yard. She didn't care at all that it was two long blocks from where she lived. The traffic paraded by and at first it was pretty difficult for me to concentrate, until I was assured by Jo that the baby knew enough not to dart out into the street. Poor babies are taught their perimeters early in life or they're dead.

The first day we went there, the boy spotted a friend and they went back to school to play on the swings. Jo and I talked until I had to go home for dinner. We were both very smart and it took us two minutes to get our math done, even though all the other kids moaned about having to spend an hour on silly word problems. The first thing Jo and I had in common was that we both thought word problems were the funniest things—ridiculous little puzzles we'd do in our heads. Much later, weeks, the black man who owned the bar watched us and shook his head and said that to him word problems were always: "If a train traveled at forty-five miles an hour from Albuquerque to Phoenix in a snowstorm, but went sixty-five miles an hour in nice weather, how many miles an hour would it go at night? Give the answer in square inches." We all laughed, especially him.

Every afternoon we talked on and on and found that we both wanted the very same things in life, could see beyond boys, and were determined to get to where we wanted to go. Our motives were entirely different, though, but I didn't know that yet; I knew it in Beirut when Jo and I parted for the first, only, and last time. At twelve you don't think about motives, except if you are Jo. Jo knew mine and hers, too. When she tried to explain to me what my genuine reasons were for acting the way I acted and doing the things I did, I was offended; I believed I was more than an adventurer. When she described her motives to me, it was her turn to be offended, because I translated them as fantasies. I hadn't learned yet that fantasies could be real. Basically, Jo and I found each other interesting. Unboring. No one else interested us. It was because we were so much smarter than all the kids we knew.

"We're lucky to be so smart, Mattie."

"I know."

"We don't really have to study for this quiz. We'll get A's."

"I know. It's a waste. If we were in Russia they'd be teaching us physics now."

In the fifties people were always talking about Russia. I remember when there was such a commotion about *Sputnik*. The day after it went over, Jo and I met at the library.

"So did you see it?"

"Yes. It was an exciting night for me, Mattie."

"Me, too. I'll bet the Russians teach their smart kids calculus instead of fractions."

"All the people from the bar came out to watch it. After somebody said, 'There it is! There it is!' somebody else said, 'Well, they beat us.' "

"White people, too, Jo. The whole island stood on our hill. *Sputnik* seemed to go by in slow motion and my mother said, 'It's as if they're mocking us.' I told my mother that nobody was mocking us, that it was going once around the world every ninety-five minutes."

"Eighteen thousand miles an hour."

"Yeah. So now they teach fractions a year early and no one can do them except me and you."

We laughed then, pretty mirthlessly, though. Now, Jo lay back in the grass, put her hands beneath her silver ponytail, and said, "Sometimes I think I have so much to offer the world because of this brain of mine, but what about my family? Shouldn't I take care of them first? Do I go make a zillion dollars and take care of them or do I try to find a cancer cure?"

"You'll make a zillion if you cure cancer, Jo. But just because you're born into one particular family in one particular community or county even, doesn't mean you owe one guy more than you do another. We're citizens of the world, Jo, smart people like us." Jo and I were pre-Gibran, pre-McKuen, pre-Bach pop philosophers.

Jo smiled. "Still, this baby is more important to me than anything else. And my little brother." The baby was eating clover.

"She looks happy to me."

"She lives over a bar with rats."

"So do you."

"But I won't get married at seventeen and stay over some other bar with some other rats." She rolled over, turning away from me.

No, Jo didn't get married at seventeen; she was twenty-three, and she didn't end up over another bar either, but there were plenty of rats. Not tenement rats, which are bad enough. Great big water rats that I watched saunter through the camps, carrying two-foot-square cardboard boxes in their mouths to do God knows what with.

But when we were twelve we didn't worry too much about our future, just that we wanted to get out and be citizens of the world. In the meantime we won an unsanctioned seventh-grade contest—who saw *Love Me Tender* the most times? We won because my mother is nuts for Elvis

Presley and took us every day, in addition to our going alone on weekends. We saw it twenty-seven times and could recite the entire script, and we'd haggle over whose turn it was to play Elvis's wife. In my room, we'd slowly kiss in the dark with our eyes closed, and when it was my turn to be Elvis's wife I really could imagine that it was Elvis's actual sweet soft lips coming down on mine and not Jo's. She was a great actress.

The next year, after the eighth-grade graduation tea dance, we went to Robert Whitfall's house and played spin the bottle. The very first real kiss of my life was that day, and it was horrible to have to kiss Gary Griggs, because he was a good friend of mine on the island, and once I'd kissed him I knew that the kiss signaled the end of backyard softball. Gary was a born athlete. He and I automatically backed each other up and never let a grounder out of the infield, or left first or second uncovered. Now that was over. Officially. He was a boy, I was a girl. Actually, I wouldn't have minded such a sad, era-ending kiss if only he could have been one half as good as Elvis.

CHAPTER
TWO

Jo and I were both accepted as day students at St. Brice's Academy in Stamford, Jo with all expenses paid. The school had a scholarly reputation, and even though I tried to convince my mother earlier that I really should go to a top prep school, she said no. She said she wasn't ready to be replaced as a mother yet. She said she'd try to be ready in four years, since when I went to college, she'd have no choice. I didn't mind, because my parents are an education in themselves. I tried to talk Jo into going ahead to Exeter, but she said her mother still needed her, too—physically, not spiritually, the way mine did. In four years the baby would be in first grade and could come home from school with the little boy. Baby-sitting problems would come to an end for Jo's mother. Our mother's needs determined our lives, much to our relief.

It was visiting day for the future freshman class at St. Brice's, a really pretty day in early May. We were sure we would love it because the academy was surrounded by green. What did we know? We assumed a school not surrounded by a sheet of black asphalt must be perfect. Jo and I were excited. We went to a few fake classes and visited the library. We looked forward to being able to hold a normal conversation in Latin someday. Then we took part in a round-table discussion in the library and a more informal discussion in the yard that was referred to as "the quad."

The quad was where we first began to grow skeptical, sitting in the middle of all that ivy. When we were in the library, most of the students were doodling in their notebooks things like "Jerry and Nancy, forever." Two were fawning over the one's high school ring that she had on a chain under her uniform. St. Brice's girls were not allowed to go steady. Publicly. One girl was making a list: Sherry Lyn, Debbie Lee, etc. I asked her what that was and she said she was thinking about names for her children. But in the quad, the girls completely ignored us visitors because they were too busy ogling and squealing over some poor janitor who happened to be passing by. The guy had sweaty armpits and was at least forty.

Jo said to me, "These girls are boy-crazy. The most intense conversation has been about what it's like to French kiss, and what it will be like to really do it."

"I've noticed."

On the way back to the library for "closing words from Mother," we passed a bulletin board. There were all the usual notices, but prominent was an announcement that said:

REMEMBER! ELVIS PRESLEY IS AN OCCASION OF SIN!!!

Jo wanted to know what an occasion of sin was.

"Well, that's kind of a temptation that might get you to commit a sin."

"What kind of sin could Elvis Presley get you to commit?"

"I don't know. Maybe it would be a good question for 'Mother.'"

"Don't you dare, Mattie."

I whispered to Jo, "I won't, but I'm beginning to think this school is an occasion of sin." Now the girls were going ga-ga over a young priest in the hallway. A priest!

"These kids are worse than boy-crazy."

"The problem is obviously the result of deprivation. They never get to see any boys. Stir-crazy *and* boy-crazy."

"I'm sorry, Mattie, but I don't think I like this place."

"Let's listen to Mother Superior before we make any rash decisions. There must be some serious students around somewhere."

Jo was smiling. "You know, Mattie, these Catholic terms for people are really wild. Mother Superior. I don't know if I'll be able to call someone who isn't my mother, 'Mother.' "

Mother walked into the room and everyone stood. I knew I couldn't call her "Mother" either. She was very big with red, florid skin and no-rim glasses. She spoke directly through her nose, which made you realize how incredibly flared her nostrils were. You could practically see into her head. It turned out that Mother was even more stir-crazy than her sex-starved daughters, who had all pretty much calmed down once the priest was out of sight.

Mother stood, towering over us, and smiled, the same way the wicked queen smiled at Snow White. "Ladies, permit me to be frank. We are all girls here so I'm sure no one need be embarrassed. Because we expect more from our girls than most schools, we have exceedingly stringent rules: a regimen of dictums prescribed first by our Lord Jesus Christ, second by the Most Reverend Archbishop Dougherty, and finally by Mother." Pause for that slow, thin smile. "We have a reputation to uphold, so these regulations concern our reputation." Mother surprisingly did not mean academic reputation. She went on to describe the now-famous Catholic rules, which were not funny at the time: No patent-leather shoes, because they reflect your upper legs under your skirt; no eating out with boys at restaurants with white tablecloths, because they make boys think of bedsheets. She went on, and I tuned her out just like when I first met Jo in the back of our seventh-grade class. I whispered that white tablecloths fell into the "occasion of sin" category along with Elvis.

By now, Mother was breathing heavily, her forehead dampening beneath the wimple. I don't think *wimple*'s the right word, but I can't remember all the parts to a nun's costume. Then she looked at Jo. Mother smiled.

"I notice some of you girls are wearing ponytails." (Only Jo.) "We feel here at St. Brice's that this particular fad is unacceptable. We feel that, well, with some of our weaker, misdirected girls that a dangling ponytail could give rise to impure thoughts. A dangling ponytail is an occasion of

sin. A dangling ponytail could cause a girl to think about
. . if you'll excuse my blunt language . . . the male penis!"

While everyone attempted to stifle their hysterics, I said
to Jo, who didn't know whether to look up, down, at her
feet, or what, "*Male* and *penis* are redundant. Let's get out
of here." It was all she needed. She stood and fled. I scrambled after her. Good-bye, St. Brice's, hello, Norwalk High.
We ran and then walked, huffing and puffing, all the way
down Long Ridge, toward the center of Stamford. Jo cried
and I waited for her to stop, but she couldn't manage it.
Just as I was about to say, "There's a Friendly's, let's get a
soda," I saw a theater marquee.

ELVIS PRESLEY
LOVING YOU

The Catholic Legion of Decency rated it one step above
condemned: "Women and Children Not Allowed" or
something like that. It was better than *Love Me Tender* but
not as good as the future and best Presley film, *Jailhouse
Rock*. When we came out, we made plans to start a committee to get four years of Latin introduced at Norwalk
High. We weren't going to let only Catholic-school kids
have that privilege if we could help it.

In the fall we ran into Linda Saunders, who went to St.
Brice's. We asked, casually, how she liked it. She said, "It's
fucking stupid." In the fifties, nobody but Catholic-school
girls said "fuck." Not even Norwalk High boys said it. Linda
explained, "At philosophy class today, we had to imagine
that we were at the edge of a two-hundred-foot cliff, about
to be raped. Sister Claudia asked, 'As Catholic girls, which
should you do? Allow yourself to be raped, or jump?' The
two neanderthals who didn't vote for 'Jump' got F's for
the day."

Norwalk High was where Jo and I were the first white
teenagers in America to be introduced to civil rights in
practice rather than in theory. In 1957, we had our eyes

opened to a concern that hadn't directly affected us, but the concern determined our lives as much as our mother's needs had.

We tried out for cheerleaders along with our good friend from elementary school, Glennis Swopes, who was a Negro. Jo, of course, wasn't prejudiced, because she had lived with Negroes most of her life and her own baby sister was half and half. I wasn't prejudiced either, because my parents had a million Negro friends, including Glennis's mom and dad, who were smart and upper middle class; a few were Catholics even, if you can imagine that. I wonder what Mother Superior did when Negroes began applying to St. Brice's?

Anyway, we tried out for cheerleaders, and the principal, who was new, made a rule that being on the honor roll would rank as a major criterion for making the squad. Norwalk High's new principal made rules that concerned the school's scholarly reputation. He taught third- and fourth-year Latin on the side. So consequently, me, Jo, and Glennis, as straight-A students, all had an edge on the others, and we were good besides, especially Glennis. After the tryouts, when we were changing, Jo and I posed in front of the locker-room mirror in various cheerleading poses, but Glennis just sat there, staring at the lockers.

I said, "Glennis, what's wrong? We're shoo-ins."

"Norwalk High has no Negro cheerleaders."

"So what?" God, was I stupid. "It's just a coincidence. You'll make it, Glennis. When you jump you go halfway to the ceiling."

She stood. "I could jump *all* the way to the ceiling but I won't be a cheerleader."

Jo said, "But most all the football players are Negroes."

"No kidding."

Glennis stalked out. In all the years we'd known Glennis, we'd never seen her stalk. Jo and I stared at each other like a couple of idiots, wondering what was going on with Glennis. She'd gone to Boston for the summer. What had they done to her there? But we were convinced she was being overly sensitive, because we had no experience with the more subtle forms of segregation.

The next week, the loudspeaker in our homeroom blared out the names of the new cheerleaders. Glennis looked at us out of the sides of her eyes as she walked to her first class with her new group of Negro friends. Jo and I high-tailed it down to the gym. Jo was always the one to take action while I gathered my thoughts in order to prepare how to put everything into rational words. With her crystal-blue eyes at their most brazen, their most silver, Jo said:

"Miss Clayton, how come Glennis Swopes didn't make cheerleaders?"

Miss Clayton smiled and invited us to sit down. All prejudiced people are polite, I have since discovered. "Girls, I've lived in Connecticut for thirty years. I have lost my Virginia accent. But I haven't lost my beliefs in the ramifications of human nature. A Negro girl would be too athletic, too . . . lively for us. A Negro girl wouldn't fit into my squad. She would, in fact, stick out like a sore thumb. Norwalk High cheerleaders are known for their precision, not their athletics."

I had formulated my comment carefully, giving my words the perfect innuendo of sarcasm, which failed to come across because of my nervousness. "Miss Clayton, the Norwalk High cheerleaders are hardly the Rockettes!"

Jo just let her words rip, though her voice was as calm as a spring breeze, unlike mine. "I quit. I don't want to be on YOUR squad. This is outrageous. This is RACISM!"

At that very moment, I knew I'd never get above a C in gym class—there went the honor roll—but I had to think of Glennis. Jo was already out the door, silver ponytail swinging. I'll be in band instead, I thought miserably, stumbling after her. Music is better for my future than jumping and wiggling my fanny in front of a grandstand. I gazed over my shoulder at the row of hangers pulled down by the weight of the heavy white sweaters appliquéd with fat blue letters. The line of megaphones stood like rebuking soldiers against the wall. I caught up with Jo.

"We'll play tuba and knock 'em dead, right, Jo?"

"Right," she said proudly. Jo had absolutely no regrets. In the years to come, no matter what horrendous decision she made, she didn't regret it, not even when she was afraid. I snuck a last glance back and saw Miss Clayton's right eyebrow rise when she met my eye. Damn. Life had never been easy and now I realized it never would be either. This was what it was like to be an adult, something Jo had known about ever since she was born.

The following football season, at the first game, Glennis couldn't take her eyes off the two tuba players in the band. She snuck away from her new friends and met us later at the snack stand.

"You guys quit cheerleaders because of me."

"No . . . really, Glennis. We never . . ."

"But I didn't want you to do that. Why did you do that?" The suave Glennis we once knew was frantic instead.

"You'd have done the same for us, Glennis."

Glennis's black eyes were sparkling in the sharp October sun. "No, I wouldn't have, Mattie. I don't owe you people anything."

"What people?"

"Glennis, what's wrong with you?" Jo asked. "Are you OK?"

She softened. "We can't . . . listen, I need to be with my own kind. I don't know my own people."

Then this big, tall Negro senior—a basketball player who was one of the six kids taking fourth-year Latin—draped his arm across her shoulders and said to us, "Glennis is ours now," and he led her away.

I threw away my hot dog. "Jo, you know much more about Negroes than me. What the hell's going on here?"

Jo shook her head. "I don't know about these kind, Mattie . . . not these kind." In college, I was told that the kind I knew about were Uncle Toms.

It turned out that Glennis had gone and complained to the NAACP about Miss Clayton, and next year a Negro girl named Ernestine became the first Negro cheerleader at Norwalk High. And that Latin-teacher principal of ours put the pressure on Miss Clayton to retire on the early side, so she did. And the new gym teacher, a frustrated choreographer, doubled as the assistant to the marching-band director, who knew a lot about John Philip Sousa and zero about marching. So we became the Grambling of Connecticut high schools. Dashing crazily about a football field while carrying a tuba is a lot more athletic than doing cheerleader jumps. Jo and I nearly killed ourselves.

But we made the honor roll.

And we were to come to know all kinds of Negroes, both of us, several years later, when we were the only whites on a busload of people going to Washington to hear Dr. King. That was when we decided to go to Africa, Jo to help blacks who had absolutely no opportunity to improve their condition, and me because it also sounded like a neat thing to do before going through the business of procuring a husband. (The feminine mystique at this time was still a mystery.)

Two years after Dr. King's march, when we were on the plane to Africa, Jo confessed to me that, as a child, she'd wanted to be a missionary nun—devote her entire life to starving, diseased black children. But the ponytail incident at St. Brice's cured her of that idea. As things turned out, however, she did it without being a nun because President John Kennedy went and gave us free tickets to the Federal Republic of Cameroon.

CHAPTER THREE

Jo and I attended the hardest college there is: Bryn Mawr. My mother proved right. It was very difficult for me to leave home for good. Jo pulled me through those first two and a half months before Thanksgiving, locking me in my room when I threatened to skedaddle to the Philly airport. My advice to all entering college freshmen from then on was: Make sure you don't go home until Thanksgiving because if you do, you might stay. If you wait for Thanksgiving to go home, you'll realize that you don't belong there, which is a good thing. Your childhood home shouldn't be a cozy nest to use as a crutch for the rest of your life.

Also, if you do give in to homesickness and go home, say for Halloween, you will be uneasy because everything will be different from the way you left it, which makes for a sense of confusion and a tendency to blame your discomfort on college. At Bryn Mawr, Jo hung on to me mightily, thereby saving her best friend from quitting college and going into the interior-design business with Mom.

Even during Thanksgiving dinner, even before my aunt's heavenly Dutch apple pie (pour heavy cream into the slits before you bake it), I found I couldn't wait to get back to that little hamlet in Pennsylvania with all the brainiest girls from the best private schools in the country plus Jo and me. By now, home was BMC, where you weren't treated like a kid, which is what you will always be treated like at home, forever.

"It's raining, Mattie."

"I know."

"So why are you going out without an umbrella?"

"Ma, it's three steps to the garage."

"Here." Mother thrusts the umbrella at me.

"I don't need it, Ma!"

"You do!"

"I don't!" Etc.

Naturally, this whole conversation takes place while you stand on the bottom step of the porch getting soaked.

And God bless the lovely person who decided to give Bryn Mawr the BMC moniker, thereby saving people from trying to speak Welsh. At Thanksgiving dinner, my relatives kept saying, "So how do you like Burn Mower?"

Even though learning is considered the greatest pleasure there is at BMC, in order to get accepted to the school you have to have a sense of humor. My first week back to BMC in September of our sophomore year, I organized a trip to the Miss America contest in Atlantic City. It was a fundraiser, actually. We had a pool, five dollars apiece to decide which state's contestant would win, and whoever won the pool got to donate the money to her favorite charity. But since BMC women are all geniuses noted for their yet-untapped powers of analysis, of the three hundred and forty-two of us who went, over one hundred guessed Miss Ohio, based on calculations of statistics over the previous ten years. We Bryn Mawr girls are great researchers. Miss Ohio, of course, won. Our one hundred and twelve winners voted together on a charity, and the real winner of the Miss America contest that particular year was the United Negro College Fund, which ended up with the one thousand, seven hundred and ten bucks.

To get back to Thanksgiving, though, my mother had converted my bedroom into a "nice sitting room," where I could entertain my friends whenever I was home. All my stuffed animals and dried corsages and playbills were in

cardboard boxes in the attic next to the Christmas orna-
ments. But even though I realized that home would now
be where I hung my hat rather than where my heart was,
I felt I had until my cat died before I really didn't belong
at my parents' house. Otis, the dear, sensitive, furry little
guy that he was, went all out to prolong that sense of
belonging I was reluctant to let go of by living twenty-two
years. I got to bring him to my real home when I got
married. The man I married thought it was all very sen-
timental and even agreed to bury him for me in our backyard when Otis died a month after the wedding, knowing
his mission was accomplished.

Jo was very happy that she didn't even have a home
anymore. As soon as she left for college and was no longer
available for child care and housework, her mother left
for Arizona to start over again for the second time, choos-
ing Arizona because she figured she'd at least save on fuel
oil. The black man who owned the bar tried to get her to
stay, but desertion was in the blood. Jo said she didn't care,
she liked my sitting room a lot better than the tenement,
but her mother left without even letting her say good-bye
to her brother and the baby. I cried about that. Not Jo.
Where a normal person would cry, Jo just tilted her chin
up that much higher. Of course, Jo never had a real home
as those in our culture know it: mother, father, brothers
and sisters all the same color, basketball hoop in the driveway, dogs instead of rats, etc. Ever. What it came down to
was that I became an adult when I went to BMC, and Jo
was very proud of me the way I managed to get through
it. For a while there, she really was afraid I'd throw in the
towel.

I would always be Jo's touchstone, and that's why she
needed me. Actually, more than a touchstone—more like
a big chunk of concrete: evidence to assure Jo that the
world that chose to bypass her really did exist. She needed
that evidence when her life was in danger, which turned
out to be all the time when we were older. But then, when
we were older that is, she stopped caring that the real world

was out there and accepted the danger as normal. It was her downfall, and my near downfall.

In the sixties, we did other things besides go to the Miss America contest; the most memorable, of course, was the march. A gang of us went down on one of the buses, and we sat at the very edge of the reflecting pool—even the water was hot—and became completely caught up in Glennis's people's dream. Even though I was greatly moved by the huge emotion of Dr. King's speech, Jo was struck to the heart by the man himself. She wanted to go to Mississippi or Alabama and get him to notice her and become his handmaiden or something, though she didn't see it quite that way.

Viola Liuzzo kept Jo from doing it. Within her fantasies Jo remained a very practical person, and she knew that if she got shot, she couldn't save the world. And the very real risk of rape was there, too. So instead, I convinced her that we could do just as much to combat racial prejudice by registering voters in Philadelphia, Pennsylvania, just as they were doing in Philadelphia, Mississippi. Thank God I won that one, because if Jo had won, and said we were going to Mississippi, I wouldn't have gone and that would have been the end of us. Unlike Beirut. Beirut was a schism, but not the end of us. Sometimes you can be closer to a person who is five thousand miles away than to one who is five feet away.

"I'm a chicken, Jo."

"No you're not. You're wise." It was true. Jo may have been smart, but she never was wise.

We didn't do badly with the registration drive. Black people in the run-down houses we went to thought we were cute. They'd come on down to city hall with us and take the oath. I always got teary-eyed during the oaths, every single one. Just like a first-rate obstetrician who feels all warm and mushy about delivering a baby even though it's his ten thousandth. A group of us registered hundreds of people and this spur-of-the-moment Bryn Mawr project (taken over by CORE in the late sixties) got me a recommendation from my thesis professor, who was an important man in the world of academe. His recommendation would get me into any grad school I wanted. What a waste. Unlike everyone else in my graduating class at BMC, I didn't go to grad school, nor did Jo. I enjoyed writing my huge civil rights thesis so much that it later dawned on me when it was time to go to grad school that I was a writer. In order to be a writer you don't go to graduate school, you write, as Ernest Hemingway must have said.

Anyway, in Philadelphia it was November, and we only had one morning class on one particular Friday and it wasn't really cold yet, so we went into Philadelphia to visit a couple of people we'd become friends with during the voter-registration drive. This one black woman who had talked all her relatives into registering with us opened the door, looked at us with deep wet eyes, and said:

"The President got hisself shot."

At first we didn't believe it, and then we were sure Jack Kennedy, the invincible, would be OK. He simply couldn't not be. But in the streets we heard over and over the words, ". . . in the head." We got scared and dashed like rabbits for the train back to BMC, even though the trains came every twenty minutes. We ran into the lounge of the first building we came to in time to see Walter Cronkite in his shirtsleeves glance down at a piece of paper. I never heard Cronkite say the words. His face said: It's over, everybody. All over. But I never allowed it to be over until Bobby was killed, too, and then I knew it was.

My parents worried terribly about me because I couldn't be cheerful again after the President's assassination. Not even at Christmas. And after Christmas I stopped writing all my famous prewriter letters home telling about my classes, my future plans, my boyfriend. I couldn't pull myself out of mourning. That one brief shining moment was just too brief for me to handle. Jo stuck by me.

"It's all right, Mattie. You'll work it out."

She knew me better than my parents did, knew that I needed more than Christmas to stop feeling so badly. But, in January, just before Jo and I were to leave for a half-a-junior-year-abroad, my father came out to Pennsylvania, and I thought from his phony everything-is-just-wonderful smile that he'd bought me a sports car after all, as he'd wanted to do but my mother wouldn't allow. He took Jo and me to dinner and ordered a bottle of Châteauneuf-du-Pape, insisting on pouring it himself into our glasses after he'd smelled the cork and tasted the wine. This meant an announcement. A car when I got back from Europe so that I could go wherever I wanted whenever I wanted, and no more of this postassassination moping around. Then he lapsed into a weird speech.

He informed us that we were about to turn twenty-one, as if we didn't already know that, and that such a milestone birthday represented an extremely important time in our lives—a time when we should be devoted to having fun. He told us we'd mourned long enough and it was time we had a vacation. While I reminded him about the next six months in Italy, I thought, shit—there goes the car.

"I know all about this trip to Italy. I'm paying for it, remember? But I know you and Jo, and the two of you will work your tails off and come home with all sorts of paper awards that are essentially worthless. Mattie, your being so upset about President Kennedy for such a long time is unhealthy. It's time to get by it, and for Jo to stop humoring you, not that I blame Jo, because of course I know how much she feels for you. I'm here to propose that you stay in Italy for the summer to have the fun you'll not have while you're studying in some musty library. Or go off to Paris, enjoy all the action on the Left Bank, see . . ."

"Dad, this summer Jo and I have plans to work with . . ."

"I don't care about those plans!" he shouted. Jo's eyes opened up to their biggest silver. "You won't be working with anyone. Not if I can help it, by God!"

"Mr. Price, that's so nice of you," Jo said sweetly—my father adored her—"but . . ."

"Don't worry about the money. I've gone from plain editor to senior editor . . ."

"Dad!" I leaped up and hugged him. We all three hugged because Jo knew what this meant to him, too.

"Now I'll earn all that money that the fiction writers should be getting . . ." Then he started to cry. My father doesn't cry. I had wondered if some day I'd ever see him cry, but I knew it wouldn't be over anything that happened at *The New Yorker*.

"Daddy, what's wrong?" I don't call my father "Daddy" either, never have. But it went with the crying.

"It's your brother," he sobbed.

"Paul?" In one second I was sure Paul was dead, but I quickly realized my father wouldn't be telling me such news while touting the value of a summer of fun on the Left Bank.

Jo said, "Is he badly hurt?"

That was about to be my question. Paul was born mature and rational and no one had ever worried about him, so he couldn't have done something crazy like drop out of graduate school.

"He's left Stanford."

"No!"

Jo looked relieved. I was relieved, but more shocked. "Paul wouldn't leave Stanford."

"He has, Mattie." My father had stopped crying.

"He has?"

"Yes." I waited. "He joined the marines."

"What?" I was leaping up again.

"You're shouting, Mattie."

"Paul joined the marines? That's incredible!" Now Jo was getting excited. She'd join the marines in a minute, but obviously hadn't considered it until now.

"But why, Dad?"

"Because he worked too hard, goddamn it! Just like you and Jo. All his life he's worked and never had fun. He told your mother he needed a break."

"The marines aren't a break. Italy is a break."

"Italy will not be a break for you, just like Spain wasn't a break for him. Paul has never known the meaning of leisure, and neither have you. Or Jo. I've failed with Paul, but maybe I can prevent your going crazy someday, too."

Then I thought of Lyndon Johnson. I remembered where an awful lot of marines were going very soon. Fighting marines, not advising marines, like Eisenhower's and Kennedy's. It was in the air. By the time Paul was taught to fight, to kill—how anyone could accomplish that, I couldn't conceive—it would be time for him to go to Vietnam.

"Dad, we've got to stop him." I'd sat back down, but now I was up again.

"Sit down. He told us the news from Parris Island." He handed me his handkerchief, already damp for the first time in its existence by his own tears instead of my runny nose.

"Parris Island?"

"Yes."

"He's already done it?"

"Yes." There was a moment of silence. "Dad, you don't have to give Jo and me this vacation. I promise I won't join the marines, and neither will Jo." Jo looked at her nails. I was about to tell her to forget any idea of joining the marines or I'd kill her, but my father said:

"You two will do worse."

"What could be worse?"

"I don't know, but you'll find it." There was, and Jo found it.

"How do I reach him?"

My father gave me a piece of paper with a phone number. Then we all said good-bye without ever eating. He reminded me that I'd do more good calling my mother than Paul. I said to Jo, as his back disappeared from view, "The hell with calling, I'm going home."

"I'll take good notes for you."

"Thanks, Jo."

I beat my father back to Norwalk because he had to stop in New York first. My mother hugged me when I walked in the door, and kept hugging me. My mother isn't a hugger like my father isn't a crier. "Let's talk, Ma."

"OK, Mattie. That's exactly what I want to do. I want to get out of this house and find a nice quiet place to talk. Your father is through talking and I'm not."

"Poor Dad."

"He's so against this Asian escalation and now his son will probably be the first soldier there to fire a gun. Paul —a marine. Our Paul!"

My brother, when he was a kid, would go hide under the porch when we'd cook live lobsters. He'd block his ears, too, as if he could hear them scream once they hit the boiling water. He rescued three lobsters one time. Grabbed them out of the refrigerator when the coast was clear, wrote with indelible Magic Marker on their backs that they were from the Woods Hole lab and to be tossed back, and set them free in Long Island Sound. My father made him cough up fifteen dollars.

My mother's idea of a quiet place was church, which makes sense, though I suggested a bar instead. No one will ever convince my mother that ladies, even escorted ladies, should be caught dead in a bar. (The Oak Room at the Plaza, doesn't count, naturally.) We went to St. Mark's. My family had all become the kind of Catholics who went to midnight mass for the pomp and Easter sunrise service out of guilt. But my mother was right. It is nice to watch the candles flicker in their little red glass cups, and to let yourself get saturated by the billions of dust particles illuminated by the diffused light pouring in through the colored glass. When I was little, I remember one beam coming through the deepest blue of Our Lady's gown, hitting directly my mother's diamond ring. I watched, mesmerized, as the shards of a rainbow danced in and out of the diamond. I once told Jo how lucky I was that my Catholic memories were becoming all the romantic ones, not the terrible ones like going to confession when you're afraid of the dark, or the Mother Superior at St. Brice's.

My mother was reading my mind the whole time, afraid to read her own. We sat in a middle pew next to the window

35

of my favorite saint, Kateri Tekakwitha, the Canadian Indian martyr. Before I learned to read, I thought she was Pocahontas. St. Pocahontas. My mother asked, "What made you stop being a Catholic, Mattie? I mean, what really happened at St. Brice's?"

I could have been knocked over with a feather. "You mean you didn't believe me when I told you I'd rather go to Norwalk High because I'd get to be a cheerleader? You knew it wasn't true?"

"Of course. I found your rosary in the garbage can. And that told me you didn't believe any of it anymore. You told me what happened with cheerleaders, but you never told me the real reason you wouldn't go to St. Brice's."

"Oh, Ma! You're so great! You never pried. You waited for me to tell you. And I never did. I wish I could be like you."

She took my hand. "You're just like your father, thank God. And I thought Paul was, too."

"Why'd he do it?" I'm nothing like my father, Ma.

"Will you tell me about St. Brice's first, while I gear myself up to start talking about Paul again?"

"Sure, Ma." So I eased her into Paul with my story of the wondrous Mother Superior at St. Brice's. When I finished, she said:

"Poor Jo. As if she didn't suffer enough with the life she's led."

"I wouldn't call her life *suffering*, Ma. She's too tough."

"No, Mattie, she isn't. It's just that she's built up a tough shell over her skin."

"C'mon, Ma."

"Mattie, someday the shell will crack and it will be her turn to need you, not the other way around."

looked at my mother. What was she talking about?

"And that poor nun! Think how repressed she must—"

"Forget her, Ma. What about you?"

"Me?"

"Your being Catholic was phony, right? What made you decide not to take it seriously?"

"I tried to hide it from you and set a good example. I was a hypocrite, wasn't I?"

"No, Ma, you were a good mother. Go ahead."

"Well, Mattie, it was when we went to visit Evelyn."

Evelyn was my mother's cousin. She became a nun and we went to St. Louis to see her take one of her vows. We all went, all the relatives, just like it was Evelyn's wedding. Actually, that's exactly what it was—a wedding. A BIG wedding. Ten postulants came down the aisle in wedding gowns and veils, except that instead of joining the grooms they lay down in front of the altar, flat on their stomachs, and were covered by a long black banner. Everybody was crying like mad except my father, but I didn't see what was so sad; it was exciting—like landing in a foreign country. I wondered what it was symbolic of. In Catholic churches everything is symbolic of something else, and nobody bothers to explain to kids just what the hell is going on. When the brides were let out from under the black banner, they went up one at a time to the bishop, who slipped a gold wedding band on each one's finger. After the ceremony, they all hugged and giggled and jumped up and down like children, which is what they were. Evelyn was the oldest —twenty-one. I was nine myself, and for six months afterward I wanted to become a nun, too—a bride of Christ. It sounded so wild. Then I saw *The Bride of Frankenstein* and I realized that if I was ever going to be a bride, it would be of a normal man.

My mother went on: "At the reception for Evelyn, everyone was talking about the recent presidential election, and Evelyn whispered to me how much it broke her heart to vote against Adlai Stevenson. The family being the way it was—I mean Evelyn's father was chairman of the Democratic State Committee—I was shocked. I asked her what changed her mind and she said it was the bishop."

"The bishop?" I figured she wrote in the bishop's name on the ballot.

"Yes. She said since she'd taken the vow of obedience, she had to vote the way she was told."

"Oh, Ma, you are shitting me! Nuns have to vote the way they're told?"

"Mattie! You're in church."

"I knew we should have gone to a bar. I don't believe it."

"It was true."

"Incredible. But, Ma, my experience was much worse than that, I must say."

"It certainly was. To say nothing of how it must have been for Jo."

"Yeah. What about Dad? Did his thing have to do with nuns, like ours?"

She smiled. "No. Dad decided it was all a bad joke when he was about ten or eleven."

"Oh boy, this is going to be good." My father tells the best stories about what life was like when he was a kid. He's tried to write them down, but he can't do fiction, and all true stories when you write them down end up sounding boring. He throws away any stories he writes, which, as an editor, he ends up doing with ninety-nine percent of the fiction he reads anyway. "What happened?"

"He was in line for communion one Sunday. A kid named Francis Dumarck was in front of him. This Francis turned around and told Dad he was going to throw up. Now, in our generation we were told that if you suddenly remembered a sin on your way to communion, you shouldn't turn around and go back to your pew, because it might cause a scandal."

"Us, too, Ma. They told us people might wonder if you suddenly recalled how you murdered your grandmother the night before."

"Don't exaggerate. Some priest must have dreamed that up because he thought it would prevent gossip, and I'm sure he was quite right. Anyway, Dad told Francis to hang in there so there wouldn't be a scandal. Then, they were kneeling at the rail and the priest got to Francis. Dad could see the host descending in the priest's hand, and then Francis's tongue stick out. But all of a sudden, Francis clapped his hand over his mouth and two streams of vomit came pouring out of his nostrils!"

I actually let out a scream, and my mother slapped her hand over my mouth just as Francis Dumarck had done to himself. We looked at each other and cracked up. We laughed until our sides hurt, and I swear Tekakwitha was laughing, too. But when we tried to calm ourselves in order to catch our breaths, we thought of Paul, and we started to cry. Unlike Dad, we're criers. We cried and cried for the first time, with my mother's head on my shoulder instead of vice versa.

"Oh my God, Mattie, he's just not a marine. What will they do to him?"

What they were going to do was to teach him to kill people, but I didn't say that. She was so upset. My brother the scholar, a marine of all things. There was no comfort to offer so I said:

"Ma, has Paul ever said when he stopped being a Catholic?"

She lifted her head. "No."

"Then let's go ask him. We'll get on the two extensions and we'll have another good laugh. Paul will need a laugh, I bet. Have they shaved his head yet?"

"Yes."

"He'll need a laugh." Paul had chin-length hair—sort of a nice little bob that hid his stick-out ears. And a headband. Imagine getting a Ph.D. in physics at Stanford while wearing a beaded headband. The sixties were truly terrific.

At home, my father was there. My mother made me tell him the Mother-Superior-slash-penis story. It turned out my mother had never told him the Adlai Stevenson story, so he heard that, too. I told him when she was done that his Francis Dumarck story was an absolute riot. He smiled. And he agreed to call Paul.

He told the base commander's secretary that Paul's grandmother had taken a turn for the worse and that Paul and she were very close and he had to let Paul know what was happening immediately. Paul got on and said:

"Well, Dad, nothing like taking a turn for the worse when you've been dead fifteen years. Unless, of course, you're talking about the other grandmother, who you told me turned over in her grave when I joined up."

"Don't be dry, Paul. Your sister needs to tell you something."

I immediately chimed in on the extension. "Paul, wait till you hear this. We're each going to tell you when and how we officially stopped being Catholics. I'm going first because mine is really sad, then Mom because hers will really kill you, and then Dad because it's the funniest story I've ever heard in my life. Then, it'll be your turn, OK?"

Silence.

"OK, Paul?"

"Ah, Mattie . . ."

"He says OK."

We told our stories. Then Paul told us his. We assumed the base commander wasn't eavesdropping. He said:

"I knew when I had sex with Mary Lou Grabowsky, and went to confession and wasn't the least bit sorry, that I couldn't be a Catholic anymore without also being a hypocrite." He paused. On three extension phones no one responded. "Are you guys still there?" My father was wrong. Paul had found recreation when he wanted to.

"Paul!" My mother shouted. "That's not true. You were only sixteen when you tutored that girl."

"She tutored me, Ma."

My mother began sputtering and I said, "Shit, Paul. Mary Lou Grabowsky was such a dog."

My father countered, "But she sure had big tits."

My mother ran from the living room into my father's den, and I down the stairs in time to see her smack my father and grab the phone from him. Forget the marines. She said to my father, "Do you mean to tell me that you knew your son was having sex at sixteen? And you never told me?" I took the phone from her.

"Listen, Paul, we love you an awful lot so be careful, OK?"

"I will, Mattie. And tell Ma that if it makes any difference, Mary Lou passed American history and wouldn't
have graduated without me."

"A fair exchange."

"I'll say."

So we knew Paul would be an OK marine and that,
somehow, he'd stay the same great person he had always
been. A couple of years in the marines couldn't change
that. A couple of years in Vietnam could change that, but
we didn't let thoughts of war creep up on us and we stayed
calm. None of us could dare to verbalize the possibility that
he might end up a dead marine.

Paul told us he had to join the marines because he couldn't
be a hypocrite. He said if you wanted to be an American
you had to go along with the rough stuff like going to
Vietnam. I didn't tell him he was being an asshole, because
it wasn't the time. I did much later as a way of cheering
him up when he was about to be sent to Panama instead
of Vietnam. He tried to get out of Panama but when your
great uncle is in politics and pulls some strings, you don't
have much choice. Even if you're in Hawaii, about to ship
out any second. But later he was glad he didn't go to Vietnam because he met this one guy who'd come back from
the war with no body from the waist down. Then he said
that what was going on in Vietnam wasn't worth the loss
of this guy's half a body, never mind the fifty thousand
guys that died.

Anyway, even though I agreed for my father's sake (along
with Jo) to spend that summer in Paris having fun, we
didn't. We had fun all right, but not in Paris. After our
semester in Italy, we went to the University of Hawaii instead, where the ratio of men to women had become 23
to 1 because of Vietnam. All the men in Hawaii waiting to
be called up felt obligated to get their sisters out there for
their friends. When they found out from Paul that he had
a sister, they never let him have a moment's peace because
I am good-looking, basically, and they saw an especially
flattering picture he had of me. Paul said it was a good

thing he didn't have a picture of Jo because the guys in his platoon would have gone AWOL to find her.

Hawaii is like having a chance to go to heaven and then getting to come back. Jo and I loved Hawaii, especially after Italy, where Jo nearly lost herself to a gigolo and where I almost lost my life for love. All right. Not love. Sex.

CHAPTER FOUR

In the little village of Aosta, above the highest lakes in the Italian Alps, we found Jo's blue-eyed, silver-blond Italians. The area is drastically remote, the roads between villages barely wide enough for a Deux Cheveaux. Northern Italy will never be much of a market for Chryslers. And these tortuous alpine roads aren't one-way, as we found them cleverly to be in Africa one year hence. In Cameroon, the road from Kumba to Mamfe (Mamfe is one of the lowest places on Earth after the Dead Sea and Death Valley) is one-way. You can go from Kumba to Mamfe on Monday, Wednesday, and Friday and from Mamfe to Kumba on Tuesday, Thursday, and Saturday. You are a fool to travel on Sunday, according to the Cameroonians, one-way or otherwise. Cameroonians take Sunday to be a day of rest, literally. In all the Bible, that's the only order they take literally. North Italians believe in living dangerously, unlike the Cameroonians, who have enough trouble just living. Also, North Italians are Catholic; hence, they don't read the Bible.

In Aosta, Jo found her relatives, the Brochettos, none of whom was her grandmother. Her grandmother never returned to Aosta after deserting her husband as Jo's Smoky Mountain family had assumed. I figure she probably just drifted off across the United States the way Jo's mother was doing. Jo hadn't heard from her mother in about six months at this point, and Jo's last letter came back, addressee unknown. Jo said to me, "Don't worry, Mattie, they'll be OK." I thought about what my mother had said about Jo's shell. Well, there sure was a shell, because I knew that Jo loved her little brother and the baby. The baby instinctively knew that Jo would be gone for a long time when we went to college. She clung to Jo like a leech. But my mother was wrong about the shell cracking. Six months since she'd heard from her mother and she tells me not to worry.

I continually stressed to myself in order to rationalize Jo's rationalizations that her sense of family was different from yours and mine, just like F. Scott's rich. I was her family now, but sometimes when I looked at her, into those North Italian silver eyes, I could see her thinking that I would drift away someday, too. But I'd come right out and tell her, "I'll never desert you, Jo." And she'd say, "Don't make promises you might not be able to keep, Mattie."

That's what Jo was really looking for: someone who wouldn't drift away, who needed her so much that she'd be an indispensable haven. Jo would give up everything to be that kind of a haven herself. On her fourth try at acquiring someone who would fit the bill, she succeeded. Her first attempt, in Italy, was a disaster, though not as disastrous as her third. In between was a normal relationship that I knew was doomed from the start—my brother did not need a haven. Before she met the Italian who she thought might fit the bill, however, she had another "problem" that cropped up. It was not a serious problem for Jo, but it threw her Italian relatives into a tailspin.

Jo's relatives in Italy were all upper middle class. They had townhouses in Turin, *pieds-à-terre* in Milan, and maintained country homes in and about Aosta. Jo, it turned out, owned a cellar in Aosta. In the Piedmont, up in those old villages, when a man dies, he leaves his house to his children, and for fun, I guess, gets to inform them in his will which room they will inherit. (Italians really do believe in an afterlife where they all sit around drinking grappa and laughing like crazy at their children reading the wills, hoping to get the parlor and not the bathroom.) Usually, just the sons divvy up the rooms, but Jo's great-grandfather only had daughters—seven. His number-three daughter, as we all knew, had run off with her soldier and wasn't around in the end to get the room assigned to her, so she ended up with the cellar—the cellar of a magnificent, three-storied farmhouse in the middle of a vineyard, which climbed tier upon tier above the little river that flowed from the icy lake cradled in the towering mountain over everyone's heads. Not unlike the terraced hills of Bamenda, which is in Cameroon, and of course, the ones behind Beirut.

Jo's cellar was full of Carema. If you find out you own a cellar, cross your fingers that it's full of Carema.

Carema is a clear red wine that does not look anything like Gallo burgundy when poured into a glass. It is the color of colonial America's ruby glass, which was made in Sandwich, Massachusetts, and nowhere else. Carema is made in Aosta and nowhere else. It is aged in oak casks in Jo's cellar before it's bottled. You open your bottle one hour before you intend to drink it and it is the longest hour in the world once you've come to know what it tastes like. (No matter what activity or conversation is going on to make that hour go by as quickly as possible, it still seems like a dozen hours, and you find yourself glancing from the ruby-red bottle to your watch every seven seconds.) Twenty degrees centigrade is the temperature Carema absolutely has to be to drink it. But I noticed that no one had a thermometer around so it couldn't be that exact.

I know zilch about wine, but this Carema was so delicious that there was nothing I could compare it to. I couldn't compare it to anything even if I did know something about wine, I'm sure. Jo said it tasted like sexual desire, but I'm sure wine connoisseurs would pay no heed to that description. A short time later, when Jo had obviously come to know the meaning of sexual desire, I asked her if she still thought that that was how Carema tasted. She laughed. I said, "It's a tie, right?" She laughed again and so did I. We both agreed that Carema had the edge.

When the Brochettos realized Jo had no intention of claiming the cellar, they were in such a delirium of gratitude that the whole time we were in Italy they kept sending Italian delicacies to us in Milan. As a special present they told Jo they'd send her a case of Carema every year via her cousin (about a million times removed) who was a visiting professor at Johns Hopkins. She told them to have the professor send the case to my father, who knows wine and who couldn't believe his taste buds when we got home and gave him his first bottle.

School started in Milan. The teachers were good, but we weren't in awe the way we were at BMC, and therefore not so wrapped up in classes and discussions. Instead of marathon intellectual bull sessions, I lost my virginity, I think. I don't really know for sure if I was a virgin by the time I got to Italy. I couldn't tell if my boyfriend at Haverford's two attempts found the mark or not. Only twice did we get to the point of entry, in the back of his car under our winter coats. We were smashed, for one, and the first time, as soon as I got my undies off, he was done. The second time, I think it did happen, but I'd passed out in the middle of our great passion. Learning to drink in moderation takes several years.

My relationship with Mark at Haverford was the thing to do more than anything else. He was nice, but we never had time to really get to know each other. We BMC/Haverford people took our studies seriously, and Mark had Vietnam to worry about besides.

Anyway, all this hogwash about "the first time" is nothing but claptrap. What matters for the rest of your life is not the moment you lose your virginity, but your first orgasm. Lucky for me, it didn't happen when I was horseback riding or having a sex dream. It happened in Italy. An orgasm can only be compared to the experience of drinking Carema, and unlike desire, orgasm has the edge over Carema.

I fell in love for the first time in Italy, too, which probably contributed to my first experience with orgasm. I fell in love with Franco, short for Francesco, and he was a student, chemistry I'd assumed, in Milan. His room was full of bottles and jars, cans and pots of stuff, Bunsen burners, and all sorts of apparatus. Something was always cooking in Franco's room. I was always cooking in Franco's room. He was a damn good cook.

He had a lot of serious friends, and for the first time in my life I had Bryn Mawr–type discussions with people who didn't just not agree with me, they didn't know what I was talking about. I didn't know what they were talking about either, but the Università di Milano rhetoric, especially the Marxist variety, was sensational. I couldn't wait to get back to BMC, where I would knock everyone out with various Italian positions on the philosophy of life. I never considered what they were saying to be radical; I just thought they were thirty years behind the times. In the early sixties we weren't into Marxism yet—the Weathermen hadn't split off from the SDS. They reminded me of the Julius and Ethel Rosenberg kind of Communists, some of whom were the previous owners of the house where I would live when I got married. I decided that some member of the BMC faculty would straighten me out on what was bothering the modern Italian student thirty years after it bothered the American intellectuals of the Depression. We mathematicians who love to express ourselves through creative writing don't fit in anywhere. I could put two and two together in a lot of wondrous ways, but coming out with four never happened.

At first, I loved lying in Franco's bed after hours of making love just watching him. He was so dedicated to his work that the university had allowed him to set up his own private lab in his room. I was impressed.

Jo, meanwhile, had also fallen in love, though with a sculptor, not a chemist. She became as dedicated to him as he was to his work. His work consisted of being a bum and living off women. He had no talent. Jo gave him all her share of the Italian delicacies from Aosta. He was very handsome, a good ten years older than he looked—he looked about thirty—and Jo couldn't see that a lot of people laughed at him. Young undergraduate girls swooned while the rest laughed. Jo began making noises about a lifetime of "supporting a great, undiscovered *artiste*."

"You're talking waiting tables, Jo," I said.

She'd give me a Joan of Arc look. "Anything I'd do for Mario would be my reward."

"Your reward? What will be his reward? Besides you, I mean. Surely he isn't chipping away at all that rock for nothing. Does he see anything worthwhile, for example, in having his work in a gallery?"

"Don't be sarcastic. He's still learning, Mattie."

"By the time an *artiste* is forty he should have sold something or had something commissioned, or at least *shown* something. As far as I can see, Mario never even finishes one single thing because some woman is always giving him a party somewhere. And where are you when he's off at all these parties? Cleaning up his studio for him, that's where. Shit, Jo, if you're going to devote your life to someone, maybe you should look around for someone who is a little more considerate."

Jo let me finish my tirade because she was thinking. "Maybe I'm meant to be a cleaning woman. Like my mother."

"Damn, Jo! Quit the martyr act. Who wouldn't be a cleaning woman for a while if it meant a great affair with someone as gorgeous as Mario? But just for a while!"

"Maybe. But Mario says his very next project will be me in bronze."

Jo had dreams, but she was no fool. She hadn't lost her noodle to this Mario. I was assured of that when she said "maybe." I stopped worrying about her. Posing nude would probably be a very valuable experience. Certainly it would be something that would wow the girls at BMC.

As the weeks passed, I began to get bored lying in bed watching intense Franco mix his chemicals. Sometimes I'd be forced to get up and go for a walk because he'd create a terrible odor. I began bringing books to his room, and I'd lie in his bed still in a sweat from his rather athletic lovemaking, reading while he worked on. He loved the company. I even wrote a short story, the first short story that I didn't show my father. Franco seemed quite surprised that I could write. He acted worried, in fact, and asked what I was writing. I told him short fiction, and he said, "Ah, good," and relaxed. He gave me a smile meant to humor me. I was a little offended. After all, I hadn't said poetry. When I look back, I realize he took me for a dunderhead. Among the things Franco taught me was that not everyone in the world knew of Bryn Mawr's reputation.

My short story was about living with a brilliant chemist who made love with the intensity and care of someone mixing something that had to be exactly right or it would blow up. The more I went over that story, the more frustrated I got because I couldn't conceive an ending. What will be the denouement here, Mattie, I'd ask myself. I couldn't go to my father on that one because he'd choke knowing the protagonist was undoubtedly me. Franco himself provided an action-filled denouement that I later tacked on to the story. Unfortunately, it gave the story a rather humorous twist that spoiled things completely, so I threw the story out.

Franco's denouement was provided the same day I got a letter from my brother, Paul, inviting Jo and me to Hawaiian orgies. He told us to forget a summer in Italy, to come and take some courses at the East-West Center at the University of Hawaii. All morning Jo and I joked about taking Hula 302 and ukulele classes. Then, off she went to Mario's studio and I to Franco. He didn't immediately sweep me into his arms, whisper Italian sex verses in my ear, and shower kisses upon my entire body. He was on the phone, shouting to someone that he didn't have time. I'd picked up quite a lot of Italian. Take two years of French in college, spend a few months in Italy, and you learn two languages for the price of one.

"Time for what, Franco?" I asked when he hung up.

"Nothing, my angel. But I must work. A project of mine is to be picked up in twenty minutes."

"Your professor is coming here?"

Again, that humor-the-dumbbell smile that I still thought was moon-eyes in love. "Yes. They come to me."

"I'll wait." I smiled, kissing his neck, and flopped onto the bed with the first book of *The Alexandria Quartet*.

Out of the corner of my eye, I couldn't help but notice that Franco seemed to be a little on the frenzied side. He kept looking at his watch, too. I took off my shirt to entice him because I didn't like him acting frenzied. He looked at me. That smile. He worked on. Suddenly, he dove under the bed, his arms wrapped around his head. I couldn't react—it was such a bizarre thing for him to do. Then, just as Franco was slowly emerging from under the bed, two of his friends came charging through the door with a large metal canister. In Italian, they kept shouting, "Quickly! Quickly!"

Franco got hysterical. He kept yelling that they'd rushed him. They kept yelling back that if he didn't spend so much time fucking the *americana*, he'd have been ready on schedule. They looked daggers at me. It was summer. Franco's two friends were dressed in strange, heavy clothes and gloves ten sizes too big. The pile of funny strings caught my eye on his table. There was a funny string hanging out of the thing on Franco's table that he'd been working on. It also had a timer on it. I leaped off the bed without even clutching my shirt to cover my breasts, flushed red with anger.

"You're making bombs! That thing is a goddamned bomb!"

They turned to me, annoyed. I was a gnat to them. Franco ignored me and went on shouting at the bomb squad. I grabbed his arm.

"You dove for cover. You would have let me be blown to bits! You shit, Franco." I began to pound on him and one of his friends picked me up and tossed me aside so he could get back to berating Franco. I glanced at the bomb. The timer was ticking softly. I grabbed my shirt and *Justine* and ran.

I ran to Mario's studio, where Jo was standing stark

naked, leaning against some sort of pillar. I never knocked. I screamed, "Emergency!" Mario gaped from me to Jo. His tongue was hanging out as if he were a Saint Bernard in the middle of a desert. I had dashed through three city blocks of Milan, bare-breasted. I put on my shirt now and began buttoning furiously, which is difficult to do when you're holding a hardcover book. I kept throwing Jo's clothes at her, too. Jo could tell I was genuinely hysterical; she shrugged at the panting Mario and let me pull her to our dorm room, which we used as a storage closet. We were never there. The dorm had a calming effect on me. Dormitories the world over, even in Milan, are exactly the same. I felt like the real me again in that asexual dorm room rather than an American student abroad. In my panic, all I could think was that we had to get out of the university, get out of Milan right away. Fanatic crazies knew I was onto them. I tried to make it look like Jo's fault that we had to leave so suddenly.

"Jo, I've got to save you from Mario. Your wanting to stay on as a waitress is a bunch of baloney."

"I know."

"You simply can't . . . what? You know? Thank God, Jo. Thank God."

"We'll go to Hawaii a couple weeks early."

"Where?"

"Hawaii! To take Hula three-oh-two, remember?"

"I didn't know that was def—"

Then, my terror suddenly hitting me, I collapsed onto my bed, crying.

"What in heaven's name is wrong with you, Mattie? Did you and Franco have a fight?"

"Jo! Franco makes bombs."

"So you've said."

I had? I looked at her. Jo didn't usually vocalize sex. She had that uncomfortable look on her face.

"My God, Jo, not those kind of bombs! He makes real bombs. I'm not talking about the ones he explodes in me. I'm talking fuses and timers here. He's not a chemist. He's the bomb maker for some kind of Italian soldiers of fortune. He's been making bombs in his bedroom. I could have been blown up. Jesus, Jo, we're going to go to Hawaii tonight."

And we did.

In the dead of night in the dark airplane, with Jo snoozing in the seat next to me, my head cleared. When it came to making love, that Franco had been incredibly intense. Small wonder. Imagine making love knowing that at any second you can be blasted into smithereens. Was it this same intensity that was to draw Jo to her Ahmad? I often wondered about that. A junior-year-abroad adventure that you don't write home about isn't supposed to be a life-style.

CHAPTER FIVE

We went to Hawaii in the other direction, so I could brag about circumnavigating the globe before I was twenty-one and also because when we arrived at the Milan airport, the next international flight out was Air India to New Delhi, "No begging in First Class," said the jokester behind us in the luggage check line. (Twenty years later, I still hadn't crossed the equator, but I had no interest, by then, in milestones.) Hawaii may be full of Orientals and steeped in Eastern culture, but it's America, no question about it. Delhi and Tokyo are definitely not. We spent the first two weeks of June in those places and went on guided tours of shrines that looked like wedding cakes and gardens full of pools of goldfish. There are more goldfish than people in Japan. We also toured Hiroshima.

The Eastern world is into little colored lightbulbs. Hindus and Buddhists light up their statuary with string upon string of G.E. Christmas-tree lights. Having been born a Catholic, I'm more naturally into candles. Everyone, everywhere, is into incense except American Protestants. One guide of a shrine tour we went on overheard my Christmas-lights observation. Very sweetly, in his pretty, Delhi-flavored English, he said to me:

"You are not understanding the vast differences between your culture and my own, which only leads to intolerance among peoples. I myself was sixteen years old before I realized that 'Jesus' was something besides the curse one shouts when one stubs one's toe."

Put me right in my place.

I was afraid to go to Hiroshima because I didn't like the thought of seeing bombed-out buildings. I preferred ruins caused by time. But, as it turned out, the Japanese felt the same way I did. Prepared to find myself standing on the edge of a crater while hearing someone tell me that this was ground zero, I was surprised to see, once again, gardens and goldfish. There was no crater and just one ruin—an old exhibition hall not far from the *Enola Gay*'s target. The target was a bridge—is still a bridge, full of cars and pedestrian traffic. They replaced the bridge, but left the remnants of the hall. The memorial to the dead killed in Hiroshima is a cenotaph. Jo and I knew what a cenotaph was because, after all, we were Bryn Mawr students. A cenotaph is a tomb without a body. Sometimes a tomb is a cenotaph simply because the family has chosen to remove the body. According to Jo, a cenotaph had to be meant to be a cenotaph. It couldn't become one. Many years later, when I met William Buckley at The Literary Guild's cocktail party for its authors, he said he didn't know for sure. But guessing, he was with Jo. I'd wished Jo was there so she could see me stump William Buckley.

In the case of the Hiroshima cenotaph, there wasn't a question of bodies. At ground zero, there never were any. People were just gone. The cenotaph was like a short, high tunnel walled off in the back. In the tunnel was a small chest with the names of the two hundred thousand people who never reappeared after the bomb exploded. Words, carved in stone, arch just above your head. The guide said the words meant, "Repose ye in peace, for the error shall not be repeated."

"Let's hope not," I said to Jo.

"Something must have been lost in the translation, Mattie, because the Japanese sure don't consider this thing an *error*." She was right, because the Japanese were looking at us the same way we later saw Americans looking at them when we went to Pearl Harbor.

The little museum next to the cenotaph was full of gruesome pictures of burned flesh, not unlike the napalm pictures that were to arrive shortly on American breakfast tables everywhere.

We couldn't wait to get to Hawaii once we'd been to Hiroshima. We slept on the plane and didn't wake up till the stewardess shook us. It was too bad that we'd missed Hawaii from the air, because we weren't prepared for the sight of Waikiki Beach. In high school, we'd spent a lot of time at Calf Pasture Beach on the Sound. We'd been to great beaches on the South Shore of Long Island, and they are truly grand. The Italian Riviera we had given a C+ because the water had an awful lot of fettuccine floating in it. We'd skipped Indian beaches. Japanese beaches were gorgeous. But any beach in the world, even those I saw after Hawaii, couldn't compare to that first glimpse we had of the shore and ocean in the ten feet of space between two hotels on Waikiki. We were in a taxi on Kamehameha Avenue, stopped at a light, and I gasped, "Look, Jo!" It took her breath away, too. The water looked like runways of lime Jell-O set between tentacles of brilliant turquoise, which we learned were reefs sitting just below the surface. The two-toned spectacle stretched out until it met the dark, purple-blue stretch of the Pacific, which in turn met at the horizon with the cornflower sky.

We gaped until the light changed and the taxi shot forward. I'd never dreamed I'd gawk at anything again once I'd seen Michelangelo's *David* who stands in Florence so stark naked, each muscle more deliciously relaxed than the next, as he contemplates his KO of Goliath. Witnessing perfect human art is a show-stopping assault upon the senses, and so is nature when she whips out the old paintbrush. The colors of Hawaii: The sea, the pale sky, the dark-green hills behind Honolulu, and the muumuus knocked us silly, though the first Hawaiian we met at the dorm was a student who went to Mt. Holyoke and said that none of it could compare to a New England autumn. We asked her where we could get a couple of those muu-muus anyway.

She also informed us of the following:

"At the last minute, we had to put you in a triple, OK?"

"Triple?"

"Sorry. Since you were the only ones we couldn't contact to ask if it was all right, and everyone we did reach said no, you got her. But she seems real nice."

"Shit," I mumbled.

"She's Japanese."

"Japanese?" Jo said, and looked at me. "Neat."

The Japanese girl's name was Louisa Yumata and we loved her. At first we were disgusted when she said she was from Chicago rather than Kyoto and went to North-western, but then we didn't care because her answer to our question, "Were you born in Chicago or Japan?" was "Nei-ther. I was born in a concentration camp in Idaho."

Louisa's birthplace was the second in a series of eye-openers (after President Kennedy) that told me America has made a lot of mistakes, some deliberate.

Louisa told us how her parents, both third-generation Americans, were given twenty-four hours to pack one suit-case between them and report to the train station outside San Diego. Louisa's mother was having a complicated preg-nancy and would be put in danger, but no one would listen to her doctor, who wasn't a Japanese-American, and who had delivered Mrs. Yumata two decades earlier. Mr. and Mrs. Yumata were told that after the war they'd get every-thing back, but when they returned to San Diego when Louisa was two, their house was the site of an exit off the new freeway. The Yumatas started over again in Chicago. Louisa's father was an insurance agent, and several of his California customers also ended up in Chicago, which was booming after the war. Mr. Yumata was also a travel agent.

"I asked him to get me to Hawaii because I couldn't handle the crisis going on at home," Louisa explained.

"Which was?"

"My sister just broke up with her boyfriend. He's Japanese and goes to Harvard. They're terrified that we two girls will not marry Japanese and then be miserable all our lives. I knew they'd agree to my coming here to study because there are so many others here. Japanese boys, I mean." We'd noticed that. "But I'm real nervous."

We said, "Why?"

She said, "I've always been protected from Caucasians by my family. You're my first ones."

God, how we loved it. Jo said, "Don't worry. We'll protect you from Caucasians, too."

"Oh, thanks. But don't protect me too hard, OK? I mean, as far as . . . uh . . . boys go." She had a real twinkle in her black eyes. "I sort of want to see what they're like."

We all laughed. "Oh, Louisa, they're like all boys the world over. They just want to get in your pants."

Then we decided we were starving, and went to find food. Over our teriburgers (teriyaki sauce on hamburgers—delicious) Jo and I asked Louisa a million questions about being Japanese. During dessert we were joined by two blondes from San Jose who told us all about being Californians. The few Californians at Bryn Mawr weren't blondes. Jo and I were the only ones that Louisa talked about Idaho to, though. We liked the California girls, but we kept remembering our promise to Louisa.

The Californians had come in on a cruise ship from L.A., and had thrown a bottle overboard with their names in it, and some marines at Kaneohe Bay found it. Six marines were coming to take them out and would we come, too?

I said, "What luck to have the bottle found so soon."

The taller blonde said, "Well, we sailed by Kaneohe Bay and someone said that's where the marines are, so that's where we threw it. The bottle didn't have a shot at going anywhere else. And someone told us it would reach shore before we would because the tide was going in."

These girls were funny. I didn't want to call Paul until the next day when I was settled in and got my emotions in order so I wouldn't spend my first hour with him crying. I hoped that one of the marines coming to take us out wouldn't be him. None were. We went to a discotheque called "The Morgue," which was opposite a real morgue, and Louisa danced with her first Caucasian. Her first six Caucasians: Southern boys who all danced with their first non-Caucasian.

CHAPTER SIX

I fell in love with a marine named Will. He was shy, and though shy boys have never really interested me because I'm so short on patience, Will was the spitting image of Elvis Presley: dark and sensuous, and also from the deep South. Very deep in Will's case, deep in a swampland. He lived in the Okeechobee swamp of lower Florida. The Pacific was the first body of water that Will had ever seen, including the Atlantic and the Gulf of Mexico. He was married. He had a baby, too, and he couldn't read or write, but he was very, very smart.

One night we walked out onto our favorite jetty off Waikiki and listened to the crabs scuttling about beneath us.

"Will," I asked, "why did you sign up for the marines?"

"Duty." Most of Will's answers to my questions were one-worders. Very far removed from discussions as I knew them.

"You think it's your duty to kill Vietnamese people?"

"Nope. Duty to do what my country says is c'rect. Pay back."

"Pay back for what?"

"Fer havin' a home an' family an' bein' left alone. My daddy went to France an' his daddy lost his leg in Belgium. My great-granddaddy was in Cuba, an' fore that . . ." When Will hadn't a one-word answer, he spoke histories.

"Are they all alive now?"

He laughed. "College girl."

I laughed, too, but I didn't know what was funny. "Really, Will. I'm just curious about your family when they're not fighting wars. Why do they want to live in a swamp? Why do you?"

"Pleasure of it."

"Oh."

"Our livelihood is that swamp, Mattie, jest like that there magazine is yer daddy's livelihood."

"Do you farm?"

He roared with laughter. "That's a good one. You are the dangdest girl I ever did meet. My daddy hunts 'gators. My granddaddy makes shoes and stuff from the hides. Beautiful shoes, he makes."

"And your great-granddaddy?"

He smirked. "He's kilt, Mattie." I must have made a face. He touched my cheek in wonder. "Weren't kilt by 'gators, don't you worry. Kilt by Spaniards."

"Oh. And what's your job?"

"I skin 'em an' cure the hides."

"Yech."

He smiled that Elvis Presley crooked smile. "Like cleanin' a fish, is all. A big fish."

Will's hands were big, too. And scarred. I stared at them, and that's when he asked me to teach him to read and write.

"Will! You can't read?"

"Nope. No need to in the swamp."

"Do you want to leave the swamp? Is that why you want to know how to read now?"

"Nope. Like it there. As beautiful and quiet as this here, Mattie, but no hotels, no lights, an' jest family."

"C'mon, Will, how could you get in the marines if you can't read?"

"Easy."

"Didn't you have to sign something?"

"I scribbled on the line."

"How did your parents keep you out of school?"

Will thought I was a riot. When he stopped shaking his head, he said, "No schools in the swamp."

"What about the authorities?"

"Saw a ranger once."

"But—"

"Boys go get a birth certificate when it's time to join up. Girls, never."

"You're kidding!" He got to chuckling again. "Will you stop laughing at me? I'm the one who should be laughing at you. You can't read, for God's sake."

"Teach me, OK? My wife ain't much of a talker. Ya know, like you are. Give me somethin' to do. Give me somethin' to do with my child. She's a smart child."

"Wouldn't your family disapprove?"

"Nobody's disprovin' in my family."

"That's wonderful."

"That's natural. Your family is disprovin'?"

"All the time . . . of everything I do . . . almost."

"Can't you jest go off somewheres, by yourself?"

"Sure. And when I come back my mother still keeps saying to either get a haircut or get the hair out of my eyes."

He reached up and got the hair outah mah eyes. I was beginning to think in his dialect. "You do have real nice eyes hidin' in there. Your mama ain't disprovin' . . . she's improvin'. Never seen eyes such a mix of colors. But you kin hide 'em if you like. All right with me."

My chest felt like butter was melting inside of it. His fingertips barely brushed the skin of my forehead and a great blush rose up and covered me. I don't blush. He leaned back against one of the boulders and crossed his arms over his chest. His arms were solid muscle, but not ugly. Like David's in Florence. He said, "And, it's borin' in our barracks. Everyone reads there 'cept me."

"Oh, they're probably just looking at the pictures." He laughed. His laugh was an aria. "I'll teach you, Will."

"Thanks."

Our first reading lesson was at the Honolulu Zoo. He learned all the sounds the letters made in about an hour. Then this giraffe distracted us. He kept letting his tongue hang out of the side of his mouth. His tongue must have been two feet long. I was embarrassed because it was really disgusting. Not Will. He was impressed.

"Cain't imagine no animal havin' a tongue long as that." He dragged me to the zookeeper's office to find out who had the longest tongue in the animal kingdom. I think he was just getting bored with saying "*puh*" and "*kuh*" and "*lllll*." The zookeeper didn't know, but he got very worried. The giraffe, it turned out, was thirsty. His water supply had been blocked. I thought Will would cry when he found that out. Afterward, whenever we were down at the west end of Waikiki, we'd always make sure to stroll over to the zoo and check whether the animals had their water.

One night I treated to tickets for a Peter, Paul, and Mary concert at the Waikiki Shell. The night, like every night in Hawaii, was balmy and dry and filled with stars. You could see the Milky Way all the time, in a wide path arcing over your head. Will said the Milky Way was even brighter in Okeechobee. It was even brighter in Africa, though I didn't know it yet. Will and I both liked Peter, Paul, and Mary in person. Will never minded that they were singing out against sending anyone to Vietnam. "They got a right," he said.

Will learned to read easily, but he could only print. I told him script would take practice. After all, it took most people years and years. No one could read my handwriting, I told him. He told me he'd practice, but I could tell he was discouraged.

Toward the end of the summer, his outfit, along with quite a few others, was shipped to Vietnam. He had twenty-four-hour notice. He came to the dorm to tell me, but I was out. I'd gone water-skiing all day with an air-force officer who owned a boat and was a jerk. We went dancing all night at The Morgue later. The next morning I read Will's note in block letters saying good-bye and thanking me for teaching him to read. I called a taxi and got to Kaneohe Bay fast, but it was too late. He was gone. I sat in some captain's office crying and crying. Two weeks later I got a pair of alligator boots from Florida. Knee-high boots that were so exquisite I never wore them. Will didn't answer my thank-you letters. But I treated those boots like a work of art, which they were.

Louisa fell in love that summer for the first time—not with a Caucasian, but a Filipino boy. Much worse, Jo and I learned. It was the kind of love affair that happens only in great literature or drama. It was a combination *Romeo and Juliet* and *West Side Story*. And also the horrible part of *The King and I* when Yul Brynner orders the young lovers to be executed. Louisa explained that his family would disown him if they knew about her. Her parents the same. Anyone who knows the slightest bit about the war in the Pacific knows that this is a completely unacceptable mix to the parents. What the Japanese did to Pearl Harbor was nothing compared to what they did to the Philippines. I didn't know the slightest bit, but Louisa filled me in on Bataan and Corregidor and all the torture. I suggested she should remind her family that she was born in Idaho, not Japan. She smiled that mystical Oriental smile of hers (she laughed like an American), and explained that George— the Filipino—was born in Maui, as were his parents and their parents. This Philippines/Japan thing spanned immigration gaps.

Unlike Louisa and me, Jo did not fall in love that summer. She refused. If she had, it would have meant marrying my brother, Paul. But Paul didn't fit into Jo's dreams. What made her determination all the more difficult for me was that Paul adored her, had always adored her, and suddenly realized she was old enough for him to do something about it. For the first time in my life, I was rooting against Jo. I knew she loved Paul, but just didn't let herself go. Jo had more controlled discipline of her emotions than anyone.

It was so nice for me to be with Paul—have him near. And it was a great comfort to our parents. Paul and Jo spent all the time together that they could and he asked her to marry him when he got out. She said no. He told me he knew she'd say no. I felt sorry for my brother. He's a nice, gentle guy. Funny how a lot of marines, most marines, were nice gentle guys, despite Parris Island.

I had a few beers with Paul one night in the revolving glass bar atop the Ilikai.

"Mattie, I'm so crazy about Jo," he said, with his neat uniform and nearly bald head. Pathetic.

"Me, too."

He sighed. "Did she tell you I asked her to marry me?"

"What?"

"She said no."

"Paul, you really asked her to marry you?"

"She told me she couldn't do it even though she really wanted to."

"You mean she's thinking about it?" This was wonderful.

"No, I mean she won't."

Paul was desolate, but I barely noticed. The wheels were revving up. "Listen, I'll talk to—"

"Don't even bring it up with her."

"Well I'm sure she'll bring it up to me. I wonder why she hasn't yet. When did you ask her? Last night?"

"The week after you got here."

"No!" I was shocked.

"I'm worried about her, Mattie. She's determined not to be a normal person."

"Don't be ridiculous. She's probably just amazed that you asked her."

"She wasn't amazed. I'm just not in her plans. But I have this terrible feeling she's on a real collision course. She's—"

"C'mon, Paul. Don't let rejection make you weird."

"She says I don't need her."

"You don't need anyone." Never have.

"Not true. She needs you, Mattie. But she knows she won't be able to need you forever."

"For God's sake, Paul, we're just best friends."

No comment. We were more than best friends. I sure as hell needed Jo. I couldn't imagine life without her.

"Don't say anything to her, OK? Unless she does bring it up."

"OK."

"Then, if she does, go to bat for me. All right?"

He reached across the table and touched my hand. When do brothers and sisters get to do that? Never. We were both teary-eyed. "I will, Paul."

"Only if she brings it up."

"Got it."

"Promise?"

"Paul!"

I kept my promise. It was tough.

Though Jo and Louisa and I suffered our love problems silently, we made a lot of noise when we had fun. Two marines and a night-shift worker at the Dole cannery haven't much time for fooling around, so after our classes together, the three of us spent our nights partying, dancing, and water-skiing with the air-force officers from the BOQ at Hickam. Kali, the Mt. Holyoke Hawaiian, and her hundreds of cousins taught us to surf. Surfing is flying without an airplane. Although I have previously thought ill of a person having her first orgasm riding a horse, which is supposed to be common among the elite classes, having your first orgasm aboard a surfboard would be damn terrific.

We wore bikinis and learned, that summer, to no longer be ashamed of small breasts, birthmarks, scars, and fine body hair, which I have a swirl of between my shoulder blades and the small of my back. The more the summer went on, the skimpier the bikinis became, until we were all tanned brown, and felt free.

Associating with Louisa was what we considered our course work that summer. She was the education; the class at the university was not. The Japanese, it turned out, have a great reverence for the babies who were born in concentration camps. They treated Louisa with kid gloves and knew immediately and instinctively upon meeting her that she was a camp baby. Between Louisa and our tour of Pearl Harbor, Jo and I received a feel for World War II, the war the generation before us referred to as "the big one," which to us had been just another movie.

We went out on the monument over the U.S.S. *Arizona*, with the gasoline seeping up out of the water, on a typically beautiful Hawaiian morning, just as beautiful as it was the morning when the planes with the round red balls on the wings zapped it. The monument itself was a white marble wall with all the names of the men who died in battle cut into it. The great white slab rose straight up about thirty-five feet above the water. It was completely covered with the names of the hundreds of boys entombed under the water. Almost qualified as a cenotaph, or soon would, according to my definition, when the bones were washed away to nothing. Every generation has its wall, and I hoped later that the one in Washington would be the last. Right then, in 1964, Vietnam was still a Sir Galahad adventure. Foolish me kept telling myself that Will was Sir Galahad when he was just an expendable cog in a very big, cruel, treacherous, and camouflaged war machine.

At the university, we managed to survive Dr. Roger Rogers's course, "Literature of the Pacific." He would lecture and lecture, oblivious to our yawns and doodlings, our readings of paperback books that did not pertain to the Pacific. Although we suspected it all along, we learned right away that there was no literature of the Pacific, with the exception of James Michener's short stories, which even he admits are "tales," not stories, though they are literature. Besides tales, Dr. Rogers taught Tahitian chants, songs from tribes in Pago Pago, and Captain Cook's log. Not literature. He took us on a field trip to see where Cook had died—beaten to death by Hawaiians who obviously appreciated Pacific literature even less than we did.

So we stood, scratching in the heat, unable to do any

doodling, and waited for Dr. Rogers's monotonous baritone to begin. All we wanted was to be swimming where Captain Cook died rather than grieving. The plaque that marked the spot of Cook's death was in a volcanic rock at the edge of a tiny cove, where the water was as clear as if it came from a tap. We took off our sandals and waded in as unobtrusively as possible, taking care not to offend Cook's ghost, or Rogers, who was known to fly into a rage when excited. We were all whispering among ourselves, waiting for Rogers to begin. Instead of the baritone, he began to cry. He dropped to his knees in front of the plaque, wept for a few minutes, and then pulled himself back up to his feet. His gaze swept across his huddle of shocked students. He raised his fist and shouted:

"Fear not! Captain Cook is among us! He has returned!" Rogers pulled flattened, brown pikake petals out of his pockets and began tossing them on the marker. We immediately forgot how sweaty we were, mesmerized by the display. "He is here with us, at our fingertips, and when we get back to class we will meet him at last." The Hawaiian students glanced furtively at each other. I raised my hand. It was the first time he had recognized a hand.

"Aha! And what is your name?"

"Mattie Price."

"Aha! From Connecticut, Miss Price. From NEW EN-GLAND like the missionaries and whalers who destroyed these islands! Who destroyed these PEOPLE!" And he thrust his finger at the two Hawaiian undergraduates quaking behind Jo and Louisa and me.

Jo whispered, "How'd he know where you're from?" Louisa edged closer. Rogers was her first lunatic Caucasian.

"It is written! All written by Cook himself. Cook reincarnated! Through the pen of the great master—the great master! The great James Michener!" We all stared, what else? Rogers waved his arm toward the bus. "Now we go back to the second half of my course to study the works of the man who is Cook risen! Come! We go!"

With that he bounded away from the rocky beach, waving a copy of *Hawaii* over his head. The kid behind us said he'd seen the movie *South Pacific* and wasn't it too bad the movie *Hawaii* hadn't come out yet.

In the back of the bus, in honor of Roger Rogers, we sang all those fantastic *South Pacific* songs: "Bali Ha'i," "I'm Gonna Wash that Man Right out of My Hair," "What Ain't We Got—We Ain't Got Dames!" I could tell Rogers didn't hear us. He was in the front seat reading the dog-eared, hardcover copy of *Hawaii*. It was the size of a Bible. Some books should really only be in paperback.

At the end of the course, Rogers gave the Hawaiian students A's, the Oriental students B's, and the Caucasians C's. The one black guy in the course, a navy officer, got a C, too.

I asked one of the Hawaiians, who was a full-time student at the university, why Rogers wasn't locked up.

"He publishes."

The University of Hawaii needs to grab any published professor it can get. It's tough for a school to be taken seriously when all of the students are barefoot.

During the last week we had in Hawaii, we took a side trip to Maui. It was much less touristy than Oahu—very New England–like, in fact, with white steeples and replicas of whaling ships. Roger Rogers probably wished Maui would sink. We had a nice, relaxing time. While there, we were invited to a party by some Peace Corps trainees who would be going to Indonesia in September. We played volleyball with them, and swam and picnicked, and they were the most lively, excited people I'd ever been with—absolutely delirious with the joy of living. Rogers would have liked them, too. They were a lot like his Captain Cook. Explorers.

Just for the hell of it, Jo and I filled out some Peace Corps forms. There was no obligation. The trainees talked us into it just in case by next June we might be interested, and then we wouldn't have to go through the paperwork. If we'd known what a tender trap Sargent Shriver had set for people like us, we would have filled out the part that asked if we'd like to request a specific country. When you don't know enough to request, you get Cameroon. People who request ask for Uruguay and get stationed in Montevideo, one of the nicest cities in the world, where they eat steak for breakfast and play baccarat all night. We did check the box that said I WOULD LIKE TO SERVE WITH A SPOUSE, FAMILY MEMBER(S), OR FRIEND(S). I filled in Jo's name, she mine. Then we flew back to Honolulu and forgot the Peace Corps. There were Paul, Will, and George to think about. We thought about them and we didn't see them. Our last week in Hawaii was pretty miserable. Jo never brought up Paul's asking her to marry him. She waited till we were in Africa. And it was terrible to have to leave Louisa.

Twenty or so years after Hawaii, I went with my son on a field trip to Washington. I guess America likes to put the names of the men who died in battle on marble slabs. The one in Washington was black, not white. I read the names, searching back and forth across the gleaming surface of the marble until I found Will's. I sat down on the grass and hugged myself, wrapped my arms around myself and hung on to my sides for something to hang on to. I pressed my forehead to the cold wall and cried. I'd known all along without admitting it to myself that Will had died because he would have answered my letters. But officially losing Will allowed me to finally concede that it was OK to still love him and to love Jo, too. Just because someone leaves you, it doesn't give you the right to be angry and unforgiving.

When we got home again, I went into the attic and got the alligator boots. I gave them to my eldest daughter and told her about Will. She cherished the boots. I found I could think about the gentleness of Will and feel very good, but I still dissolved when a shred of memory of Jo skittered across my mind. And I continued to force her out until the morning I read about her husband in *The New York Times.*

CHAPTER SEVEN

Upon returning to BMC, the first thing we found in our mailboxes was a letter from Lyndon Johnson, thanking us for our Peace Corps applications and informing us that we would be hearing from him again soon. So, our senior year at college was punctuated by correspondence from the President. Around Christmas, he sent us engraved invitations to serve our country as Peace Corps volunteers in the Federal Republic of Cameroon. Out of the packet, as if in answer to our unspoken question, "What is Cameroon?" fell a brochure. A beautiful color brochure, travel-agent variety. On the cover was a picture of the most adorable little African children, all sitting at rickety desks in a run-down classroom, smiling.

"Where the hell is it?" I asked Jo.

"Is what?"

"Cameroon?"

"In the armpit, I believe."

Jo was right. We studied the atlas on her bed. The country was a tick above the equator on the west coast of Africa, just under the great hump. Geographically, we were immediately intrigued; Cameroon had savannas and jungles, mountain ranges and grasslands, and its northern tip reached up to just touch Lake Chad. There was a thirteen-thousand-foot volcano on the coast and just off the coast a tiny little island owned by Spain called Fernando Póo, pronounced "Poe," according to our geography professor. Neat.

But we didn't answer the RSVP. Lyndon was talking two years and we were thinking it would be really fun for maybe a month. Then we got a telegram asking us to please notify the State Department if we were interested in attending the Peace Corps training program for West Cameroon at Columbia University from June 17 to September 3.

"Mattie, was the active volcano in West or East?"

"West. But I'm not going."

"Me neither. But, Mattie, it says if we go to Columbia and finish the course of study, we're still not obligated to go overseas. And we'll earn twelve graduate credits. From Columbia!"

So, all right, I let her show me the enclosed course of study. When it comes to teachers for their training programs, the Peace Corps sure doesn't fool around. We recognized the names of experts in the fields of political science, American history, African studies, etc. There would also be language and culture studies with Cameroonian students presently attending American universities, and lectures with Cameroonian diplomats from the U.N. Every teacher listed had a million letters after his name, except for Gus Piedemonti and his assistant, Stonewall Jackson Washington, from the Columbus Avenue Mobil, who would teach Jeep and Honda maintenance.

At dinner, we passed all the stuff around to our gang. Everyone voted. Eighty people said, yes, go, and two abstained. Bryn Mawr students are a little conservative in that they prefer their thrills to be vicarious. The two abstentions said they abstained because they were so jealous, since they were unable to consider such a possibility, and why should Jo and I have such an adventure just because we were more impulsive than most? By dessert we were promising to send mimeographed letters to the entire class of '65. I didn't want to break their hearts and suggest that perhaps the villages of West Cameroon might not have mimeograph machines at the ready.

Back in our room I said to Jo, "OK, let's go to Columbia. We'll still carry through with our grad-school plans after the summer. Imagine, the Big Apple, no charge. It'll be an incredible summer. We'll get a million twofers. We'll see Streisand in *Funny Girl*. It'll be great. Columbia!"

"Well, I'm going."

"Of course we're going."

"I mean to Cameroon."

My stomach turned over. "No, Jo, you're not. Do you intend to have your twenty-second birthday party under a banana bush in Cameroon?"

Jo's eyes were especially silver. "Banana tree."

"Shit."

"You give great parties, Mattie, even if it will have to be under a banana tree."

"Swell. And who will you invite? Lumumba?"

"I think he's dead, but if he isn't, why not? Although I doubt he'll be able to make it."

"Funny, Jo," I said as she led me to the library. We opened up the reference encyclopedia, volume C, and read.

Three years earlier Cameroon had gained its independence and all the colonials left. The one college and half-dozen secondary schools were under British control in West Cameroon, and the teachers left, too. Naturally, the British, as well as the French in East Cameroon, hadn't trained anyone to take over. So who would teach all those stranded kids? President Kennedy to the rescue. He recommended the spots be filled by recent American college graduates, whom he would train to be teachers. For Cameroon, such a suggestion came right in the nick of time. The little Cameroonian students in our brochure never missed a beat.

We read on. Before World War II, all of Cameroon had been a German colony, spelled "Kamerun." That fact would turn my world, my life, my heart, my relationship with Jo, topsy-turvy. Nazis hid out in places other than Argentina and Bolivia. There is no way I could have known this, though. You get a lot of information from the Encyclopaedia Britannica, but not all.

So Jo and I graduated from Bryn Mawr, Jo, *magna*, and a week later we went to training in New York; my goal was to make Jo realize that we should fudge out in the end and go on to Ohio State, as planned. We had been accepted into the African studies Ph.D. program, which seemed a shrewd choice, since we'd be gaining an awful lot of background at Columbia. But I couldn't convince Jo that I would only be going to the training program, not to Cameroon. She'd just say, "At least you're not a boy. Better Cameroon than Vietnam." My father had a bad time of it when we finally did go because he'd believed me when I told him I wouldn't let anyone send me to any heart of darkness. I needed big-city lights. As for my mother, like most mothers, mine would make a great fortune teller. She knew exactly what I would do. My mother got to casually segue out of her role as mother by replacing care of her children with care of my father when he conceded that, almost overnight, his children were gone, gone completely off on their own, on opposite sides of the world, one in each hemisphere.

Peace Corps training.

Forty-two recent college graduates, thirty-nine of whom were between the ages of twenty-one and twenty-two, living together in a Barnard College dorm on Broadway. Talk about prolonging your adolescence. These people truly were the last frontiersmen; everything we saw in the trainees in Hawaii was there and we were no different. They were wonderful, idealistic, adventurous, happy people. The only three who were not quite the norm were a retired couple who were tired of gardening, and a guy named Michael, who was a few years older than the rest of us. I could tell that, like me, he didn't really want to go through with this Peace Corps business. I was doing it because I couldn't stop myself from trailing along after Jo. He had ulterior motives.

During training, I decided he was cute. He was, and soon I found out that Michael was probably the youngest person in Europe to survive the death camps. Actually, he was rescued from the "commuter" train from Munich to Dachau before it reached its destination. Michael made me want to write a book, once I'd learned his astounding background. Not short stories, but a novel, and I started one. I wrote almost a whole book during my two years in the Peace Corps. I didn't put all the pieces of it together, though, until many years after.

I was attracted to Michael not only because he was cute, but because he was so mysterious. Since my Italian bombardier, I had begun to realize that certain men attracted me because they were intriguing. Will had been especially intriguing. Michael helped me to stop missing Will, whom I'd missed during my whole senior year at Bryn Mawr. I hardly dated, but not because of missing Will so much as that there just weren't any intriguing men in Pennsylvania that I could find.

As the days of Peace Corps training blended one into the other, an exhaustive mash of course work and studying and language and not enough hours to do it all, I became more and more intrigued with Michael. I attempted to charm him. But he held me off, which was a very difficult thing for him to do, because I could tell he liked me. I can be very likable when I want to be.

Jo advised, "Mattie, find another tree to bark up. Better yet, spend more time studying or you won't be able to manage culture shock." Jo knew how shocking an unknown culture could be. The tenements of South Norwalk, full of black people, are a far cry from the Smoky Mountains. "That Michael dwells continuously on something awful. I can tell. Let him be, Mattie, he's busy."

I felt that Jo was right, so I stopped running into him —accidentally on purpose, as we used to say in junior high—but I watched him. I turned Peace Corps training into a science lab, and Michael was my subject. And amazingly, one day as I watched him, I saw someone following him.

It was a Sunday. We were three weeks into Peace Corps training and everyone had taken the Day Liner to Bear Mountain. I'd decided not to go because I wanted to be alone for a day—read the whole Sunday *Times*, think, write. And I'd just gotten my period. The thought of running in and out of the ladies' room on a tourist boat, changing one Tampax after the other, was depressing. Jo went. She was apologetic, but I said, Don't be silly. Jo was thriving on every bit of this training business as if she were training to go to Mars. I left my room around eleven to get a Coke from the machine in the lounge. The lounge was off the hallway, down a few steps—a dark, cool place to sit around and read in on a hot day. A very hot day. New York City heat is a tangible thing with a grin. Just as I reached the doorway, I heard Michael on the phone inside. He was screaming at someone. He was cursing. Michael never did either, scream or curse. I heard him slam the receiver down and then he bolted out of the lounge and out the front door, without seeing me gaping stupidly at him from the dim hall. He didn't shut the big cherry door behind him either. I looked outside. He was rushing through the Barnard gate. That's when I first noticed this short, fat bald man. He wasn't hard to miss, lurking so preposterously in the dense hedge that surrounded the dorm. He was in white shirt-sleeves, and suspenders held up his baggy, European trousers. He waited a moment and went down the sidewalk after Michael.

I ran to the elevator and pushed R for roof. The elevator made no stops, but it still went ten times more slowly that it usually did. The roof was black, hot and sticky. I ran over to the metal railing that edged the roof's perimeter. There was Michael, still rushing along. The old fellow followed him toward the subway station. The instant Michael disappeared down the steps, the man ran, charging into the station right behind him. The guy was agile. I turned around, my back against the view of Broadway. The opposite view was the Hudson, blue and choppy, all kinds of little sails bobbing atop it. Probably very breezy for anyone on board a boat. Even the Day Liner. I was sweating.

As soon as Jo got back, I told her. She said, disdainfully, that I was bored and looking for intrigue. "No wonder you're a good writer, Mattie. You see things nobody else does." Then she told me to come to the West End bar for a drink. That's where they were all going. We loved the West End. LeRoi Jones was always there in the back, surrounded. Time to tie one on. But I said no, I still had cramps. And I felt hurt by Jo. I couldn't guess why she didn't believe me.

"C'mon. You'll forget all your cramps by your third beer." I knew that was true, but I wanted to wait for Michael. I didn't tell her that. Everyone left for the West End, and I hung around the front door, not even going to the ladies' room for fear I'd miss him, expecting yeoman's duty of the Tampax. I didn't miss him. He came back a little after ten, a bit drunk. I staged coming out of the elevator to get a Coke in the lounge.

"Hi, Michael."

"What?" He jumped.

"Are you OK?"

"Of course I am. Where is everybody?"

"West End."

"Why aren't you?"

"I thought I'd wait for you. I wondered where you were."

"Shit," he said. "Mattie, leave me alone, OK? You're very sweet. Very pretty. Do you know what I want to do? Go into the lounge and sit with you on the sofa and neck. But I've got a lot to think about. This is a weird time for me. A lot is happening and it takes up everything, OK?"

He sounded awfully sober for someone who was definitely drunk. He was swaying.

"So who was that guy following you today?"

He stopped swaying. "What guy?"

"The one who looked like Isaac Bashevis Singer, only chubby."

Michael grabbed me by my arms, turned me around, and pushed me down the steps into the lounge. He threw me onto the couch and stood over me like a madman. This must be rape, I decided. He leaned down, grabbed my arms again, and pulled me toward his hysterically angry face. The dorm was empty. Nobody would rescue me. I started to involuntarily cry. It wouldn't be as bad as rape, but murder was still awfully tough to face. When I was crying, he realized what he was doing. He let go of me.

"Oh God, Mattie, I'm sorry." I fell into the cushions. "I can't have anybody know about any of this." He was even more relieved than I that I wasn't going to be raped or strangled. Then, still standing over me, he placed his hand on my head, like a bishop, like the pope. He stared at me.

"It was an accident that I saw that guy following you," I said. I sounded very in control, though I wasn't.

"Yes."

He was thinking. I waited. He sat down beside me. I had nothing to say that made much sense like, "Oh, forget it." So he said:

"Mattie, will you please forget about it. Will you be a plain old friend like you've been and just forget it?"

"Michael," I answered, "don't you like me?"

His troubled face broke up and rearranged into its normal face, which rearranged itself into a smiling face. He laughed. "I do like you. How could I not?" He put his arm around my shoulder, but I don't think he noticed that he had. "It's bad timing. Real bad, OK? I have something so important to do. I can't get . . . this is such a stupid way to say it . . . I can't get involved with you."

I sat forward so that his arm stayed on the back of the couch and not on me. "Well . . . I have something important to do, too. Help a Third World nation stay on its feet. So, good-bye." I struggled to my feet. The sofa had no springs and I was sitting at knee level. He yanked me back down, half on his lap.

"Listen, we'll get together sometime soon instead of now. How about that?"

"Maybe."

He smiled. He was Michelangelo's *David* for sure. It appeared to me that we kissed. *Smooched* is a better word, because it was quick, a punctuation mark at the end of a sentence. I was worried about him and, of course, I was dying to know what he was up to. I wanted to kiss some more, but I couldn't scare him off either. "Michael, let's go down to the West End with everyone and have a drink."

"I've drunk enough tonight."

"Then what's one more?"

"I don't think so."

"You'll blow your cover if you don't." I smiled. He didn't, but he sighed sweetly.

"OK, Mattie, but as much as I'd like it, you can't become a part of my cover."

"I wouldn't want to. I have my own problems."

"Yeah. Saving the world."

"Shut up."

He stood and pulled me up out of the sofa. I'm tall; Michael isn't. We were eyeball to eyeball. And then our eyes were closed and I found that kissing Michael, serious kissing, was like sinking into quicksand. He held me in his arms after the kiss for a brief moment and stepped back. "Let's go."

We did. Cover for what, I wondered, after my head cleared. For what? I wanted desperately to ask, but I didn't.

We caused a lot of raised eyebrows when we walked into the West End hand-in-hand. I laughed at everyone and told them I was merely holding Michael up because he'd just gotten back from many beers with some old college buddies. Jo looked askance. I went to the bathroom.

I sat with Jo and our friends and Michael went off with a couple of guys to the pinball machine. It was two in the morning before people started drifting out, and I dawdled, and Michael dawdled. Jo was a little anxious, I could tell, but she left without me, and Michael and I were alone in the bar, in a corner with two more beers. It was one of those times when you find someone you want to tell your life story to. Like Will wanted to tell me. Michael said what he told me wasn't part of the cover, it was just how he was born. He told me he'd been taken off a train between

Munich and Dachau by a young woman who had given her baby to someone for safekeeping. His mother had died in labor just minutes earlier. The woman who saved his life escaped from the train and made her way to the Swabian Alps. The details were absolutely extraordinary. He was smashed. He said the man responsible for everything was named Wilhelm von Hiltz, and he was still alive. How can I rest, he asked his beer, not me, knowing this crud is still walking around free?

The next day, I went to the library instead of classes and there really was a von Hiltz, a colonial governor of Kamerun. But he'd died just before the war. He did have a son, born in Kamerun. Mother—Pauline Schlimmer. The son returned to Germany in 1918 to the family schloss in Bavaria. And that family schloss was later used as a rest house for the Führer before the Eagle's Lair was built not far away. The whereabouts of the Baroness Pauline and her son, Wilhelm, were presently unknown.

Michael figured this von Hiltz guy had gone back to his birthplace to hide out. To Kamerun!

I checked out a book of pre–World War II maps. I checked out *Baby and Child Care*, Dr. Spock. I checked out so many books I had to make three trips to the dorm to get them there. I ran to the bookstore and bought a new notebook. Then I went to my room and wrote the story of Michael's birth as well as the birth of von Hiltz. Without even realizing it, on July 17, 1965, I started writing a book in the style of popular thrillers, which I loved to read.

I created the details of von Hiltz's life in the German colony. I wrote character sketches of the baron and of Pauline Schlimmer. I made her the baron's mistress. I drew a parallel between the sterilized care for Pauline during the birth of Wilhelm and the gory mess of Michael's birth. And I built the beautiful schloss over Buea, the one mentioned to us in one of our classes, a replica of the baron's schloss in Bavaria that he'd built to persuade Pauline to accompany him to Kamerun.

I created Michael's adoptive mother, a young Jewish girl

who witnesses his birth, who saves his life after handing her own baby over to safe hands. I named her Elisabeth. And I had this girl and the baby make their way, hidden in the back of a truck, to Ulm in the Swabian Alps. An old man directs her to a flat plateau, high above Ulm, where a British spy plane lands. She and the baby are rescued and taken away to Great Britain.

CHAPTER
EIGHT

Jo shook me. I had fallen asleep from the effort of writing down all that Michael had told me, and especially from making up all those details. Jo read it. And when she was done, she hugged me.

"It's so good, Mattie. It really is."

"I've never done anything this long. Is it really?"

"Oh yes. What happens?"

"You know what happens. Michael grows up and joins the Peace Corps."

"No! I mean what happens in your story?"

My story. "I don't know."

"Well, when you do, hurry up and write it down because I'm dying with worry."

"Oh, don't worry about me. I'm—"

"Not about you, Mattie . . . about Elisabeth. About the baby."

Jo wasn't worried about craft and imagery and leit-motivs. I decided not to show my novel to my father because those were the things he worried about. Plot was more fun. I'd have to do some kind of outline and figure out what exactly would happen to Elisabeth and the baby.

"Ready for dinner?"

"Yes." I was starved.

Jo studied hard during Peace Corps training, and learned

so much that several professors asked her to consider Columbia after her Peace Corps service. Not only would she be a brilliant graduate student; what professor wouldn't want a research assistant who was a silver-blond, silvereyed, Italian? Jo seemed to become more beautiful every day. And she was eating more. A little more. Just enough so that, as Jo was about to turn twenty-two, her body went from an adolescent's to a woman's. I'd look in the mirror at myself. No change.

But she was really determined to help Third World people become part of the First. I wanted adventure. Maybe that's why I wasn't changing. Jo's body was responding to her mind. Mine had nothing to respond to. In the Peace Corps, we both got what we wanted, I more than I bargained for, Jo less.

Two guys were drafted out of our training program. They went to Vietnam. Some draft boards were less tolerant than others. I couldn't remember their names when I went to see the wall, but I hoped they made it because they were nice guys. Maybe they went to Canada, I decided, after seeing Will's name.

I learned more in those three months at Columbia than I did in four years at Bryn Mawr. I learned about the real world, though I didn't know the depth of Kumba Lake, or the length of the Tiko River, the way Jo did. I was forcibly immersed in the reality of Cameroon's struggle to survive. The country's effort to leap out of poverty, to educate its children, was inspiring. I would fall asleep at night wondering how our whacky group of sixties Americans—committed, but still whacky—could convince the Bakweris that the thing that made them so sick was the little snails along the edge of the water where they swam. Schistosomiasis. But I believed, being committed, that we would convince them. I'd say to the Cameroonians, Teach me how to get a chigger out of my toe, and I'll show you a chart that will explain schistosomiasis. American cartoon-pictures of snails, and teeny-tiny eggs, and the eggs hatching in some blood vessel in your arm.

I don't know exactly how or when it happened, but I couldn't wait. We all couldn't wait. Cameroon, here we come! And as we waited, we began to see that we weren't all the same; we were very different from one another—represented every race, every religion, and we ran the gamut of political feelings. There were those among us who were a little more conservative than others of us, and when we got to Cameroon and the conservative element got chiggers in their feet, they panicked and went to the Peace Corps doctor, who thought that the small white bump just under the skin was as easy to take out as a sliver. Then he'd pierce the bump with his sharp little scalpel, and the bump would burst—the membrane containing the egg sac thinner than American doctors thought they could possibly be. Breaking it would lead to an infection, so the Peace Corps doctor gave you a Band-Aid and ten days of penicillin. Whereas the village doctor—witch doctor, as we'd tell the folks back home—would take a shred of rock-hard bamboo, cut through the fine top layer of your skin without your feeling it, and lift out the egg sac whole. He'd smile, you'd smile, and then you'd give him a bottle of aspirin as payment and you'd never even need a Band-Aid.

We learned a lot about ourselves. We had to see a psychiatrist once a week, individually, all during training so others could learn about us, too. Lyndon wasn't sending kooks to Cameroon. It was tough seeing a psychiatrist because this was prefeminism. The shrink told me it was difficult for him to deal with so many abnormal girls. He said girls at my stage of development (i.e., recent college grad) wanted to get married and have babies. They didn't want to go off to Africa for two years. This was normal behavior for boys (i.e., Ernest Hemingway). He was really curious to know what went wrong in our childhood to cause us to do something so neurotic. In those Freudian days there were two groups of neuroses, male and female. There were three or four neuroses typical of males, and eight million typical of women.

So we were supposed to pussyfoot around with this psychiatrist and his cuckoo assistants because if they suspected a trainee was unstable, the trainee was out. I assumed that meant if I punched one of their smug little faces I would immediately be considered unstable. It was truly grit-your-teeth time.

"Oh," I said chattily, "I'm just putting that hubby-and-kiddies stage of my life on hold for two years. I want to see the world."

"Wouldn't a trip to Europe for the summer suffice?"

"Gee, I don't have the money."

"You know, Mattie, we think of men as wanting to pull up roots and go out and see the world, not pretty girls."

"How about ugly girls? A lot of us are ugly, actually." Smile, Mattie, and keep gritting.

This one clinician was kind of cute and in the wrong profession for sure. I made him laugh. During one session he asked me to lunch. He took me to the Algonquin because in my questionnaire, under "hobbies," I'd put in "creative writing." It was very sweet of him and told me a lot. He drank several Bloody Marys. That told me a lot, too. During dessert—my dessert; he had another Bloody Mary—he said, "We're just jealous, you know. Dr. Goldfarb and the rest of us, we're jealous. We don't have what it takes to do what you're doing. Here you are, just young girls, not the least bit chicken like us. You'll be great at this Peace Corps stuff, all of you. Good luck, Mattie."

The guy was practically crying. Of course, he was drunk, but besides, he was really upset. I patted his hand. Nothing worse than a twenty-five-year-old who's already a stuffed shirt. "Listen, Dr. Abbott, will you do me a favor?"

"Anything," he sniffled.

"If you really want to see some healthy psyches, why don't you get us some time in Columbia's swimming pool—say, twice a week. God, it's a hot summer."

He did. I bragged at our first biweekly splash party that they could all thank me. They did. Michael wasn't there. I had to drag Jo because she wanted to study for a malaria test. Actually, she was afraid of contracting malaria. Jo was so mature. None of us worried the least bit about catching all those dengue fever, bilharzia, schisto things. I told Jo to stash a couple of cans of Off in her suitcase and she'd be fine.

The best part of our training program was when we met Cameroonians. One afternoon, our whole group was bused just like Cub Scouts down to the U.N., where we got to meet the Cameroonian ambassador and his staff. Their robes flowed, their black faces beamed, and we loved every one of them. We were told to call the diplomats "Honorable Mr. So-and-So," but they all had robes and we couldn't tell who were the secretaries and who were the diplomats. This sweet little Mormon girl with freckles asked one of them, "I'm sorry, are you honorable?" These Cameroonians sure knew how to laugh. After that, they kept asking us if **we** were honorable, too.

Then, they got us a place on the floor in the General Assembly and we got to listen to a debate about a harbor in Ceylon. After the session we sat in the delegates' chairs. I got to be France and I put on my little earphones at the horseshoe table. A comedian in our group finagled his way to the Russian seat. He stuck a big blob of gum on his cheek to resemble a Russian wart, took off his shoe, and began pounding the table, shouting, "We will bury you!"

We were all thrown out, but the two Cameroonian attachés in charge of us laughed all over themselves. They said, "Ah, you Peace Corpse! You bring the real U.S. to us. Very funny people, you U.S."

Then we told the Peace Corps staff member to get rid of our tour bus, we'd make our own way back to Columbia. We took the two Cameroonians to a pizza joint where, between them, they dumped the whole jar of red pepper on their slices of pepperoni pizza. We'd been told that West African food was hot and spicy. Now we had an inkling as to just how hot and spicy.

When training drew to a close, and we had some idea of the teaching positions available in Cameroon, we all hoped for that part of Cameroon we'd been most intrigued by. I wanted the coast of Cameroon because I love water. And I wanted Michael nearby. He was still as intriguing to me as the Cameroonian shoreline. We all knew Jo, as the smartest, would be placed at the elite College of Bamenda, West Cameroon's only school of higher education. They needed someone to teach American culture, history, and literature. She hoped desperately that she'd be assigned to the college. As it turned out, she was. And I got the beach. We were both happy, but cried, too, knowing we would be separated for the first time since seventh grade by not too many miles, but by a thirteen-thousand-foot mountain and a rain forest that was so dense it was selected to be the setting of a Tarzan movie twenty years later. I told Jo that she was lucky to be going to a place of such supposed beauty—the rolling highlands of Bamenda, which were purportedly a replica of Scotland, only better.

They were.

CHAPTER NINE

We got to go home for five days before leaving for Africa. We cried at our impending parting, but Jo cried for an extra reason. My brother, Paul, on his way to Panama, asked her not to go, to come instead with him. Then I cried because Paul was so heartbroken and Jo so staunch, but mostly because Jo really did love Paul, though, unfortunately, in the same way she loved me. We were her family. I tried to get her to change her mind even though it meant my going to Cameroon and her not. I didn't know if I could get along without her, but at the same time it meant her children would be my nieces and nephews.

"C'mon, Jo, maybe you only *think* you love him like a brother. He's a sexy guy." I kept from her the conversation I'd already had with Paul in Hawaii. I was surprised that I could keep something from Jo that easily.

"I'll never love any man more than I do Paul, Mattie, not in the way that I do."

"But he adores you."

"I want something other than adoration. Paul doesn't need me."

"Why would you want him to? You want to be your husband's mother?"

"Of course not. I've been enough people's mother." She looked down into her beer.

"Meaning me?"

"Don't take it wrong, Mattie. You've mothered me, too. We've been everything to each other—mother, sister, friend. . . . I want someone who needs me in order to do something great. Something fantastic. Something that will make the front page of *The New York Times*."

"Paul will probably do that . . . when he discovers a new nebula or something."

"I agree. But he won't need me to do that. Paul will never need anyone and I'm not going to spend my life at awards dinners listening to people tell me how proud I must be of him."

"What about making the front page of *The New York Times* yourself? You guys could be the Curies."

"I'd rather be the backbone of the team. I don't want limelight. There are too many people where I've come from who I want never to hear of me again."

"Oh." She was worried about being blackmailed by all those Smoky Mountain people. "What a bunch of shit, Jo. Behind every great man lies a drudge."

"That's right."

"You want to be a drudge?"

"If that's what it takes, then yes. I'm used to it at least." She gave me her "let's end this" look and smiled. "You'll be the household name, Mattie. You're the one with the talent. I'm just smart."

"Ha!"

"You'll see. Pulitzer Prize winner."

"Oh sure." That was exactly what I intended to be, actually.

"So how's Paul going to handle all this?" I said, more to myself than to Jo.

"I've told him that if we're both free at the end of the Peace Corps, we'll try to take it from there."

"You figure he'll have found someone else by then."

"He'll have to. He loves sex."

"God damn Mary Lou Grabowsky."

"What?"

"Nothing. Jo, are you sure you're not throwing something too wonderful away?"

"I have to find a brand-new life. I have no one, really. I'm going to start all over again."

"What's that supposed to mean? What about me?"

"Mattie, I don't think I'm ever going to come back here."

"To this country, or Connecticut?"

"To this country."

Damn.

"You'll have your own life with a new family and there really will be nothing here for me."

"I hope you know what you're talking about because I sure don't."

"I really do."

"Good."

My father stuck his head in the kitchen and said, "Ready to go, girls?"

We stared at each other over our beers, across my mother's authentic metal kitchen table from the thirties, and we clutched hands. We were girls again ... the two of us together ... scared stiff as we took our next step out.

The whole way to the airport I absorbed every familiar sight, holding back the panic. Not only would I not see any of it for two whole years, Jo wasn't going to come back with me. Even though I believed her, it didn't stop me from vowing that it wouldn't happen. Then I tried to think of Paris. We had an eighteen-hour layover there on the way to Africa. Paris, Paris, Paris, I kept saying to myself.

At Kennedy, we were immediately informed by our beaming Columbia liaison that Pan Am had introduced a new flight direct to Dakar, Conakry, Abidjan, and Douala, Douala being in Cameroon. Twenty-two hours direct, he kept saying. In the VIP lounge, where Pan Am so kindly sequestered us, knowing full well that we would mutiny, we mutinied. But it helped us a lot. Instead of being nervous all the way to Cameroon, we bitched. Bitched about each and every Paris sight we'd planned on seeing for eighteen hours. Instead of Montmartre, we were getting Conakry.

In the departure area, my mother and father seemed very small as they waved good-bye to me after I'd peeked over my shoulder even though I promised myself I wouldn't. Jo saw, threw her arm around my shoulders, and dragged me along. From the plane I spotted them walking, leaning into each other, outside the Pan Am hangar. My mother had changed to pants for the ride home. Now they really were small, tinier than ants, and I felt such a pang in my heart. I looked away. What was I doing on this airplane? Whatever was I thinking of when I joined the Peace Corps? I never joined the Peace Corps. I fell into it.

I saw Michael leaning over the guy in the seat next to him so that he could look out the window, too. Michael's mother had been in the departure area also. She looked like his older sister, her eyes as determined as Michael's. Now, lying back into my cushy seat, I thought about how she was sending him to find this Nazi who represented the destruction of her home, her family, her life. Michael was thrilled to be able to do this for her. I hated Michael's mother. He wasn't meant to be a fanatic. He couldn't help it that he'd survived, that she'd saved him. I was wrong. Real fanatics aren't much different from the rest of us. And sometimes a fanatic doesn't necessarily stay a fanatic. I learned that in the person of Ahmad ibn-Burash.

Pan Am fed us every three hours as we flew backward into time. Night lasted just a few hours. The closer we got to Africa, the worse the food. Nobody could sleep. Thirty-eight recent college graduates on our way to a country where the women's breasts were uncovered. That alone was enough to make us gag with fear and tense anticipation. So my friends slept, or drank, or played cards, or read *Cry, the Beloved country* (Jo). I wrote. I had to make a tough transition—getting Michael and his mother out of England and into the United States at the end of the war.

Hours later I stopped writing even though I didn't want to. The plane was making its first stop. I would be touching

Africa in a few minutes and I was slightly more interested in what was happening to me than what would happen to my fictional Michael.

It was dawn in Dakar, and all the runways were deserted: an empty airport surrounded by a flat misty jungle, dark and—if you were Joseph Conrad—inviting. We could have gotten off the plane to stretch our legs, but none of us did. We just watched. We were waiting for Cameroon. Our Cameroon, too loyal to get out of the plane until we got there.

Coming into Douala we had to fly into a shroud so thick we couldn't see the mountain. The great estuary surrounding Douala gave up thick masses of dense moisture. It was the rainy season, we knew, but we didn't know that the rainy season meant living underwater. That was what it was like getting off onto the runway in Douala; we were heading into and under the brackish estuary itself.

They shoveled us through the rain battering the airfield into little planes that said CAT on their sides. It meant Cameroon Air Transport. Mixed with the rain was invisible volcanic ash. You could feel it. This was not American rain. It was African rain. It excited me. Without anyone being aware of it, our resident Mormon went to the bathroom and never came out. She holed up until an American official from the embassy came to see that she flew right back on the same Pan Am jet that we had come out on. The African rain did not excite her one bit—it crippled her. We thought Mormons were used to that sort of thing. Then again, she was the only one of us who drank orange juice at breakfast instead of screwdrivers.

From the CAT planes, Mount Cameroon showed its face for a quick few seconds, just enough to welcome us. It was a deeper shadow in the shroud, an apparition that was not something even remotely real. No one remarked on it either, it happened so fast, each of us imagining that our adrenaline was playing tricks on our brain.

We flew to Buea, five thousand feet up the mountain— the toy capital of West Cameroon; the entire town had been built by the Germans above the malaria-infested estuary. Buea was blanketed with musty smells, the atmosphere full of mold. The Germans had gone back to Berlin during the rainy season. I could understand why.

The Buea Mountain Hotel was perched on the edge of a mountain ledge that held the town, a pocket in the mountainside. We knew that in a few weeks, once the rains left, the view would be spectacular. Now you could see just a few yards ahead of you. We were told that if we wanted to see the mountain, it would appear early in the morning. The rising sun would successfully burn off the fog for a very short time and reveal the volcano; then both would be gobbled back up again by the thick mists.

Everyone set their alarms for five A.M., but shut them off and went back to sleep. The first night in Buea we'd sampled palm wine in a town bar, the Tip-Top. Mountain-viewing was postponed. But, unlike everyone else, I wanted to be stationed in Buea. I didn't care so much about those Scotland-like hills of Bamenda. I wanted to be near the ocean, as I've always been, even if the Bight of Benin, lying around the base of Mount Cameroon, was flat and tepid, without mussel and slipper shells in the sand. And the mountain intrigued me. I wanted to live on the side of an active volcano. I'd said that to my father. He laughed and told me I was an active volcano.

So, with my head throbbing with a new African variety of hangover, I stepped out of the dark hotel corridor into the wet garden. Old fog dripped from the big green leaves that hung all around. It was pitch-dark, but I could make out the white tables and the bright folded Cinzano umbrellas. I opened one of the umbrellas and it sheltered me. I waited.

A little bit of light broke into the garden from somewhere and I saw someone else standing just a few feet away from me. It was Michael. I didn't want to disturb him. In fact, I didn't want to disturb myself, but when the mountain slowly developed above us, like a Polaroid picture, I couldn't help myself. The immense hulk got bigger and clearer and blacker and I whispered, "Michael." He jumped a little and turned. "Isn't it scary?"

I heard him breathe. "Yes. It really is."

He was glad I was there. The mountain brightened slightly to dark-green before fading away, first to a shadow, and then it was gone. As big as the mountain was, its summit was hidden behind ridges high above us. In pictures it was a Napoleon's hat rising out of the coast. Up close, it bulged and broke, and as far as Michael was concerned, hid secrets in its crevices. As if someone had pressed a button, the show ended, and now the dim Buea morning began.

"Still want to be stationed here?" I knew that was what he wanted because this town was where von Hiltz was born.

"I will be here." He caught himself. "I think."

I didn't let it go by. "How do you know you'll be here?"

He cleared his throat. "There's a post here available and they need a man, preferably someone older. I fit the bill. Teaching in the prison farm. I found out about it and asked for the job."

"How'd you find out?"

He smiled. "Same way. Asked."

"I'd like to be here, too, or at least near the coast."

"Well, maybe you'll get Victoria."

"I hope."

Directly below Buea, Victoria was on the water, a small city really, supposedly bustling. I wasn't interested in bustle. I liked Buea. Probably because I liked Joseph Conrad. If Professor Roger Rogers were around, maybe he'd tell me I was Conrad's reincarnation. I chuckled, too softly for Michael to hear.

Later on, amidst pandemonium, our Peace Corps director announced posts, and after each announcement everyone fluttered through their papers and their maps, exclaiming about what a great place it was. Michael became the first schoolmaster at the Buea prison farm. People kidded him about going to jail. "Hope you like stripes, Mike." Jo was going to the college, as we knew she would, and she beamed. I wasn't assigned anywhere. The director called me over. He told me I wouldn't be teaching. It seemed that since the country's population of secondary-school graduates was growing so rapidly, these young people needed a library. Would I mind trying to set up a public library? I was the only one who had worked in a college library. I didn't mention that all I did was send out overdue notices.

"Where?"

"Right here. In Buea."

"I'll do it."

Jo congratulated me. How lucky I was, everyone was saying, to get to actually make something that might be around forever. Just like the Peace Corps brochures. The director, who'd memorized all our names from pictures, told all of us:

"Martha here will have an office right in the hotel. And she'll live in one of the little cottages where the hotel workers live. It truly is the kind of job we in the Peace Corps get excited about." Then he started telling everyone what a challenge I'd have finding a piece of land and getting the government to help.

While he spoke, I wondered how I would manage. Find a piece of land. This was going to be good. Maybe I'd be the first person fired from the Peace Corps. Take a rest, our director told us all, and then we'll get a convoy going down to Victoria for some supplies and have a nice swim before heading out to our posts.

"It doesn't rain quite so badly along the coast as it does here. Does anyone mind swimming in a bit of a drizzle?" he asked.

"Noooooooooooo . . ."

I didn't rest before the good-bye splash party. I hurried back to my notebook so I could try and get Michael to the States. The weather made me feel just like Graham Greene.

Michael's mother was given a job at Oxford. Cleaning. I wasn't thinking of a charwoman, but more of Jo's mother. She met a professor and he fell in love with her. They got married. A few years later, when Michael was a little boy, Elisabeth's professor took an offer to teach at Yale. They moved from Oxford to Bethany, Connecticut.

It was Michael who distracted me. I saw him across the

lounge leaving the hotel. I stretched and rubbed the back decided to join him, but instead, I ended up following him. He wasn't very good at noticing people who followed him.

He turned out of the hotel drive and started down the road toward Buea-town. The cloud bank broke into round, stout balls, and the sun's rays fought their way through the spaces, bouncing off the fine mist and casting magnificent rainbows all around. The perfect arches shimmered for just a few seconds before the clouds meshed and swallowed them up again. I knew that sun showers were common in Buea as the rainy season drew to a close, but no one had warned us of the beauty they created. We were only prepared for mud, not rainbows. The sun's equatorial intensity, when it peeked through, felt like an electric blanket. I looked up, but the mountain remained hidden.

Michael avoided the numerous potholes and the crooked, gaping fissures filled with hip-high bands of bright-green elephant grass—the same grass that edged the rain forest on either side of the road. A mile from the hotel was a traffic circle—a roundabout—where two stony dirt roads extended from the base of a sign painted with two arrows: The south-pointing arrow said POST OFFICE, the north BUEA-TOWN. Michael headed toward town. He stopped a Cameroonian and the man pointed up the mountain. He took a dirt road—two tire ruts, actually—that probably went up to the prison farm. There was nothing else above the town.

Buea. I took it all in and I remembered the lessons. Buea, the state seat created by the German colonizers high above the heat, humidity, and mosquitoes of Victoria. The seaward side of Mount Cameroon enjoyed an air temperature that never varied from that of a delightful, Alpine spring. During the assailing rains of summer, before World War I, a leisurely cruise back to Germany set sail each year, leaving behind only a skeleton force to deal with the Bueans, who barely managed to survive on the only food that refused to rot in the yearly soakings—cabbage.

Even though a few German administrative habits passed

on to Cameroon's next troop of colonists, the British and French, who conveniently divided the area between them, splitting tribes at will, the Germans were the ones who left substantial physical remnants of their presence. In the center of the roundabout Michael passed, hidden in a tangle of six-foot-high weeds, was a bust of Bismarck, staring condescendingly down upon everyone who passed his marble pedestal. His stone eyes were realistically piercing, and his fat moustache, suddenly stylish again, finely carved. He went unnoticed by Michael, who might have spotted the blackened statue if the sun had been shining at that moment, as it was when I walked by. In the sunshine, reflected rays of light danced on the needle sticking out of the top of the helmet, and except for this occasional, high, dazzling diamond, the statue went ignored, not only by Michael, but by all but a few Bueans who had forgotten that the ugly thing was there. What I didn't know was that those few Bueans who knew it was there revered the thing—at least according to Michael's father, whom I would meet. Not the professor I'd made up—his real father, who also survived the Holocaust, the husband of the mother who died on the train.

Michael moved on past a tall, pillared building constructed entirely of river stone. It had once served as a homey maternity ward where unhappy *hausfraus* delivered their babies under expert medical care, while Cameroonian women waited in long lines outside the door with a shred of hope that the German doctors might give them some medication for the babies in their arms, dying from diseases brought to them by their colonizers.

Suddenly, to the northwest, on another ledge just east of Buea-town, a mirage appeared. Michael stopped, and so did I. The clouds parted and a dwarf castle from a German fairy tale appeared, so authentic that it might have been lifted right out of a Bavarian forest, and it was seemingly suspended in air beyond the tiny African town. It hung over all heads, all buildings, all trees: above all of Cameroon but for the great mountain itself. It was now the residence of the prime minister of West Cameroon—kind of a governor's mansion.

I had pictured the schloss just as Michael had—Michael had dreamed of it, in fact, but neither of us could have imagined the power it had over its surroundings. What we couldn't see, but what we knew was there, was the large scrolled letter *P*, embedded in the great wrought-iron gate. Now it stood for prime minister. A funny little story from training. Soon Michael would climb up there, take a tour of the boyhood home of a Nazi, a monster—perhaps an engineer of the Holocaust.

The schloss faded away. Michael gazed into the clouds where the ghostly house now hid itself from view, and his lips moved. I wondered which curse he had chosen for the occasion. Or a vow maybe.

I went back to the hotel. It was not time to run into Michael. Besides, I didn't want to think of the evil that had once ruled this lovely place. I put myself in my mother's shoes as I walked back, taking a different route by the post office and other government buildings. Now where was a good spot for a public library? Damned if I knew.

Before we were dispersed toward Kumba and Bamenda and Nkambe and Tiko and all the towns whose names now rolled off our tongues with ease, we went back down the mountain in the Jeeps and motorcycles that were issued to us—one to each school. I got a little Jeep since I would, hopefully, be carting books around. Michael got a Honda 250 to get him up and down the mountain.

We arrived at the black-sand beach, which was bordered by coconut palms filled with monkeys. We played touch football, and the monkeys imitated us, raining the beach with coconuts. When we swam in the hot, calm Bight in the fine mist, the monkeys laughed at the sight. Except for the monkeys, it reminded me a lot of Hawaii. The Hawaiian monkeys were in the Honolulu Zoo, not at the beach. I thought of Will and the thirsty giraffe.

Michael had reappeared in time to join us. He would

have a neighbor in Buea after all. Me. And he didn't like it. I told him I'd been given a little rag-top Jeep to cart my books around in—what books, I had no idea—and that if he ever needed a ride to Victoria to get supplies I'd be glad to give him a lift. He said no, that he'd manage in the local market.

He did, too. Michael wore native shirts and ate egusi soup and foo-foo corn. Once in a while, I'd see him zip by on his Honda and he'd wave. But he hardly ever left the prison farm, and he surely didn't invite me up there for a visit. I pretty much forgot him, and my novel, too. My notebook ended up in a drawer, the first thing I put in what eventually became a junk drawer just like the ones at home: full of matchbooks with one match, batteries, tape, toothpicks, and rubber bands. Plus one unfinished novel.

My father opened an account for me at Barclay's Bank. I felt a little guilty, but there was a hotel on the sea in Victoria run by a German couple who were great cooks and who had an ice cream machine. I'd go down there once a week on my dad's money and eat like a maniac, and then the German would come and sit with me during dessert and pour me a schnaaps. "On the house," he'd say, and laugh, pleased with his command of the English language. I liked to think he was Michael's Nazi, but he was too young. A few British expatriates and this particularly annoying, though very gorgeous, Italian who represented AGIP, began to notice my weekly visits. One evening he joined me, and picked up the tab. My father's money accumulated because there was nothing else for me to spend it on. Except the movies. Ten-ten francs to get in. About a cent and a half.

Every Saturday night, wooden folding chairs were set up in the town meeting hall for all the Bueans to watch the latest film from India—in Urdu, no subtitles. The films were hilarious, consisting mostly of costumed maidens with bells on their fingers and toes, showering rose petals down upon the heads of fat little babies dressed in turbans and robes. The Cameroonians laughed themselves silly, and so did I. One week, the man who ran the show somehow got a copy of Alfred Hitchcock's *The Birds*. The townspeople were so frightened, especially for me, insisting that I was Tippi Hedren. I told them that even though I looked just like her (I look absolutely nothing like her), she was an actress but I was just me. They were doubtful and worried about me for weeks afterward, checking on me quite often to make sure I hadn't been eaten by birds. Birds are scarce in Buea, so there was that fear of the unknown, too.

In the building that held the meeting hall was a conference room that nobody ever conferred in. The government official I spoke to told me I could use the room for my library if I liked. He was skeptical.

But once I had that room, things seemed to fall into place. The local carpenters started building shelves, the Peace Corps office in Yaoundé sent me a typewriter, and Bryn Mawr students and alumni began sending books. All the kids in Buea-town unpacked and stacked books. Kids love stacking things. I typed catalog cards and grew to detest the Dewey decimal system. The whole thing was fun—working, living there in Buea, and taking long walks along the mountainside. Someday, before leaving, I'd climb the mountain. Someday. But it was like being a New Yorker who never goes out to the Statue of Liberty. I never climbed Mount Cameroon. Michael did.

I ran into Michael once at the post office. I told him about the German who ran the hotel in Victoria. Michael knew about him, knew he was from Berlin, and that his wife was actually Dutch. His wife's family had thrown her out when she married him and they'd come to find their place in a Third World country where they could be successful. I was amazed. He'd sure checked the guy out. Wrong German. And no, even though he'd like to go down and have dinner with me at the Victoria hotel, his prisoners had exams coming up, and he worked with them in the evenings. Sorry, Mattie. I said, "OK." I kissed him good-bye on the cheek. I don't know why. He wavered, he looked into my eyes, and then he said sorry again.

I felt bad. I liked him. That night, I took my notebook out from the junk drawer, and Michael grew up, a little Jewish boy from England in the goldfish bowl of a university community.

CHAPTER TEN

I visited Jo for Thanksgiving. I told all my Cameroonian "librarians" about this special holiday that I wanted to spend with my best friend. They'd never heard of a festival that only lasted one day. They told me to stay a week and really celebrate. I decided three days. The day before Thanksgiving, the carpenters of Bonjongo, a village outside of Buea, presented me with a remarkable gift for my library, which I kept telling them was their library. These carpenters were actually artisans who did beautiful carvings, even though, for me, they made fine, smooth shelves. They were really a cooperative and sold their artwork through Save the Children. They'd been very curious about this picture I had of a card catalog, and when I explained that a person could find any book in the library by looking into the card catalog, they whispered, *"Juju, juju . . ."* and looked at each other, eyelids lowered, crazy about the mysterious.

I told them that I'd asked the embassies in Yaoundé to donate a card catalog, but hadn't gotten very far. All the embassy people said they would inspect my premises and if they determined that what I'd done qualified as a library, they'd consider my request. This one particular carpenter from Bonjongo could see I was really disappointed. Cameroonians can't stand to see anyone disappointed.

So the day before Thanksgiving, a huge lorry pulled up

in front of the library building, filled with the entire population of Bonjongo, all beaming like mad. The carpenters, the *mamis*, the kids, and a few goats. Cameroonians never travel without a few goats. Sort of like a few living thermos bottles of milk for the kids. In two minutes I looked like Yul Brynner's girlfriend in *The King and I,* surrounded by kids dancing around, though mine were in their shirts and had bare bottoms. (Bare bottoms meant they weren't toilet-trained yet.) The adults hefted over the side of the lorry a solid mahogany card catalog with little brass pulls molded into tiny alligators and curled-up snakes. The pulls, and the attached rods going through the drawers, were so meticulously polished that they looked like 24-karat gold, not brass.

The thing must have weighed two tons, and the grain of the wood was designed by God. My card catalog was more magnificent than any piece of furniture I'd ever seen. I couldn't help myself, and burst into tears, causing terrible consternation. Cameroonians never cry with joy. They have so much hardship that their tears are always sorrowful. They thought I hated the card catalog. They started apologizing for the mistakes they must have made copying the picture. Finally I was able to explain how much I loved it and went aroung hugging all the carpenters, and then quickly hugged all the women and children, because in Cameroon hugging is considered sex.

They left, giggling, shaking their heads over this crazy American, oversexed girl who had no husband though she was past her prime. For the entire two years I was in the Peace Corps, women would sympathize with me that my father had failed so miserably as a husband procurer. I would try to explain the American method of courtship, but they didn't get it. They'd always secretively ask me if I was barren, Miss Mattie, or diseased, Miss Mattie. This Miss Mattie business killed me and I finally took to calling them Miss Ashad or Miss Grace, depending on whether they were Christian or Moslem, and consequently, they didn't spend so much time worrying about my marital status. They just laughed at me instead.

Before I left for Jo's, I wrote a letter home asking my mother to send me Johnson's Pledge for my new catalog. but she wrote back and told me you don't touch Pledge to such a fine piece of furniture. She said that if the finish was as beautiful as I described I should just dust it off every day. Amazingly, I did. Every day for two years I dusted it, giving the job over only to my most trusted worker when I went on vacation.

It was illegal to take my Jeep on a personal trip, but the Peace Corps didn't send any law-enforcement officers out to check on volunteers. Just doctors who came around every six months to try to cure us of mild dysentery, which we all put up with because we refused to boil our lettuce before making a salad.

The ride to Bamenda was stunning. I kept stopping to take pictures. My father had been to Scotland, and later he said yes, it definitely could have been a road through the highlands. The altitude was seventy-five hundred feet, the weather was dry, and the temperature in the mid-seventies. The sky was bluer than the Hawaiian ocean. Long-horned cattle grazed and small villages popped up here and there amidst little pine copses surrounded by fields of corn. Too bad the Bamenda road was such a wreck of stones and potholes. Or my Jeep springs not more functional. The first thing I said to Jo was, "My back kills. Where's the bathtub?" When you're a teacher in the only college in West Cameroon, you get a bathtub. My first real bath in ten weeks.

In the back of the kitchen I soaked in the tub, and she kept heating water to replenish it when she wasn't sitting on a stool next to the tub. We talked all night. In the blue glow of the Tilly lamp I told her every single thing I'd done for the last two and a half months. When I was done she told me she definitely wasn't going back. She was going to marry an African and stay. I controlled my desperation to tell her I wouldn't let her do that, and instead asked if she had anyone in mind.

"Yes. He's a banker."

I panicked. A Cameroonian banker. A Cameroonian

banker is not like an American banker. When you go to
Barclay's Bank in Cameroon, the conversation goes like
this:

"Hello, Miss Mattie. Good day."

"Good day, Mr. Enobot."

"How is your family in America? I hear you received a
letter yesterday?"

"They're all fine. And yours?"

"All well, thank Allah. Has your father located a husband
for you yet?"

"Not yet."

"Your father is a poor man, yes? Or is it that he has
many daughters?"

"Many daughters."

"So sorry."

"I'd like to cash my check, Mr. Enobot."

"Very well, then, tomorrow." Big smile.

"What about today?" Bigger smile.

"Ah, we have closed."

"But it's quarter to four."

"Yes. Closing time."

"Closing time is at four."

"Yes." He's smiling again. I'm not.

"Oh. Well, could I just have change for a hundred-franc
note?" They don't make change in the market, which would
be my next stop.

"As a guest of my country, I will do it for you even
though we have closed. Do you like four twenty-five-franc
pieces, or ten tens?"

"Ten tens."

"So sorry. I have just eight ten-franc coins left today. I
will have some more tens tomorrow when you come back."

"Then give me the four twenty-five-franc pieces."

"But you prefer the tens. I do not wish to disappoint."

"But, Mr. Enobot. I need rice and vegetables in the market."

"Ah. Then you must come to my house for dinner. My
wife will kill a chicken in your honor."

Etc., etc., etc.

"What banker, Jo?" I hoped it wasn't Mr. Enobot.

"The French National Bank is going to set up a branch in the West. A legitimate bank that does things like make loans. The man in charge is just back from Oxford this summer and has been doing a great job getting everything organized. His name is Jean-Pierre. His family is in government. They live in Yaoundé, and he will live here in Bamenda."

"What part of the government is he in, Jo?"

"Ah . . . Jean-Pierre's last name is Duna."

At first, I didn't say anything. Why should I be surprised? No man could resist Jo. Not even the vice-president's son, that's for sure. "Jo, you're going to marry Vice-President Duna's son?"

"Yes."

"You don't love him, right?"

She stood up and began to pace. "No. I love Paul, remember? But I like Jean-Pierre. He's very sweet."

"Sweet?"

"Yes. Sweet. He—"

"Is there something intrinsic in 'sweet' that would help me understand why you're considering marrying him?"

"Don't be caustic. And I'm not considering. . . . I'm going to do it."

"Jo, this is crazy and you know it."

"What's crazy about living in a beautiful house in Yaoundé—wait till you see Yaoundé, it's fabulous—and there will be servants, and I'll get to spend my life with all those neat Frenchmen, and—"

"What's so neat about Frenchmen? All they do is make love and drink wine."

"Mattie, Jean-Pierre will be in government himself someday. Who knows? I might be the first lady of Cameroon."

"Since when have you wanted to be the first lady of anything?"

"All my life. You just refuse to recognize this about me. Through Jean-Pierre, I'll have the power to do things about the famine in the north. Things like that."

"As an African wife? A Moslem wife yet? You're dreaming."

"Yes, I am. And French Moslem is a lot different from African Moslem. Jean-Pierre has been educated in Paris. He's lived in France since he was seven."

"I've never heard of anything like this working out."

"There's King Hussein's British wife."

"Hussein and Duna . . . there's a wonderful comparison. Duna is from a little village and is only in power to balance the real power, which is Christian. He'll be out in a couple of years. Then what?"

Jo wasn't listening. She had it all planned. Except there were certain realities she wasn't taking into consideration. As she'd just said herself, Jo didn't consider, she just did.

I met Jean-Pierre that night. He was very sweet. And it was true, he was very French, too. He kissed my hand and talked for a half hour about the special wine he'd brought in my honor. He had no charisma whatsoever, unlike his father. He also had six brothers. No way was this particular son going to inherit the throne from his father. Jo had picked the wrong brother. Jean-Pierre adored Jo, of course. Neither of them considered the realities.

Jean-Pierre had a surprise for us. In the morning his father's plane would pick us up, and we would attend a Thanksgiving party he was giving in Yaoundé. His parents were to host several Americans, he said, and we were included.

"Jean-Pierre," I said, "this all sounds so exciting. But all I've brought with me are this skirt and another one and two dirty shirts that I'd hoped I'd be able to wash. I haven't had time."

Jo said, "We'll wear African dress."

I choked on my wine. "Sure, Jo. African dress. If I tried to wrap myself up in a length of cloth it would all fall down to my ankles in a minute. African women know how to keep their weight shifted and there's never a slip. Every European woman I've seen wearing African wrap ends up picking one end of it out of her soup."

Jean-Pierre's face turned from mahogany to ebony, which is an African blush. Jo said, "You can wear my dress." (We'd all brought one "good" dress to Cameroon.) "I'll wear an African wrap. I've learned the knack."

Eventually I went along with them because I'd heard so much about Yaoundé—the name alone has such a magnificent African ring—and I might never have a chance to get there another time. It's a long way inland. You have to fly to get there. You can drive, preferably in a Land Rover, but you have to bring your own gas.

That night, after Jean-Pierre left, I lay in my sleeping bag on the floor by Jo's bed. "Jean-Pierre is sweet, Jo. Very gentle. I like him."

"Thanks."

"But I sure wouldn't marry him."

"It isn't you he wants to marry."

"And he'll never make the presidential palace either."

"Behind every great man there's an even greater woman."

"Poor Jean-Pierre. All he wants to do, I think, is go back to France and drink wine."

"That's true. I have my work cut out for me."

Jo really didn't know how to connive. This wasn't going to work out, I could tell. "You know, Jo, somewhere between living over a bar in South Norwalk and living in a palace, there are other real nice places."

"Mattie, if you want to live in a four-bedroom colonial in Darien, fine. You'll still have my love, friendship, and respect. I prefer palaces or tenements. Both offer me something special. I've already decided. If my plan with Jean-Pierre doesn't work, I'm going to Mississippi."

"Not Mississippi again! Shit, we've been through this already."

"There's a clinic there opening up funded by SNCC."

"A clinic. So when did you become a nurse?"

"I'm sure there will be more important things to do there than nurse. There will be political transactions necessary for someone to do. Somebody white, probably."

I rolled over and went to sleep, disgusted. Jo, the great white queen. Maybe I'd forget writing Michael's story and start on Jo's. I began to think I should have pushed harder for her to marry Paul. I preferred to have Jo safe and unhappy than vice versa, which is how things sounded they might turn out. But it was not to be. Not with Jean-Pierre anyway.

Yaoundé was a real city, sort of like a miniature Paris. It had discotheques, couturier shops, hairdressers, and pastry. It had a cathedral with a black Madonna and wide boulevards. I went into the Peace Corps office to see the director.

"Hi, Mr. Jones."

I could see his mind racing through our photograph handbook. "Ah . . . don't tell me . . . you're . . uh . . . Martha Price!"

"Mattie. Nice to see you again."

"Mutual . . ." Now I could see his brain going—who's this? She's not an East Cameroon volunteer. What's she doing in Yaoundé?

"How's the teaching going?" he tried.

"I'm setting up the library in Buea."

"Of course! I hear it's going great guns."

"My alma mater sent me three thousand books. That helped. And—"

"Remarkable. But what are you doing in Yaoundé? Not ill, I hope."

I was about to tell him that I was checking on getting some supplies from the Cameroonian ministry of education, but why lie? This wasn't school. "I'm a guest this evening at the vice-president's residence. Jo and I."

"Joe . . . let's see . . . Joe . . ."

"Jo Parsons."

"Oh, of course. That Jo. A romance brewing, I understand."

I said nothing. It was none of his business. He cleared his throat. "Well, if two Peace Corps volunteers are invited to dinner at the VP's house, I think it's perfectly in order that they should go. Uh . . . how did you manage to get to Yaoundé?"

"Jean-Pierre Duna flew us."

"Ah." His brow furrowed. Then he said, "My wife and I will be at the Honorable Duna's dinner, too. It will be quite nice for me to have you and Jo there to chat with. I don't get to talk to the volunteers that often. Face to face."

"That will be very nice. Mr. Jones, do you people have a slush fund?"

"Beg pardon?"

"I have a dress that I borrowed from Jo but she's a little bigger than me. Could I take out a loan on my next paycheck to buy a dress? I mean with the American ambassador there and all."

"The slush fund isn't big enough for a dress, believe me." He grinned a fake grin. These up-and-coming diplomats all had the same clean grin. "I have a better idea. Especially after all the wonderful things I've heard about that library. Hang on a minute."

He called his wife and described the situation. She was in the office within minutes and gave me a hug. The poor woman was forty years old, had two teenaged kids that she missed horribly, and she couldn't speak French. Naturally she couldn't speak any West African languages either. She would always drop the volunteers little notes on pretty blue notepaper, asking how we were doing and could she help us with anything. She needed to mother and we all needed to be away from mothers.

"Mattie, you just have no idea how I miss taking my girls out shopping. Let's go buy a dress. My treat."

"Oh, I wouldn't want you to—"

"And what about your friend? She has something appropriate?"

"She's wearing African." Mr. and Mrs. Jones exchanged looks. "But don't worry. We volunteers get away with that sort of thing. The Cameroonians think we look cute."

"Is that so?" said Mr. Jones. "Well, have fun, girls."

We did. She bought me new underwear, too. My own bra and pants were gray from the hard water. And new shoes.

There were twelve for dinner. I sat between Jean-Pierre

and a USIS jerk. He was definitely CIA, but God only knows what there is to spy on in Cameroon. He talked a lot to everyone about how the South Vietnamese were begging for more help to stop the Communist barbarians. He told us how Dr. Tom Dooley wrote that a busload of children had their pinky fingers cut off because they wouldn't inform on their parents. I couldn't stand it. I placed my hand on his thigh under the tablecloth. He was a real stuffed shirt and spent the rest of the dinner coughing and staring at me, trying to figure out how to get me to stop. I'd had a lot of Jean-Pierre's favorite wine.

Jo looked ravishing. Bright African colors look exciting and wonderful against black skin, but those same colors have quite a lot of appeal next to silver-blue eyes and icy hair, too.

As he passed a large platter of mush to Jo, Vice-President Duna said, "The yam foo-foo is especially good at this time of year." He looked at Jo. The white African queen started to agree and I chimed in ahead of her, "You mean foo-foo corn." I could tell the difference without tasting because my Bueans at the library always brought one or the other for lunch. (Jo's fellow Bamenda teachers at the college brought tuna sandwiches.) You mix the cornmeal or yam meal with boiling water until you get this heavy ball of something like thick wallpaper paste. Not unlike polenta in Italy, except the Italians bake the ball and slice it. The Africans break off lumps of it, and dip the lumps into stew.

Vice-President Duna gazed down the table at me. So did his wife. She was having trouble with her fork and salad. Although we were having Cameroonian food as appetizers before the turkey, and although in East Cameroon you get your salad just before dessert *à la française,* when Americans come to dinner they just put the salad bowls out there and you can have it when you want it. The Cameroonians never eat salad at all. They call anything green "grass." I was once asked why I ate the food of a grazing animal, in fact. The veep's wife was trying to be polite as she disgustedly pushed the leaves around her bowl. It was time to loosen the party up.

Usually, when you eat foo-foo you can't help but be loose, since the Cameroonians eat it with their hands. I scooped a big blob of foo-foo onto my plate and pulled off a walnut-size wad. Then I kneaded it in my right hand just enough to get rid of the glutinous elasticity. (Always use your right hand in Moslem countries because your left hand is for toilet-related activities. Guess which hand is called the man-hand and which is called the woman-hand?) Then I dipped it in my stew, which was a tomato-pepper, peanut-oil combination. I popped it in my mouth.

"Delicious, Madame Duna."

She giggled and pulled her head wrap lower down on her forehead. She was young and very pretty, and managed to look that way even though she had eight children, the oldest twenty-six. She was the kind of person a Cameroonian president needed as a wife. I looked at Jo and she looked away.

Then the vice-president, with his little look aimed at Jean-Pierre, said, "Your brother in America—my third son," he explained to the rest of us—"is at Howard University. He tells me he has fallen in love with a fellow student and wishes to marry her. A Negress." What else, I thought, at Howard. "I have invited the girl for a visit. Perhaps Miss Price and Miss Parsons can show her their neighborhoods in both the south and north of West Cameroon. I want the girl to realize how difficult it will be for the people to accept her. Even though she is an American Negress. Miss Parsons can show her our ways of dress and Miss Price can show her how to eat foo-foo."

Mrs. Duna and I laughed. I was sure this Howard girl probably loved salad. Black or white, no American should be marrying any of Duna's sons.

"Honorable Father," said Jean-Pierre, "if Charles marries an American girl, she will not exactly be living in a bush village."

"No, she won't. Not now. But if there is a fall from power,

an imbalance between the Moslem East and Christian West, or if there is worse—the sort of thing evident now in Nigeria—we may all be back living in our home village. Grateful for any home, perhaps."

"We have a very stable country."

"It would seem so. Now."

"I don't think we need to worry, Honorable Father."

Honorable father ignored him. "Jean-Pierre, have you brought your two American friends to our home village? Perhaps they would like to meet your aunts and uncles . . . our cousins."

"I had planned to do that in the future."

By now, Madame Duna and I were squeezing and dipping our foo-foo furiously. The ambassador and the Peace Corps director could feel the tension, since that's the one thing they were trained to do, but they didn't know where the tension was coming from. The USIS guy next to me was eating his salad like a grazing animal. And he kept asking the servant for more wine. Smart move.

When we got back to Bamenda, Jo was a little more realistic about Jean-Pierre. She was very unhappy, but all the same told me she looked forward to this visit from the Negress at Christmastime. Just the person Jo felt she needed to speak to. Not me. That was hard on me, but I understood. I told her it was OK because I'd decided to visit Fernando Póo for Christmas. I told Jo that she and the American girl could use my cottage at the hotel as a home base for touring my "neighborhood." Jo said she was sorry we wouldn't be together for the holidays, but we would both be doing what we needed to do. And I did need a vacation, for sure. Our second Christmas in Cameroon we would definitely go off together for the last time before she married Jean-Pierre, she said. Maybe the Sahara or someplace like that, to buy some artwork. There was a guy, supposedly, in Kano, who drew outlines of people's feet and made antelope-leather sandals for two dollars, any color. I'd have my mother send me her outlines. She'd love that.

I climbed into my little Jeep and said good-bye to Jo. Good-bye, instead of all the things I really wanted to say. Hopefully, she and the Negress were smart enough to face reality together and tell each other what I wanted to say to Jo.

The night I got home I was very tempted to go up to the prison and invite Michael to my cottage for a Thanksgiving drink. But I didn't. I'd been in Cameroon a very short time out of the two years. I had to get used to being either alone or with just Africans. I didn't know what saved the rest of the people in my group, but writing saved me. (Jean-Pierre certainly wasn't saving Jo. What was?)

I wrote a big scene. Elisabeth telling Michael about his roots. About Wilhelm von Hiltz's roots. And then I turned Michael into a driven man: researching, interviewing, finding out everything he could about von Hiltz, until he finally convinces himself that the old baron is back in Kamerun.

CHAPTER ELEVEN

At the end of three months in the tardigrade country of Cameroon, where one comes to appreciate the intrinsic pleasures of putting off till tomorrow what could have been done today, the library prospered—the fastest-moving project in Peace Corps history. It was Christmas, and the library could easily have been opened, but the Bakweris have a need to savor developments as slowly as possible. Who knew how many decades it would be before another development occurred?

Every Bryn Mawr book was read by at least ten people before getting placed on the shelf. "Working" meant a crew of people sitting on the library floor reading. I mentioned that my next step—once the books were shelved in Dewey decimal order—would be to procure furniture from the government. Two weeks of serious discussion followed: What kind of furniture would be appropriate? Catalogs from government offices appeared, filled with expensive, heavy furniture that would look correct in a hundred-year-old law firm in London. Eventually, I appointed a furniture committee so I could get back to cataloging the new books that the Bryn Mawr students kept sending. The committee found a Sears catalog with lawn chairs. The vinyl strips of the lawn chairs were the three colors of the flag of Cameroon. Before I went on my Christmas break, I left orders to write a letter to Sears asking for a donation and to have the entire village sign it. I knew they'd spend the week seeing to it that every Buean read or had the letter read to him while I had my vacation in Fernando Póo.

I took a seven-hour mammy-wagon ride to Douala. I lived enough Africa in that trip to last a lifetime. I had kids in my lap, babies in my lap, and an infant so tiny in my lap I'd swear it was born after the trip had gotten under way. There were chickens and bush dogs, each indispensable to the trip. Halfway there, everybody got out and boiled eggs for lunch. The scruffy little bush dogs served as pampers for the under-three set. The dogs fought over one kid who had severe diarrhea. It was one of the most disgusting sights I'd ever witnessed, but then I'd never changed diapers either, so maybe bush dogs made more sense.

Ten years later, I learned in my La Leche meeting that the only waste breast-fed babies produce is the butterfat in the milk, which they can't quite digest. I decided then that those gross little bush dogs probably had a better diet than many Third World people. I never mentioned the buttermilk-loving dogs to the La Leche ladies, though.

There was the perennial goat tied to the roof, along with everybody's bags and baskets and my Louis Vuitton suitcase. The goat baaed the entire seven hours, poor thing. He had to stay on the roof because bush dogs don't eat goat shit. Once an hour like clockwork the driver would stop and yell, "Peace!" That's the pidgin pronunciation of piss. Every other hour, he'd yell, "Sheet!" and everyone would barrel out and obey his command. Bouncing wildly on a springless African version of a Greyhound bus does stir up the digestive tract.

The mammy-wagon wasn't an express. Every single village or hunter's hut would bring us to a stop, and everyone would come out and greet each other. Most of the people who got on for the short haul got back off at the next village. It took a good hour to cross a makeshift bridge over a small river. We had to unload the whole wagon and

then watch it go across first. Very big cheer when it made
it to the other side. The goat put up an incredible struggle
when she realized she had to get tied back up on the roof
again. A goat can be as loud as a helicopter landing.

I passed out to all the kids the purple Tootsie Pops Paul
kept sending me. When Paul and I were little he'd take all
the purple Tootsie Pops out of the bag before I could get
to them and then he'd say, "Sorry, kiddo, no purple ones
again." Now he felt guilty. My first week in Cameroon I
got sick from gorging on purple Tootsie Pops and I'll never
eat another one. The kids sucked them, looked at them,
sucked them, waved them around, and stuck them in their
hair. Just like American kids. The first little guy who discovered there was something softer and even stranger-
tasting on the inside went berserk with his good fortune.
Every kid started crunching though the purple candy to
see if he would have the same great fortune. The shrieking
was ear-splitting, and then they all started calling me "white
juju woman." Their parents just laughed and laughed. Then
the kids played for two solid hours with the little white
sticks. They made up about a thousand games with those
sticks. Toys are where you find them in Cameroon.

At the end of the journey, compliments of my father
who read somewhere that I should do this, I passed out
to the adults Kennedy half-dollars. Mass crying and breast-
beating ensued as they sang, "KeneDEE, KeneDEE!" I began to realize that they'd never spend the money, which
made me feel bad because fifty cents goes a long way in a
Cameroonian market.

I spent the night in Douala and flew out the next morning to Santa Isabel on Fernando Póo. Twenty minutes. No
goats. Just four passengers and the pilot. The three other
passengers were a French couple and their teenaged
daughter. The three looked upon me with great disdain,
and the pilot made a pass, as all pilots of small planes
everywhere will.

Santa Isabel was a little Spanish town with a beautiful
cathedral at the west border of the plaza, which itself was

lined with palm trees and gardens. Old Spanish men played checkers on little benches and duennas dressed in black trudged along behind strolling couples. In twenty minutes I had made a remarkable leap from one culture to another, neither of them mine.

The Santa Isabel hotel was built on the floor of what had been a fort on the end of a peninsula facing Cameroon. The fort was built for whatever reason forts are built, but was later used to fight off pirates who wanted to steal slaves from slavers and sell them themselves. We were surrounded by old rusty cannons and sentry posts. The peninsula was actually a cliff high above the sea, and since it was between the wet season and the dry, the hotel gave its guests a stunning view of the great mountain looming out of the sea at the foot of the Cameroon coast—like a gray ghost. It was impossible to fathom the little town of Buea almost halfway up its side. I found I was homesick. For Buea.

The hotel had a kidney-shaped swimming pool. I took one look at it and knew I would have a wonderful week. Lying by a blue pool near the sea and taking an occasional dip is my idea of paradise. I'd brought twenty-five books to read. I couldn't wait.

I went up to my room behind a thin black boy dressed in white, who toted my suitcase as if it were full of feathers, not books. Once in the room, the boy opened the curtain, exposing the luxurious Bight of Benin spread out before me all the way to the gray mountain. The patio below was a pattern of colorful tiles, and from the edge of the patio came the splash and chatter of the lounge lizards. Out on my balcony I could already feel the equatorial sun burning away the Buean dampness from the skin of my arms.

Before my flight from Douala, I'd run into a little shop and bought a French bikini. I put it on and was nuder than in Hawaii. The bikini was made of turquoise twine. I'd put on a little weight since coming to Cameroon but I felt more voluptuous than plump. French bikini tops are basically two tiny arcs of fabric-covered foam with a strong, heavy wire underneath that allows your breasts to defy gravity and the natural tendency, when you are relaxed on your back, to fall into your armpits. Now when I look at pictures of Marilyn Monroe, I know I looked a lot like that in Fernando Póo. Not actually plump, but absolutely no muscle tone whatsoever. Nobody in the fifties thought of Marilyn Monroe as fat. She was, though, according to the standards of eighties bodies. I grabbed my terry-cloth robe and stuck my feet back into my sandals. I had the second book of *The Alexandria Quartet*. God, could it be nearly as wonderful as *Justine*?

The French from Douala and the British holiday-makers from Lagos ringed the pool; they ignored me as I draped my robe over a chaise and spread baby oil all over my body. There was a red float in the center of the pool with no one on it. I guess they were all too lazy to make the effort to climb aboard. The hotel keeper was tending a short bar with three stools under a raffia overhang. He was a jolly, moustached Spaniard who laughed continually. I asked if I might use the float.

"*Sí, sí!* And you take my hat, *señorita,* to protect your lovely nose."

He took a big Mexican sombrero affair from his head and plopped it on mine. "*Gracias,*" I said. I looked like an idiot, but nobody knew me.

"And do not float too long. Stay under the shadow of the palm. The sun is very high."

"*Gracias,*" I said again. That was the extent of my Spanish.

He laughed. "*De nada, americana.*"

I slipped into the water, which was chilled to perfection, and in two strokes I reached the float and heaved myself aboard. I lay flat on my stomach, unhooked my bikini top as the women lying on the lounges were doing, and drifted into oblivion. I felt like I was in a toaster oven, so I took the manager's advice and twirled my fingers in the water, propelling myself to the end of the pool shaded by an overhanging palm. I closed my eyes and fantasized about staying forever on this gem of an island. À la Jo. Would I really mind being married to a Spanish cocoa-bean grower if I could have this? Hmmmmm.

A deep voice three inches from my ear said something in Spanish. God must have heard me and sent me just such a cocoa man. Before I lifted my sombrero I asked God for just one thing—make him gorgeous. If it was now instead of then I would have added, Julio Iglesias's twin brother. I turned my head, smiled my best pass-receiving smile, lifted my lazy lids, and found myself eyeball-to-eyeball with Michael.

His good-looking Jewish face broke into a murderous scowl. "Son of a bitch," he said. "Are you following me or what?"

I was shocked. I paddled over to the pool ladder and climbed out, holding on to my bikini top for dear life. I wasn't trying to be Marlene Dietrich, but I did a superb one-handed job of throwing my robe over my shoulder and storming off. I felt all those people around the pool staring at me. I was so embarrassed I wanted to kill Michael. Damn it, I thought. Marlene wouldn't have had tears in her eyes.

I stood in my room, dripping on the tile floor, wanting to fling myself across one of the high white French beds. But it would get wet. My bikini top was hanging askew from my neck. There was a puddle forming around my feet. I tried to retie myself into the tangled turquoise twine. I was so frustrated that I came close to shouting at the top of my lungs for Scottie to beam me back to Connecticut. Then I heard Michael shouting instead. He was just on the other side of my door.

"Mattie, open up. I'm sorry."

He said he was sorry a half-dozen more times. He admitted that he'd been nasty and that he needed to explain. Please and sorry, over and over. I let him pound on the door while I tried fruitlessly to come up with a really clever obscenity to hurl at him. None that I knew were obscene enough. His tone changed.

"Mattie, you have the most gorgeous rear I've ever seen

in my life. Where'd you get that bathing suit?"

Now I couldn't help myself. To hell with clever. "Shut up, you conceited shit." *Shit* packed a lot of venom. For me.

He banged on the door again. "Come out and call me names. To my face."

"Leave me alone, Michael. Just go away."

"I have a peace offering."

Cute. "I'm not interested in peace. Not with you. Good-bye."

"It's a bottle of white wine. Compliments of Señor Calderón, who hates to see fighting in his swimming pool. And I can tell by the label that it's a great wine. Let's see . . . 'From the Cask of Amontillado,' it says, '1834.' Great year. Not as great as this year . . . 1965 . . . the year I met you. It—"

"Drink it your goddamned self!" Could he tell my voice was giving away my very forgiving nature? Even if the words weren't?

"Do you think I'm some kind of an alcoholic? I can't drink an entire—"

I whipped the door open and sailed past him, shoveling myself back into my beach robe. I strode down the hall. I was pretty sure I'd gotten the bikini top to rights.

He caught up with me. "I really am sorry."

He was. "I know."

"I'm very messed up."

"I know."

"You do?"

"Not entirely. Tell me about it over the wine."

He smiled. "OK." He put his free arm around my shoulders. He looked down at my breasts, not quite covered by my robe and definitely not all the way back into the bikini. He looked away. Intriguing guy. Obnoxious one minute, a gentleman the next. I tied the robe more modestly about me. Let him wonder about me, too.

Downstairs we were in time for lunch. The hotel lobby was also a dining area. Each table held a red cut-glass vase with a candle in it. The ivy growing around the pillars was woven with Christmas lights. It was Christmas, after all.

People from the pool drifted in, nodding to each other, loving the way Americans could spit in each other's eyes one minute, and act like old buddies the next. Would Americans ever learn romance? Yes.

After lunch, we changed, met in the lobby again, and walked through the afternoon and into the dusk, down along the crenellated wall that bordered the narrow road into Santa Isabel. We shopped in tiny dark stores, their doorways hidden under scrolled balconies. We drank *café con leche* from tall glasses at corner bars. We went into the cathedral and it was full of poinsettias. There was a stunning baroque crèche to the side of the altar, and I lit a candle. I told Michael that it was the one wonderful thing about being a Catholic child—escaping into the quiet, eerie world of a cavernous church, its gloom made all the more tangible by the banks of candles, the sunlight outside turning the stained-glass windows into the original, all-time light show.

"And the smell, Michael . . . incense, burning candle wax, the oil of the oak pews . . . wonderful."

He said, "It's disgusting."

At first I couldn't really say anything. I'd been selfish. But then I said what I'd always felt about what was going through his mind, even though it might make him scoff.

"You know, Michael, I think that if all the time and drive and effort and money that went into the Holocaust—killing six million Jews—instead went into Hitler's war machine, Hitler would have won. The Jews he killed gave their lives for the survival of the world. I know how melodramatic that sounds, but even though the destruction of those innocent people is unimaginable to me, I don't have any trouble at all imagining Hitler winning. Winning Europe, Russia, and then crossing the Atlantic and invading Norwalk, Connecticut. If the Nazis hadn't come up with such a plan . . . for the final solution, I mean . . . then they'd have come up with the atom bomb first. Before us.

I believe it. I believe that your family, all those families, saved mine."

He was staring at me.

"I know how simple that sounds, but—"

"No, no. I hear what you mean. But I have imagined the Holocaust, Mattie. My mother saw to it. And all I know is that when my mother looks at me, she doesn't see me. She sees what's gone. She sees all her dead relatives and her home that she grew up in. She doesn't know how she's alive. But when she sees me, she sees her chance to find out how it happened. All the answers. And her possible revenge."

"I see you, Michael. Let me help you."

"No."

"Why not?"

"Too dangerous."

"What's too dangerous?"

"Nothing."

So I held his hand, and we walked back to the hotel and up the flight of steps and down the long corridor to his room. On the high white French bed we whispered until our whispers became kisses and Michael had no choice, through the night, except to reveal his secrets. The whispers and kisses and secrets passed back and forth between us like osmosis. There is another way of making love without having a fear of bombs in the back of your mind. There is the dreamy awareness of matched body temperatures, meeting and not parting for hours on end, just flowing along like the warm ocean outside. Michael and I did not melt together, but we were connected, the way people in Buea feel connected to the estuary by the nearly invisible perpetual mists. We could actually taste each other.

What happened to us in the next few days on Fernando Póo, I wrote about. I wrote while Michael went off on strange errands to "tie some threads up." What a wonderful place to be a writer—sitting on a balcony, or beside a pool on miraculous Fernando Póo. It was what could be considered a perfect honeymoon (perfect except for the fact that the bride and groom weren't married). We explored Santa Isabel, we swam, we nearly drowned at the base of the peninsula cliff, and Michael, in between times, made his dashes into town, which added mystery, which I loved. I had a lot in common with the Bakweri tribe of Buea, West Cameroon. To explain things away with, *"Juju, juju . . ."* was wonderful.

I didn't know yet what I would have happen to Michael and Elisabeth between the time she saved him and the time I met him, but someday I would fill in the gap. Now, I just tried to write from a detached point of view about what was happening to Michael. And to me, though I changed my name to Mary, Mary being the name that came right to mind. I didn't want to waste my time thinking of a better one. It took me a month to come up with Elisabeth. Many years later, when I was putting all the pieces of my story together, and filling the gaps, I realized that I couldn't really remember what part happened and what part I'd made up, it was that fantastic.

CHAPTER TWELVE

On the morning of Christmas Eve, early, I watched from Michael's bed as he picked up the envelope someone had slipped under the door. I made believe I was asleep. He ripped it open and stood reading for a moment. Then he went into the bathroom. I heard him tearing it up, and then the toilet flushed. I sat up. He turned on the shower. I left him another note, telling him to knock on my door if he wanted company for breakfast. In just my nightgown I dashed down the hall between his door and mine, but everyone was asleep. I took a shower, too, and while I was getting dressed, he knocked.

We went downstairs and had an "English" breakfast—eggs, rolls, muffins, toast, sausage, thin slices of grilled beef, ham, sausage, stewed tomatoes, marmalade, tea, and my first kipper. We looked across the table at each other stuffing our faces, and we both smiled with food in our mouths. Outrageous.

I said, "Surprised you have any appetite left."

He grinned. "On the contrary. I've worked up a tremendous appetite."

"I'm in love with you, Michael," I said without meaning to. I couldn't help it. I was.

"I'm in love with you."

"You don't have to say that."

"I said it because I mean it."

We buttered more rolls and I thought, What the hell, I'll ask him about the note. After all, he's in love with me. But he said first, "I have to run into town for something."

"You do?"

"I need some shaving lotion."

"Oh." What a lousy liar he was. I could always tell lies with panache because writers are professional liars. So I didn't ask him anything since I could tell he wasn't lying when he said he was in love with me, so why make myself obnoxious? Anyway, I felt like being alone. To think.

I basked by the pool, reading instead of thinking. And I was sick of writing, sick of making dozens of little notes all out of order, all disorganized. I just wanted the real Michael for now. Creating takes as much out of a person as playing tennis in ninety-degree weather when it's humid. Michael wasn't much of a pool-basking person, so it was a nice, guiltless time. I wondered how Jo was making out with the black girl from Howard. A black sister-in-law for Jo. Not the kind of thing she wasn't used to.

I went back up to my room and took a long, cool shower, until I heard this bashing at my door and Michael yelling my name just like the day before, only louder. He was twisting the doorknob back and forth. I wrapped up in a towel and ran to the door.

"I'm coming."

When I opened the door he leaned against the doorjamb and gaped at me. Sweat was pouring off him. "You're OK," he gasped.

"Of course I am. What did you do? Run all the way from town?"

"Yes." He dragged himself by me and slumped into a chair.

"What did you think happened to me?" He didn't answer. I got him a glass of water. He drained it and pulled me onto his lap.

"You were in danger, Mattie. You are in danger."

"Just tell me where you came from."

"A friend of my father's."

"What father? I'm sorry. That didn't come out right. I mean . . ."

He picked up the glass. I went and got him more water. He tried to explain everything to me all at once. I let him talk instead of asking him why he was so afraid for me.

"I'm talking about the dead father, not the man my mother married. He was John Graham. But the dead one . . . he's alive. He made it. That man in New York . . . that guy you followed . . . he works with . . . never mind who he works with. He wanted to tell me I was crazy to look for von Hiltz. Then, while he was giving me all his dire warnings, he began to stare so hard into my eyes that I thought he was maybe a little mad. Insane. He seemed to lose track of what he was supposed to be saying to me and out of the blue, he asked me where I was born and when I told him where, I thought he was having some kind of heart attack. You know, his eyes were bulging.

"Then, they . . ." Michael stopped. I wiped off his forehead with the corner of my towel. He went on. "He . . . the man you saw following me . . . at the end of training, he called me again and told me someone needed to meet me. I went to this bar in Greenwich Village and I knew it was my father as soon as I looked at him. And he knew it was me. He told me I looked exactly like my mother except I had his color eyes. It was a long time before it occurred to me that here was my opportunity to find out who the hell I was. Instead, I asked him to find the baby that my mother—the mother who rescued me—had given to some church deacon in Munich.

"But he told me that that baby was dead. The deacon gave him to some Jews who ended up dying on the same train as my real mother." Michael was starting to cry. "So my real father went to see my mother to give her the news and to tell her that he'd added the name Pieter Schutzmann—her real baby—to the records at the memorial in Israel. He thanked her for saving me."

He was really crying. He took an old chewed-up picture

out of his pocket, and held it up for me to see. It was a baby, a couple of months old, smiling so hard that he must have been gurgling out loud when the picture was snapped. "I'd given them this, thinking it would probably help in locating the baby. It didn't help. They already knew. My real father had turned over every rock looking for my mother, and later me—in case I was alive—but all he found was the baby Pieter." He put the picture back in his pocket. "My mother will want it back."

I just put my arms around him and waited till he finished crying. It took a long time, and the whole long time I was trying to sort it all out. I couldn't. "So who are you, Michael?"

He smiled a little. "Oh, Mattie. I'm still me. The family that this Benjamin—my father . . . his name is Benjamin . . . told me about still isn't real. Not yet, anyway. But I'm a German Jew and my family lived for generations in Munich. They were successful, but they wouldn't go to Holland at first. Then they didn't because of the fact that I was to be born. There's just me left and my father. He lives in Israel. He says he's stopped trying to do—professionally —what I'm trying to do right now. He told me to forget von Hiltz. He kept saying, No proof, no proof. Well if there's no proof, why the hell is he so worried about me? What has proof to do with it? There's never been proof, only witnesses."

I couldn't stand it. "Michael, what did you think happened to me? What did they say to you?"

"Some guy, some emissary of Benjamin is in Fernando Póo. To tell me that if people begin looking for me—try to stop me—they will become aware of you. Very smart. They scared the wits out of me. By using you. Mattie, we go back tomorrow. We can't stay together anymore. Until this is over, the Peace Corps, all this . . . then we will get back together. We can't be together anymore."

"But I'm not worried, so why should you be?" When I said that, in a silly little voice, I knew that I'd been humoring him all along. To write my stuff about him. But I didn't believe a word of this von Hiltz business. Not really. Not till now.

"Good. I don't want you to worry about it. I don't want you to think about it. We have another year and a half in Cameroon. We'll get back together then, or when I find von Hiltz—whichever comes first." He tried to smile. I tried a new tack, figuring, Why stop humoring him now?

"And what if you do find him? Up there on the mountain?"

"I don't know."

"Tell the Israelis? Or that guy—the short bald guy in New York—that he's up there?"

"No."

He said it very emphatically. "You want to get him yourself, don't you?"

"Yes."

"Then you'd better buy a gun and shoot him in the back because if he sees you first, he'll shoot you."

"I want to talk to him."

Michael was crazy. "Talk to him?"

"Yes. I want to ask him if he did it."

"You'll still need a gun. In case he says yes. That is if he's really there. If he even exists."

"He exists, Mattie. I just found that out a half an hour ago. But forget it all, OK? Forget everything. Make believe I didn't say what I just said. There is no von Hiltz, OK?"

"OK. How about a nap? Take a shower and go on down by the pool."

"I'm not in the mood . . . for the pool. But I will take a nap. Will you be at the pool?" His forehead creased.

"No. I'll stay with you. I have letters to write. Señor Calderón told me there would be a special dinner tonight, outside on the patio. We'll go down early and drink beforehand. To celebrate. We might never see this place again and it's so beautiful."

"You're beautiful." He looked up at me. He was a mess. "But, Mattie, it will be our good-bye dinner. At least for a while. I mean it. I don't want to mean it, but there's just no choice."

I didn't answer. I couldn't because I didn't know what I was going to do. But just being Michael's distant friend again was not my plan. I had to reformulate my plan.

Our last evening on the patio of the Hotel de Santa Isabel was a fantasy. I was glad. I wanted to be normal. Maybe normal was what I was hoping for all along and all the von Hiltz stuff would just be for my book. If only Michael really didn't believe that this ex-Nazi was up there on our mountain. But he did believe it. I needed to talk to Jo. Thinking about talking to Jo made me worry that that Howard girl was still there. I went back to my Diamanté. Nothing like Carema, but still wonderful.

I wore the dress the Peace Corps director's wife had bought me. Dinner was delicious except for one course, brains. Everyone bubbled with Christmas spirit, which is corny, but still special. Off to the side in a dark corner, under the palms, two men in black were moving a couple of chairs about. Then they sat down and began to strum guitars. Classical guitar with two guitars sounds like a hundred if the musicians are good. Their playing became louder and faster-paced, and the tempo rose and rose until the music turned furious.

All of a sudden, this stream of light shot down from one of the balconies, creating a flat round disc at the feet of the musicians. Then, bursting into the luminous circle, came a flash of red satin and bare skin. Castanets and heels clicked in a whirling staccato that brought everyone to their feet, applauding wildly.

The flamenco dancer was an expert: spinning and stretching her entire body into an arc, and then spinning again. Our eyes were riveted to her, and the dance became more and more sensuous—her arms overhead, her strong, narrow back rippled with muscles. The audience was afraid to move, and didn't, not even to sip a drink, until the dance ended, and when it did there were riotous, demanding calls of "Encore!" Along with the *bravas*, no one wanted to lose the sexual surge she'd infused, and she acquiesced in a final crescendo of wild dancing and equally ferocious music.

Later, Señor Calderón walked the dancer to each table under the strings of colored lights, introducing his beautiful flamenco dancer daughter, who was home from college for Christmas. "Hi there," she said to us.

"You were fantastic," I said.

"Thank you."

They moved on. "Michael, that's who you wanted me to be on the float in the pool that day you yelled at me, right?"

"She'd have been a close second."

Michael was such a nice guy. Crazy, though.

CHAPTER THIRTEEN

We flew back to Douala. When we left the plane, we were invited to the VIP lounge at the airport, where we were told that all the Peace Corps volunteers in West Cameroon were in Yaoundé. There was an emergency that required we all be brought together. Michael panicked that there was a coup going on and we would all be sent home. But the official who was in charge of us said, "No coup." He laughed, too. "This is not Nigeria." Of course he didn't know exactly why we were expected in Yaoundé. And when we got there it still took us quite awhile to find out because we walked into a luncheon where all the volunteers were assembled and their heads turned all at the same time:

"Well, look who's finally arrived!"

"How was Fernando Po-oh?"

Someone began singing, "Hello, young lovers, wherever you are," and they all joined in, which made it too funny to be embarrassing. We tried to protest. "We just ran into each other there. Really."

"Oh, sure!"

"Ran into each other. Isn't that adorable?"

They were merciless. Jo told me they would have thought it was just a coincidence that Michael and I were in Fernando Póo at the same time, but she said the glow surrounding us gave us away.

It was so good to see everyone again, to be in a roomful of nothing but Americans, all yakking at once, full of gossip and stories and rumors. We were in Yaoundé because we had to have measles shots. An epidemic had broken out in southern Nigeria and even though we'd all had measles shots in training, we were to have another "just in case." In case of what, we didn't care—it was a great excuse to celebrate.

Almost everyone was able to stay a couple of days, because the schools were still on Christmas break. Michael got his shot and took the next CAT plane back to Buea. And I humored him right up until he left. I knew there wasn't any ex-Nazi hiding on Mount Cameroon, but it was something he had to get out of his system before he'd let me back into his system. That was OK. I wanted to spend time with Jo while there was a chance. I needed to tell her everything. And I needed to hear what was going on with Jean-Pierre. We were on our backs, one to each single bed, listening to each other—Jo with her eyes closed, me staring up at the ceiling.

"So what's he planning to do about this von Hiltz guy, since he's so sure he's going to find him?"

"That's exactly what I asked him. He has no idea. He hasn't reached that part of it yet. I think that deep down he knows it's all bullshit. He's really messed up, Jo."

"Well, it sounds like he's been through a lot in the last year. . . . I mean the coincidence of finding his father is incredible. Maybe he just needs to delude himself. I think we all need to do that sometimes."

Aha. Reference to Jean-Pierre. "No more dreams about first lady of Cameroon?"

She smiled sadly. "I just feel my life should have more meaning."

"Being in the Peace Corps is a lot of meaning."

"Not enough."

"So how's Jean-Pierre taking this?"

"He's back in England. Said he couldn't live in a country a hundred and fifty years behind London."

"Brain drain."

"Yeah."

"You can't really blame them, though. I mean, if you go to medical school in Paris, why would you want to come back to the bush and treat yaws?"

"I think that's precisely what you should want to do. I told Jean-Pierre he was a traitor."

"Not very nice, Jo."

"I know."

"What about that girl from Howard?"

"What do you think?"

"Back at Howard."

"She lasted twenty-four hours. She told me she had even less in common with Africans than she does with white Americans."

"Well, Vice-President Duna's probably happy."

"He made a pass at me in Yaoundé when Jean-Pierre left."

"No!"

"Men are really rotten."

"Not all of them."

"All of them. Every one."

"What about Paul?"

She rolled over and opened her eyes. "Paul is not rotten. He's an angel. Not my angel, though. I'm sorry, Mattie, I wish he were."

"But, Jo, couldn't—"

"Please. No more Paul."

I sat up. "Jo! Are you crying?"

"No." She was. So I did, too. And something inside of me kept telling me how selfish I was not to comfort her. I didn't want to let go of the role I was used to—Jo taking care of me.

"I'm sorry, Mattie."

She was sorry. *I* was selfish. But she found her angel. Exactly one year later. In Beirut.

A measles epidemic in an underdeveloped country was the most terrible thing I ever faced in my life, but maybe because I did have to face it, I was able to maintain myself in Beirut twenty years later. What happened in Beirut and the measles epidemic were almost a tie in horror. It would have been a tie except that I had a personal stake in Beirut—Jo. Here in Cameroon, it was happening to my neighbors, and that was almost as horrible.

And through me, the epidemic brought Michael closer to his von Hiltz.

The Buean officials and clerks—anyone with money—sent their kids to the north, out of the coastal path of the virus. The prime minister didn't take any chances. In time of danger, just as the Germans did who had occupied his house fifty years earlier, his offspring were sent directly to Europe. Consequently, there were very few children under the age of five left in Buea. A handful. No one worried about the older children; once you reached five and survived all the other diseases, it was expected that you could survive anything. It reminded me of what a nun had taught us in catechism class: that even though Herod killed the Holy Innocents, it was really not thousands of babies, as we all imagined. Maybe there were two dozen infants in Bethlehem at the time. No more.

Those infants left in Buea died very fast and with very little suffering. First they got a fever, and a day later, a rash, and then instead of getting better day by day as little American babies would, they got worse. Slowly, their body temperature rose, leaving them without the strength or the medication to fight the fever. It was as if they were caught in a calm ebb tide. They drifted off and away and no one knew how to swim, though God knows, they tried to hold on to them. And there were no rescue boats. The parents and relatives and friends stood on the shore setting up such a wail that I was sure God would hear and bring those babies back. And after the wailing stopped, the ceaseless funeral drumming began, twenty-four hours a day, for a month. An African funeral dirge played on drums is beyond any describable sound. Misery.

Only the strong survived. None, in Buea, were strong. Everyone spoke of the child in Kumba or the child in

Mutengene who made it through. These children were looked upon in great awe, even though they were permanently damaged—all deaf, or blind, or worse.

Someone told me that Katharine Agboran, whom I'd taught to type, had not sent her children away. Mrs. Agboran was a very smart lady, and had taught herself to read and write. All day, she'd slip the cards in and out of my portable Underwood. Once in a while, I'd see her bite her bottom lip and I knew she'd made a mistake. Mistakes devastated her. Once she invited me to her house, and she and two other women and I practiced tying scarves on each other's heads. Although Mrs. Agboran had friends, she was ostracized by her tribe. Her husband had died, and she did not want to go to her brother-in-law's village to live, which was the custom. People think this is polygamy, but it's not. Only if the sister-in-law chooses, does she become her brother-in-law's extra wife. But Mrs. Agboran wanted to stay in Buea and she came to me for a job. I told the ministry of education that I'd needed a typist and had found one on my own, so they agreed to give me a salary for her. She was seventeen.

When I heard that her two babies weren't sent to the brother-in-law's village as I'd assumed, I was also told that the brother-in-law had made a threat; if she sent them, he'd keep them. They'd be his children, not hers. He said that to save face. He was worried about them alone, with just their mother, in what his people thought of as "the big city." While the little children were beginning to die of measles, I wasn't concerned about Mrs. Agboran's children. I was sure she'd sent them to the north. But then she didn't come to the library and I began to worry that maybe she hadn't risked losing her children to her brother-in-law. Finally, I couldn't stand listening to the infernal drums anymore, and I went to her house in the strangers' quarters.

At her front door, I called, "Mrs. Agboran?" very softly. The wailing was even louder in the town itself. I had been so worried that I hadn't realized how late it was. Not quite midnight. I tiptoed into her living room and could see a light under the bedroom door. I peeked in. Mrs. Agboran and her two friends were huddled together on the end of a cot where the two babies lay. The boy was Christopher and he was almost three and the baby's first birthday had been a week earlier. The baby was a sturdy, pretty baby with bowed legs because she stood all the time, holding on to the edges of things from the time she was five months old. I had told her fretting mother that her legs would straighten out when she was older. Her name was Grace. The women were shivering. I began to sweat. The children were covered up to their chins, nestled together. Their lips were cracked and swollen and the skin of their faces was like gray crepe paper. When they'd been alive, the babies had had deep, brown skin, smooth and silky, like that of all babies. The children had dried up.

I sat down, squeezing myself beside Mrs. Agboran, whose cheeks were tight lumps. I put my arms around her shoulders. She wasn't shivering—it was more like quivering—and then she vomited all over her lap and mine. I felt myself fainting. I guess her friends got me out of there and cleaned me off. Two men appeared at the door to escort me home. One of Mrs. Agboran's friends said, "Sometimes there is nothing to be done," and I thought, in America, there is always something to be done. Something always.

I stayed home alone for a few minutes and then I ran across the parking lot to the hotel, where there was a phone. It took me two hours to get a line to the Peace Corps doctor in Yaoundé.

"Calm down, Mattie," he kept saying over and over, while I ranted about measles shots. Every American got measles shots and we didn't even need them. Why couldn't we have given measles shots to these kids? He told me that the World Health Organization was working on that, and I wanted to know why the Peace Corps wasn't working on that. What was the sense of teaching people math if they were dying of something stupid like measles? It took a long while, but I eventually calmed down.

While I was speaking to him, a fellow named Ngoundu, who was the bartender, came up to me. He had two waiters standing behind him who were his relatives. I'd never seen Ngoundu not smiling.

I told the doctor to hang on. "What's the matter, Mr. Ngoundu?"

"My last boy—Enubu—he is sick. Do you have medicine for him, Miss Mattie?"

My hands began to shake. I could hear the doctor calling me and I put the phone to my ear. "Listen, Mattie," he said—he was a nice guy, relieved to have this "public health" job rather than the alternative, medic in Vietnam—"the best thing you can do in a situation like this is if you find that there is a child with measles who has not lapsed into the advanced symptoms of the disease, give him water and aspirin and cool his skin down with wet cloths. And get other people to help you. I'm convinced that some of these children could get past the fever with very little." I stared at Ngoundu the whole time the doctor spoke to me. "You still there, Mattie? You OK?"

"I'm here."

"Just aspirin. If the child is too sick or too young to swallow it, dissolve it in water."

"OK."

"I'm sorry, Mattie. I wish I could do something, too."

"I know. Thanks."

I hung up the phone, and turned to Ngoundu. I could barely keep up with him as we went around the back of the hotel and beyond the gardens to where the hotel employees were housed. I'd seen Ngoundu's boy. He was twelve and a famous scholar among his friends. By "last boy," Ngoundu meant that he used to have other children, but didn't anymore. They had died in infancy.

A horde of people surrounded the door to Ngoundu's room. They parted for us, and inside another small crowd of sobbing people surrounded the bed where Enubu lay. It was very hot and stuffy in the room. I put my hand against Enubu's cheek and it was afire.

"Mr. Ngoundu," I heard myself say in my mother's "take

charge" voice, "the boy must be cooled down. The people must leave and the window and door opened."

"His mother will stay."

"Yes."

I looked at the woman kneeling on the floor by the head of the bed. She was an older woman, and she hung on to the edge of the boy's blankets. She said to me, "I think it is late. He has stopped sweating just now."

"Please, *Mami,* we must take off his blankets and make him cold. Mr. Ngoundu, we need a lot of water and a glass and some cloths."

Ngoundu went out and his wife uncovered Enubu. He was small and wiry, a strong child. But the virus was deadly, and though he was twelve, he had never developed an immunity to this strain of the disease. He began to shiver, and his mother leaned forward.

"It's all right, *Mami,* he should be cold."

"Yes, miss. Excuse me. I do not know this illness."

I took the little bottle of aspirin out of my bag. Ten tablets. There had been twelve. I had taken two for a damn headache. Ngoundu handed me a glass of water and I dissolved an aspirin in it. From the open window and door, the sorrowful faces, so much blacker than I remembered them to be, watched. I told the *mami* to soak the cloths in the water and wipe his face and arms and chest. I lifted his head in my arm and dripped the aspirin and water into his mouth. It dribbled down his chin.

"Let me, miss. I am used to feeding babies."

So I took on the job of swabbing down the boy, and as soon as the cold cloth touched his skin it became warm. The *mami* spoke to the boy in their own language, and I could see that he was conscious, though barely. She was pleading with him to try to drink. He seemed to be making a feeble effort. A convulsive shiver passed along his body.

Ngoundu said, "He is so cold, miss."

"No. He is so hot." I don't think I knew what I was saying, but I knew how Ngoundu felt. I had the same urge to cover him up and hug him so he'd stop shivering. I think

I was hoping that the shivering wasn't some kind of convulsion. I watched Enubu's throat rise and fall. Some of the aspirin was going down. When the water was gone, I filled the glass. "He must keep drinking," I said with some great authority that came from somewhere.

I leaned over the boy's face to replace the wet cloth on his forehead and his eyes snapped open. He said, "Jew!"

His parents' heads snapped to attention. I swayed. Then I controlled myself. I said, "Enubu, I am Miss Mattie from the library. I am helping your mother to drive away the fever."

His eyes closed, but he mumbled again. He said, "The Jews!" His parents' facial muscles actually jerked.

I smiled at Ngoundu. "This is what we call delirium," I said, in some strange little sing-song voice. "He says things we cannot understand. It is the fever speaking." Cameroonians personify everything. I was trying to divert them. And then as clearly as if he were in perfect health, Enubu said, "A package is here for the old man. Shall I take it, Papa?"

The faces in the window were wide-eyed.

"Miss, he is dying," his mother said.

"No he isn't. He has tired himself from trying to speak. He is sleeping. He is fighting against the fever. We are hearing his nightmares. Why don't you lie down, *Mami*, and rest." She was still on her knees. "I will bathe him and give him the water. You rest, too, Ngoundu."

They exchanged glances. Ngoundu said, "We want to be touching him when his ancestors take him."

I looked at my watch. It was four o'clock. I looked at it again when dawn broke. The three of us never stopped taking turns trickling water and aspirin into his mouth. Two women came in with trays of food. They apologized to me for not having "white man" food. I stood up and took the trays and told them I loved Bakweri food. One said, "Miss Mattie, we are very happy to have Enubu one more night. Our drummers waited. It is a blessing to have him this long."

I tried to get Ngoundu and his wife to eat, but they were hanging on to their boy. He looked more reposed than ever. They stared at his chest, which continued to rise with each breath. I felt his forehead.

"I think he feels cooler, *Mami*."

"True. For the last few minutes. I am frightened that now he is about to die."

Great tears formed in her eyes and I thought she must be right. She knew. And then Enubu spoke again, though his eyes didn't open.

"*Mami?*"

I heard the *mami* gasp. "I am here," she said clearly, and firmly, her English perfectly accented.

"The aunt has made my favorite food." Now his eyes did open. "I am hungry."

His parents didn't move. I placed my palm on the boy's forehead. It had become even cooler, and it was also growing damp. He was sweating again. I turned to Ngoundu. "I think the fever is gone."

"Gone, miss?"

"Left him. Gone away. Feel his head."

He didn't have to. The *mami* stood up. She threw her arms around one of the women who had brought the food, her sister. "Your soup, Tata. Your soup!"

Pandemonium broke out. Everyone began hugging and leaping around as Enubu's aunt fed him spoonfuls of soup. I leaned against the wall and sank down to the floor. My legs had stopped holding me up. Then I began crying, and just as when I cried over the card catalog, I threw everyone into a panic. There was silence. The *mami* came to me now.

"You are hurt, miss?"

I sobbed in her arms while everyone began buzzing, explaining in English and Bakweri that I was an American and when Americans are happy they cry instead of laugh. And one old man explained to his friend in pidgin, "How for these American white men? They happy—they cry, they sad—they make monkey-face."

That made me stop crying. The *mami* pulled me up and led me to Enubu's bed. Now he was propped up on pillows, sucking on a piece of papaya.

"Enubu. This woman has saved your life. Your life is hers, that to which you owe everything."

"Why does she cry so hard, *Mami?*"

"She rejoices. It is the way of America."

He smiled at me. "Thank you, miss. I have been to your library often."

"I know you have." I smiled back.

CHAPTER FOURTEEN

When I was ready to leave Ngoundu's home, he asked if I would like an escort to my house, but I told him no, that I was going to see my friend at the prison farm. Ngoundu's expression froze for a second, and then he told me to remember that his house was my house, all he owned, mine, all he could do for me, he would do. As I walked away, I thought that he owed more to whoever made Bayer aspirin than he did to me.

The adrenaline shooting through me got me up the steep winding road that crossed the ledges above Buea. I walked past the prime minister's house, past Pauline's gate. The smell of roses filled the niche in the mountain, roses planted by Pauline, imported from a Munich nursery, two dozen varieties. I'd been in the schloss. The only thing left of the Germans was a chandelier in the ballroom, which had over a thousand crystals hanging from it, but it wasn't that exciting to see because, unlike in the days of the German colonials, there were no slaves to spend day after day on tall ladders, polishing each piece. When the baron was told to return to Germany posthaste, he hadn't the time to have it dismantled.

At the prison gate a guard had to call for Michael, who came out to the sentry post a few minutes later, sleepy-eyed. He was shocked to see me and more shocked at the way I must have looked. And all at once, the adrenaline was gone and he and one of the prisoners practically carried me to his rooms. The rest of the prisoners watched from small windows. They weren't barred. Michael said there wasn't a one who was a real criminal. They were there because of land disputes or because they were "ostracized." Ostracized meant they were outcasts and had no land to farm and couldn't find a job in the market. It was more of a poorhouse than a prison.

I sat on Michael's bed drinking his instant coffee, and started with Mrs. Agboran's dead babies and went on through my hysterical call to the Peace Corps doctor and on to Ngoundu. He kept reaching out to me and I kept signaling him away because I had to get it all out to prepare myself for what I would find so impossible to say. Then I said it.

"Michael. He's there. Here. Right here."

"Who's here?"

"Von Hiltz."

"I know it. But—"

"No you don't know it. You've been dreaming he was here. If you really believed it you'd have had some sort of plan. Well, you'd better make a plan, because you've been right all along. I humored you. I thought it was fun. I thought it was . . . I don't know . . . I thought it was fiction. Now I'm warning you that this is scary. Really scary."

Michael kind of puttered around for a few minutes, wiping water off his sink with his back to me. Then he said, "Please tell me what you found out. And how you found out."

"Enubu, Ngoundu's boy, when he was delirious, he screamed at me. He said, 'Jew!' Then he said other things. Asked his father if he should bring the package to the old man. I couldn't understand too much.

"Michael, none of this made any sense before. How could some guy live on a mountain for twenty years? I mean he has to eat. Someone has to take care of him. I'm sure the son of a baron isn't going to spend half his life camping out and living on porcupine meat."

"What did Ngoundu say when his son said these things?"

"He got real nervous. And he looked funny when I said I was coming here . . . to see you."

"Ngoundu is his brother."

"What?"

"He's von Hiltz's half brother."

How could such a thing sink in? "Michael, I don't understand."

"Von Hiltz's father had a regular harem. The children born from his concubines were von Hiltz's playmates—his own little personal slaves. He even brought one back to Germany with him. They lived together all those years in the schloss—the one in Bavaria—and I think they still do live together somewhere up on the mountain. And the others—the other half brothers and sisters—like Ngoundu, are able to read and write and survive without families. They and their children are their own little tribe. Ngoundu's wife is an Ibo, her own family in Nigeria slaughtered. She got to Buea the same way my mother reached England with me—the will to survive. They have jobs working for Europeans at places like the hotel."

My brain stopped. My eyes closed. "I'm going to sleep," I think I said. And I slept for ten hours and never felt Michael take off my sneakers and shovel me under the blankets. When I woke up, Michael and I fought. We fought and fought. Back and forth we argued.

"If there is proof that he's here in Buea, why don't you just call in these famous Nazi-hunters of yours to go get him out?"

"They won't. He's too small. He's not the Angel of Death or any of the Nazis you read about in the papers all the time. And there is no proof. According to the Israelis, maybe it was his idea to use the trains, maybe it wasn't."

"His idea to use the trains. What trains?" I was babbling.

"My mother heard that the train she was put on . . . the train where she found me . . . the one to Dachau . . . but my father . . . this Benjamin guy . . . he says von Hiltz was never directly involved in killing Jews. Not true. He was directly involved in killing my mother. My real mother. In killing my adopted mother's son. He worked hard on his project. I know. I've found out. I spent a whole year in Munich finding out. It was premeditated murder."

I think I said something like, "Munich?"

"Mattie, the first camps weren't built to exterminate Jews. Dachau was a work camp for political prisoners, captured spies. They became the infamous death camps when von Hiltz worked out the tranportation plan. He organized the whole thing from his little castle. Just one more mad German baron. There sure are a goddamn lot of them, aren't there?

"I was there. In the little lake by the Starnberersee. I was there, too. I've been through his papers. There were letters. He bragged."

"You have letters?"

"No."

"But I thought—"

"They've disappeared."

"Oh, Michael! From where?"

"From here."

"Damn."

Michael went to his sink, the only place where he could get away with having his back to me. "Benjamin didn't believe me either. But I think that's because he didn't want to think about his wife anymore. The one who died giving birth to me."

A spasm went through his shoulders.

"I'm so sorry. I am."

"And I found out how he came down from his Bavarian mountain to go to Munich to watch the operation. He got to be a big cheese. He liked the attention because he was a nobody. A useless nobody. The final solution became a simple solution because of von Hiltz's little suggestion. Instead of worrying about what to do with six million murdered people throuhout Europe, von Hiltz's trains moved them out of the cities and villages first, and then exterminated them. Very neat and clean and very convenient for everyone to say, 'Gee, I didn't know they were killing the Jews. I thought they were just taking them to work on farms. Or in factories.' As if that were perfectly all right. Fucking Germans. What a lot of shit."

"Michael, couldn't you convince the Israelis of all this?"

"Yes."

"Why don't you?"

"You gave me the reason, Mattie. In Fernando Póo. Because I want to personally wring his rotten neck."

I wasn't Jo. I didn't want to be in on this kind of stuff. He took me home on the back of his motorcycle. We didn't say anything. We didn't kiss good-bye. He could see right through me. He knew I didn't want to get involved. I didn't love him enough. He was so right. I couldn't ever love anyone that much.

But I was worried about him. It helped to write now, more than ever. I wrote about this sweet, innocent guy searching for a mad baron.

What would really happen to Michael, I didn't know. I didn't want to know. I started a dozen letters to Jo, each sounding more ludicrous than the one before. I needed to see her, but I didn't think she'd understand. How could she, if I couldn't?

I helped Mrs. Agboran come back from the dead. I bought her a chartreuse chiffon scarf. It was six weeks since the children had died. The scarf brought the first smile to her lips. Her friends laughed, in front of her, for the first time. I played dumb. I knew it was the scarf a prostitute would wear, but they wouldn't hurt my feelings by telling me. Each of us tried it on, taking turns tying it around our heads. They thought I was the most naïve human being alive, and once again they began to make suggestions about how I must write home and encourage my father to find a husband for me.

When I saw Mrs. Agboran smile, I decided I needed to smile, too, sick of worrying about Michael, trying to decide if I might really be a little crazy after all. Was this Benjamin for real? Maybe Michael had hallucinated him—maybe the whole thing. But I'd heard Ngoundu's boy, what he'd said. I wished I could convince myself that I was the one hallucinating. I took my little Jeep down the mountain one night to the hotel in Victoria. I sat at the bar, not at a table in the lounge. I didn't order ice cream either. Scotch on the unboiled rocks. I knew I'd meet someone, hopefully not the Italian from AGIP. I was there for half an hour, on my third Scotch, when a man sat down next to me. He looked like an American astronaut. Gus Grissom. He was a mercenary on vacation from the Congo. Right. I never batted an eyelash.

He got drunk, too. He told me about killing rebels and making a hundred dollars an ear. If I wrote the things this guy was telling me, my dad would say, "It's virtually impossible to make soldiers of fortune believable." My dad wouldn't say anything about Michael's story because I'd never show it to him. He'd say something about how thrillers written by women wouldn't wash. And how could I tell him that—except for some necessary drama—the story was basically true? Basically going on right now. Had no end. I was very afraid of what the end would actually be. But I couldn't think about it anymore.

I told the mercenary how I needed to go to Bamenda to visit a friend. I would do anything to get there. He said he was going north. Did I want a lift? A four-seater CAT would be waiting for him in the morning in Tiko. He looked at me. I said, "OK."

At the bar, I did need to see Jo badly, because someone else besides me was telling my body what to do. So the first thing I told her when I did see her was that I had had sex with someone to pay back a favor. "I am officially, Jo, somewhere between mildly promiscuous and a hooker."

"Well," she said, studying me, "you look exactly the same way you did the last time I saw you. Not like either of the above. Except for the hangover. You have a really bad headache, right?"

"Yes."

"Then I'll get two aspirins and in twenty minutes you'll

be back to normal." She gave me an efficient smile. Aspirin. I'd have to tell her about all that, too—to make sense.

It was like being a kid and going to confession. Like a priest, Jo could forgive anything. Instead of two Hail Marys, two aspirins. When she came back with the aspirin she said, "Do you feel any different, Mattie?"

"No."

"You don't feel guilty about being unfaithful. I mean . . . I mean to Michael."

"I wasn't unfaithful to Michael. I'm not in love with him anymore. I mean, I love him, but I don't feel romantic about him the way I did. It went away. He loves something else more than me and I feel like being adored. You know, Jo, when men fall in love with you, they adore you. I want to know what that feels like. I'll do anything for Michael but I'm not going to love him anymore."

"You can shut it off, just like that?"

"Yes."

"So can I."

"Like with Jean-Pierre?"

"Yes."

"You didn't shut anything off, Jo You weren't turned on to begin with."

"I've decided to go home." I think my mouth opened but Jo was still talking. "My mind is made up. I'm going to find my family. All of it. My father, too." She and Michael really were made for each other. "And, Mattie, I mean I'm going home now. I've got plane reservations for Monday."

"Get up, Jo," I said, "we're going for a walk."

I dragged her out into the high Bamenda hills. We walked under the night sky, which in Bamenda is soft, black, and with stars so bright you notice them. It was how Will described the sky over the swamp. An equatorial night on high hills away from any artificial light took my breath away as much as the sea around Hawaii. We walked up past the Fulani's permanent encampment. The Fulani have big round mud houses with perfectly pointed thatch roofs.

In the dark they looked like little circus tents. A baby cried and its mother crooned one of those Fulani lullabys that sound like angel music in a Christmas movie extravaganza.

"I'm not doing enough here, Mattie."

"Enough what?"

"I'm not making the most of my life." Where had I heard this before? "I have more to offer these people than what they actually need. Cameroonians are happy people. They have so few material things, but they have everything."

That's when I told her what a measles epidemic was like. What dead children were like. Every gruesome detail, while I bawled. It was impossible not to, thinking of those little kids of Mrs. Agboran's.

"All this shit about how happy these simple people are even though they don't have television sets. Jo, they have less than nothing. They're happy because some of their children are alive despite such terrible odds. How self-righteous we are to admire that kind of so-called happiness."

It didn't take much else to change her mind about leaving, but it helped when I went on to wail about having been jilted for a Nazi baron.

"I should have told my mercenary last night about von Hiltz, Jo. He'd have run up the mountain in two seconds, found the guy, and marched him down to whoever wanted him. Maybe the Israelis would have given him a nice price He sure got a nice price from me. Shit. I'm scared."

"I know."

"Not for Michael, for me. Do you know I liked sleeping with that guy and not caring about anything? I liked it. Don't leave me, Jo."

"OK, Mattie, I won't let you do that again."

"Thanks. You'll stay?"

She didn't think it was necessary to answer the rhetorical question. "Did the mercenary ask about Michael?"

"I don't think he asked me much about anything. All I remember is him and me in some hotel bed, screwing our brains out. God, it was fun."

"Oh, Mattie!"

"I'm sorry. It was. Yes, he asked about Michael. He asked about the volunteers around Victoria. He asked about the one at the prison." I stopped. Jo's eyes were very big. "Jesus, he did ask. Oh my God, what did I tell him? I can't remember."

"He must have been an Israeli. Someone watching out for Michael."

"What if he's on the other side? What if he's flown back and killed Michael? What if he's an assassin working for some cell of ex-Nazis in Paraguay or somewhere?"

"That's insane."

"But what if? Michael sure thought I was in danger. I just don't know."

"Mattie, people do realize that if an American volunteer is mysteriously killed, the Army Corps of Engineers would be out here in two seconds."

"Jo, the Army Corps of Engineers dredge sand to put on Coney Island."

"You know what I mean."

"Is it possible to call the prison from the college?"

"Yes."

We ran all the way back to Jo's college through the silent black night. A lot like a summer night in Connecticut, only different insects. Jo grabbed a key from her house and we unlocked the administration office's door. It took about twenty minutes to get through to the prison. Michael was fine. He thought I was calling from the hotel. I didn't tell him I was with Jo. I told him I couldn't see him again except as a friend. He agreed that that would be best, but he loved me. Then we both couldn't hang up. He kept talking about another time, another place, and I was thinking about Humphrey Bogart, and I knew that Michael had to find his Nazi. If he didn't, he wouldn't find himself. And that's what we were all doing in Camelot. Trying to find out who we were. Big cliché. Big truism. What people were we that we went running off around the world? Why weren't Jo and I doing what all our classmates at Bryn

Mawr were doing? Michael knew what he was doing. Jo thought she knew what she was doing. I didn't know what the hell I was doing.

So I returned to Buea, Jo stayed in Cameroon, and Michael found Wilhelm von Hiltz.

When I went back, I avoided Michael. He didn't make much of an attempt to see me. A few notes left at the post office and I sent a few back telling him I was so involved with the library that I couldn't meet him for a swim in Victoria. When a group of volunteers got together for a party, Michael didn't go. It was a relief. I wrote essays on the exotic scenery in this remote area of the world that had really become home to me. My father really liked the essays, although he pointed out that they were a part of a greater whole that would come as I matured. He sent me Isak Dinesen's diaries. My father didn't accept the fact that we were basically middle-class people, he and my mother and brother and I. We considered ourselves Roosevelt, New Deal, union types at heart, who found ourselves in affluent Fairfield County with affluent-people kind of jobs and schooling. I wasn't Isak Dinesen. And even though I was writing a thriller, I wasn't trying to be John Le Carré either. There was my blue-collar heritage winning over my white-collar background. As a writer, I intended to be something new. I didn't tell my father this because it would injure his ego. He was an editor at *The New Yorker*. He knew better than I what I was, what I should be.

I told Jo all this, in letters, and she agreed with me, supported me, and told me that someday I would represent a whole new kind of writer. I was very lucky to have Jo. No one would ever understand me as well, believe in me as much.

Time on the mountain moved slowly while books on my library shelves increased in number. Bryn Mawr alumnae sure loved to contribute books. Great books, too. The library was becoming famous. I enjoyed this period of peace, but wasn't prepared for its abrupt end. Michael had an accident. I say "accident," but I don't know what it was.

One evening I was walking back to the hotel just as dusk settled in. There was this incredible roaring and I thought the volcano was going up, but people were definitely running toward something, not away. They were running to the hotel, where a helicopter was landing. We all thought the president was arriving. I got there as they lowered a stretcher out of the helicopter into the parking lot. The stretcher was for Michael.

He was on the floor of the lobby of the hotel and he'd been beaten up. His face looked like it had been run over by a truck. The Israelis had come for him in a helicopter. They were about to take him out of the hotel just as I got there, but I made them stop. I knelt next to Michael and started saying he had to see a doctor or go to the clinic first. There was a lot of commotion as two men tried to keep the kids back in the parking lot, but they were already scrambling like bush babies up the side of the helicopter and into it.

This one man standing over Michael picked me up by my shoulders, and I looked into his eyes, and they were Michael's eyes, which I now realized were so beautiful. Light-brown, almost mulatto topaz—they were that clear. It was his father. I didn't know that I was hysterical until I heard the words he was using to get me to calm down. Accented commands that I ignored. Finally I could hear Michael saying, "I'm OK, Mattie. I'm OK."

I looked down at him from his father's arms. "You're not OK. You look awful. What did he do to you?"

Michael's father sat down on the floor, pulling me with him, not letting go of my arms. "Michael is telling you the truth. He is just badly bruised."

"His cheekbone is broken. I can tell." I felt as though I couldn't breathe. I'd gotten a good look at Michael's eye and I couldn't look at him again. His face under his eye was caved in.

"A cheekbone heals itself. It's for protecting your eye. The cheekbone did what it is there to do. His eye is fine.

152

He'll be fine. But now, I've got to get him out. He has found secrets that are dangerous to many people. He needs protection from us. Only you can help us."

It was like a movie scene that went wrong. Cameroonians chattering everywhere. The hotel manager trying to restore order. Police arriving with their little shorts and batons, having no idea what to do about an illegal helicopter parked at the hotel.

"Mattie, can you understand me?" Michael's father asked.

"No, I can't."

"Listen to me. The Peace Corps doctor is on his way. With your director. They expect to evacuate Michael to Munich because they know he's been badly injured. You must tell them when they get here. You must tell them that Michael is an Israeli citizen and that the Israelis have taken him to Tel Aviv for treatment."

"And how do I get out of the cuckoo house after I tell him that?"

I heard Michael say something like, "Hum," which was a laugh. I looked at him. He was really hurting. I scrambled down next to him and laid my head next to his and told him I loved him. I felt his hand touch me somewhere. His father dragged me back up. "I'm sorry, we must go. Just smile when you explain what happened to Michael. You are too attractive for them to doubt."

I looked back at his Michael-eyes. "I'm not attractive, but I'll tell them whatever you say."

Michael mumbled. His father became concerned. I told him Michael was saying I was too attractive. They put him on the stretcher. I walked along with it to the helicopter. Before they lifted him up, I said, "Did you get him, Michael?"

Michael lifted one thumb up. I kissed his mashed face. Once he was inside, his father took my head in his hands and said good-bye. I thought he would crush my head. That was his way of being hysterical. And then they were gone and the fat Danish hotel manager appeared and half carried me into the hotel lounge and started pouring brandy down my throat. The whole time I sat there shaking and drinking he was telling me that the Bakweris who lived on the mountain and took care of von Hiltz did this to Michael after he shot von Hiltz—until Ngoundu arrived to make his black half brothers stop. And Ngoundu asked Michael what it was he wanted and Michael said von Hiltz's correspondences.

"And now we have addresses in South America that will lead us to people who we need to find, some who we never realized existed."

And the whole time I listened to this fat man, I kept thinking, Who the hell is this guy? He was part of "we." Benjamin's "we."

The circuit of Nazi-hunters are a very small group, but they cover the world. That's what Michael told me a year later. It was probably too farfetched to put in my book. I didn't ask the Dane where Michael got the gun. It didn't matter.

When the Peace Corps doctor and Mr. Jones arrived, I was completely drunk. I told them that someone evacuated Michael already to the hospital. Then I passed out, so the doctor had to take care of me. When I pass out, I pass out good. I slept for twenty-four hours, and woke up starving to find the director had gone back to Yaoundé and I was in a hotel room with just the doctor, who was sound asleep in the other bed. I went down to the kitchen and ordered two huge breakfasts. Ngoundu brought them. I asked him how his boy was. He told me, "Well," and asked me if my friend, the prison teacher, would be all right. I said, "Yes." Even Steven.

I woke up the doc, and he and I ate together, and I told him what Michael's father told me to say. He said OK, if Michael's an Israeli citizen, fine. He's in Tel Aviv? Fine. Director tells me to handle this, fine. I'm handling it. The doc said he'd write a report, file it, no one would read it, fine. As long as I was sure Michael was going to be OK, fine. Fine, fine, fine. I loved his attitude. He had no attitude.

154

After we ate, he said, "So what do you do for fun around here, Mattie?"

One thing about doctors—the first thing they teach them in medical school is not to get emotionally involved with the patient. Physically involved is understood. I took him swimming at the Victoria beach. We kind of ended up necking in the water. I reminded him that I was his patient and wasn't it a no-no to get emotionally involved. He said, "That's right. No emotional involvement." Then he said, "Have I given you a breast examination in the last six months?"

"No."

He, no doubt, said, Fine. I was glad Jo wasn't around to not let him.

CHAPTER FIFTEEN

Our second Christmas in Cameroon approached. In training we were told that we'd stop missing home once we'd finished our first year in country. This was true, except for potato chips. I'd have done anything for the opportunity to sit down with a good book and a large-size bag of potato chips and then finish both by the time I went to bed. Other people dreamed of rare steak. Not me.

The Cameroonians I came to know at my library and in town were more and more loving toward me as the months passed. They adopted me once they'd resolved themselves to my spinsterhood, coming to the conclusion that American women remained children twice as long as Cameroonian women. Since they were such a tolerant people, they came to accept that, but it didn't stop them from trying to take advantage of a solution to my tragedy if the opportunity arose. Mrs. Agboran, now pregnant—by whom, I didn't ask—stopped to see me one morning as my friend Phil, from the French college in Victoria, was leaving. He'd slept in his sleeping bag on my floor before climbing the mountain. Most volunteers saw my living quarters as part of the tourist attraction, and almost all of them climbed Mount Cameroon, starting with a rest on my floor. Mrs. Agboran assumed I'd slept with him and was very pleased at my progress.

156

Phil was a charmer who loved all women, but was monogamous by nature and had a girlfriend back home waiting for him. I found it comforting to have a male friend whom I could be myself with. Phil was sort of like having Paul around to talk to.

"He is a nice fellow, Miss Mattie," Mrs. Agboran told me once Phil had charmed her. "Would he consent to be your husband?"

She had no qualms about inquiring into my personal life. "I hope not, Mrs. Agboran. I told you, I'm not going to get married for a few years. I'm tired of men anyway."

This was an enigma to her. People don't think of each other in Cameroon as things to become tired of. "But you let him sleep the night. You must at least like him."

"I didn't sleep with him, Mrs. Agboran. He just needed to stay here so he would be able to climb the mountain, first thing."

"He is sick then?" She didn't buy the mountain-climbing business.

"Yes." It was easier to say yes. Let her think poor Phil had gonorrhea. The explanation satisfied her and we went to the library together. When Phil came back down the mountain to stay another night, he had someone in tow whom he'd met climbing the mountain. I told Phil about his gonorrhea and he got all embarrassed, which was an abnormal reaction for Phil. He loved sexual jokes, innuendoes, puns, etc. He was embarrassed because the guy with him was a Franciscan monk. Brother Pat was one of the assistant Peace Corps directors in Nigeria, the only clergyman in the State Department, actually. He'd been sent to a meeting in Yaoundé with our director and decided to climb the mountain while he was in the area. He laughed at the gonorrhea story politely.

The three of us had a nice dinner of rice and yams and four cups of Royal chocolate pudding Louisa had sent me for Christmas. She sent it from Hawaii and her Filipino sent his regards. Louisa was getting a master's in Asian studies from the University of Hawaii. I mixed evaporated milk with water, and the pudding worked except for an aftertaste of baby formula, which is what evaporated milk always makes me think of. Brother Pat told us he'd arranged a pilgrimage to the Holy Land at Christmas for American Embassy and USIS people, and that if we ran into any foreign-service types to let them know about the trip. Brother Pat had a few more slots to fill to keep his charter price at four hundred dollars. I told him I knew two people who'd love to go and took his Lagos address. Afterward Phil said, "You wouldn't really, Mattie, would you?"

I said I didn't know, but I did. Phil told me I was crazy. I reminded him if I got caught and sent home, I didn't have Vietnam to worry about like he did.

I had four hundred dollars. We all did. The Peace Corps gave its Cameroon volunteers one of the highest living allowances in the world because there were no stores selling Western food except in Yaoundé, Douala, and Victoria. Peace Corps Washington didn't count the village markets as stores. But that's where we bought all our food, and I was getting fat on what was basically a vegetarian diet because of the Buea town baker, who'd learned how to make all kinds of French bread from his former French employer.

So I wrote to Jo, told her to forget whatever plans she'd made for the money sitting in her account, and told her to get a money order from Barclay's Bank for the trip. She did, and with only a small argument. She warned me not to mention the trip to a soul because it was bound to get back to the director and he really could prevent us from going. And the guy was such a rules man that Jo was right—he'd stop us, especially after what happened to Michael.

When the doc got back to Yaoundé, he sent me a note to tell me Jones became "amusingly" crazed when he read the doc's report. As for our leave applications, I told Jo not to worry because we'd do them at the last minute, and besides, the director never took time to read all those leave applications. He was too busy with his French lessons. He just signed everything. Official policy encouraged us to spend our vacations touring our own country or bordering countries, but the written word said that you could actually go anywhere, as long as you didn't leave your continent. That rule went into effect in the early years of the Peace Corps because volunteers in Africa would send home for money and zip off to Rome or Paris for a long weekend.

I told Jo that my geology professor at Bryn Mawr had said there was some question as to whether the Middle East could genuinely be considered part of Europe. It could be part of Asia, but because of the Great Rift-Valley it was, in reality, part of Africa. There is so much latitude in the letter of the law, I told her, especially from a geological point of view.

As it turned out, a complication did arise, but it came too late to cause any problems. When I applied for my exit visa, the Cameroonian who stamped my passport introduced me to a Cameroonian lawyer who was in line directly behind me. He invited me for a drink at the hotel. He was a nice guy, but married. He got even with me for giving him the brush by announcing at a Christmas party in Yaoundé, attended by Director Jones, naturally, the following:

"I have a feeling that even though Mattie from Buea may be in the Holy Land, she probably isn't praying. Hahaha." He was right, the rat; I was at a disco that very night.

The director's secretary told me that Jones made her go to the office with him right in the middle of the party to check out my application for travel, and there it was under "Countries to be visited": LEBANON, JORDAN, AND SYRIA. He was so beside himself that he went through all the other applications and of course found Jo's, too. But we became minor stuff when he found out about these four guys who went to Johannesburg, which was a complete no-no, continent or not.

My friend Jo had worked very hard since Jean-Pierre left, and she really did need a vacation. She was going a little crazy, too, teaching for standardized tests that were developed in England. The minute she'd get into some subject, get great discussions going, her students would jump up and shout, "Please, miss, this is not to be found on the test." She told me she really got mad once because she had to spend six weeks teaching her biology classes all about birds in England. The curriculum gave her three days for reptiles. Cameroon abounds with reptiles and you can go months without seeing birds. "I don't know why there aren't any birds here, but anyway, tough!" said the students. "No snakes on the tests, so just keep telling us about the breeding patterns of magpies."

Jo worked all summer writing a report for the ministry of education on how they could go about developing their own, more relevant tests. She got a letter back from the minister's British secretary, telling her that since the dream of West Cameroonian students is to go to England to study, they'd have to have the same background as students educated in England. Jo doubted the minister ever saw her report.

"There's a good cause for you, Jo," I said, hopefully.

"Too dull a cause, Mattie." She persuaded a dull volunteer who taught in Bamenda to work on it instead.

And I was so sick of cataloging books.

It took us five days to get to Lagos overland. We went to Calabar, the first town over the Nigeria border, and got on an enormous ferry, packed full. The stone docks had been loading stations for slaves, and the river to Enugu was even more out of the heart of darkness than all the other African scenes put together. It was very wide, yet the jungle canopy covered it in a great green arch. We took a million pictures instead of thinking about how the slaves must have felt as they were carted down that beautiful, calm river to the terrifying sea.

At Enugu we got out and took a mammy-wagon from one town to another, carrying suitcases on our heads because we always got such a laugh out of the African *mamis* who did it so gracefully. As we searched out government guesthouses, which the Nigerians had inherited from the British, we slowly made our way across southern Nigeria to Lagos. The guesthouses were wonderful; they all served high tea at four. Only once did we have to stay in a "local hotel," because the town guesthouse was full. The hotel had no doors and the walls of the rooms were only six feet high—several feet short of the ceiling. People, mostly kids, stared at us all night through the space where the door should have been. Folks were either making love or coughing all night long, but fortunately, our neighbors—on the one side the tubercular case and the other a prostitute and client—never decided to look over the wall at us. After that, we would call ahead and make reservations at the next town's guesthouse.

Once, in the middle of absolutely nowhere, we came to a barbed-wire fence with the U.S. flag flying far behind it. It was a satellite tracking station, manned by two suicidal southern guys, who were so glad to see American women that they broke out champagne and Chef Boy-ar-dee frozen pizzas. They immediately assured us that they wouldn't rape or take advantage of us, but please could they just give us a couple of quick hugs. They were very funny. We suggested dancing after dinner instead of hugs, and asked why they didn't date Peace Corps volunteers in Nigeria, and they said the "girls" were warned in training that the sex-starved NASA guys would make them sex slaves. And the two of them were quite offended because they were genteel Birmingham boys who had credit with the local prostitutes besides.

I could have spent my entire vacation with those guys. They treated us like two visiting moon maidens. In the morning they even brought us breakfast in bed. Their beds. They insisted on sleeping on the floor. They were a two-man southern fraternity and begged us not to leave them. But we had a plane to catch. In those twenty-four hours that we were with them, no satellites got tracked. Not a one.

We promised them we'd stop on the way back and we

intended to. They made all these incredible plans for what they'd do for us when we returned. It would have been a lot of fun, and they must have wondered why we stood them up. They knew we liked them. Actually, just I stood them up, having completely forgotten them, because Jo never came back at all. A few months later, I did remember the guys from NASA and wrote notes to all the women volunteers in my group that if they wanted a wonderful vacation to go to Onitsha, Nigeria, and visit the two adorable fellows from Birmingham behind the only barbed-wire fence I'd ever seen in Africa.

We flew with Brother Pat and all the Americans from USIS and the lower echelons of the embassy over the Sahara and were fortunate enough to witness sunset on the great desert from the air. The sand was rippled just like the sandbar beneath the waters of Long Island Sound at low tide. It was so grand and vast, with a life of its own that I couldn't fathom. Even though I knew there were Bedouins, and other people in and out of history books who peopled the deserts, I couldn't imagine anyone living on what lay below me. Desert people must be some sort of sand swimmers, I thought, and it was no wonder they were constantly on the move. It was not a place where you'd stop, and stay, and say, Well, this piece of sand looks nice and cozy—let's build a nice house. What people were willing to shift, back and forth, interminably, just the way the ground was doing?

In the dead of night, the lights of Beirut reached up to us and drew us down. And as soon as we were out of the airport, I could feel myself heading for a city. I love cities, and cities on the sea are a special wonder to me. All that energy, and next to it, all that inscrutable water.

Beirut was beautiful. City lights infuse me with energy, and Jo and I went walking as soon as we checked into our hotel. There were bars and movies and restaurants, stores and drugstores, all open. But best of all, Jo and I discovered *souks*—big open markets with mounds of spices, little brass cups of thick coffee offered everywhere, yards of Damascus brocade—pure silk, and run through with strands of 24-karat gold. Cheap, too. Very cheap. An Arab city. But just like in New York, things finally became quiet at the first light of dawn, and Jo and I ate breakfast in the coffee shop of the Hilton. An American breakfast. We had eggs and pancakes, both. Then we hailed a taxi. The driver spoke English, French, and Arabic, and he took us back to the hotel, telling us he was now eight thousand, two hundred and forty-seventh on the waiting list to immigrate to America. He'd converted, too. He said he belonged to a Congregational church so that he'd be more acclimated to America when he got there. He was giving up everything he was to leave. Jo and I couldn't understand it. Beirut was magnificent.

We asked him to show us where the American Embassy was before he brought us back to the hotel because my passport was out of pages. He drove down a long, wide, perfectly curving boulevard that skirted the Mediterranean, and pointed out a great white building surrounded by plush green trees with fruit on them. It was a majestic building, shimmering in the light from the sun, which first glanced off the sea. It was yet to be sabotaged. Bombs with addresses on them would not arrive for two decades.

Beirut was the most cosmopolitan of cities, with all the languages singing back and forth, church bells, and the call from the minarets five times every day. A peninsula at the north end of the city jutted out into the sea, and on it was a sprawling casino. Inside was a room called the "American Room," full of ear-shattering slot machines and a ring of men screaming at the dice to come up with the right numbers. The "European Room" was smooth: blackjack and roulette and baccarat, as quiet as library reading rooms. The casino nightclub was showing the road show from the Lido in Paris. I called it the All-Bosom Revue. We American pilgrims, including the monk, clapped the loudest at the music, the colored feathers, the spangles, and the rows of rouged, pink nipples.

After the authentic French nightclub, we went to an authentic Arab nightclub, with a belly dancer who weighed about two hundred pounds and had at least seven or eight bellies, all undulating in different directions. She had little tiny feet. She picked on poor Brother Pat, because he really was so adorable with his round bald head, and round little glasses, and a round little belly of his own. She came dancing across the floor, climbing across the laps of several people, and then sank to her knees in front of Brother Pat. She reached up and took his head as if it were a melon she was plucking from a tree and cuddled it into the deep crevasse between her two apocalyptic breasts. He came up, gasping for breath, as she finally released him, flicking one great hip in his direction as she searched out her next victim. I've never seen anything as funny since, in my life.

One afternoon, while the pilgrims napped, Jo and I went to see *Doctor Zhivago*. It was in French, but Omar Sharif was still gorgeous.

During the next few days, we went to see real pilgrims. We went to Old Jerusalem, Bethlehem, and Galilee—all those places that are now Israel. None of them were then. In the middle of the Way of the Cross, Station Number Six, Veronica Wipes the Face of Jesus, we accidentally stepped into an Arab candymaker's shop. Light-haired women create a stir in Arab countries, and with Jo's hair being silver, they couldn't stop fawning all over her. Next thing, we were making candy with the candymaker and his two apprentices, and then we went through a black curtain in the back into the owner's house. There were women wearing veils and they brought us coffee and we had a million kids in our laps inside of three minutes, chattering just like African kids. I wish Americans could giggle like the rest of the world. Those Arab candy people were the best gigglers of all.

Of course I wondered, once I was home again in the United States, and once the years had slipped by, what happened to the Arab candymaker and his family and his friends. At least they didn't live in those warrens in front of the Wailing Wall. All those little houses, according to *Newsweek*, were bulldozed in order to make room for all the Jewish tourists who had waited such a long time to put their prayer notes in its cracks.

On Christmas day, we rented a car to take us up to the mountains, where we saw the cedars of Lebanon covered in snow in a little grove. The oldest trees in the world until the California redwoods shoved them aside. We brushed the snow off our thin sweaters and had Christmas dinner in a chalet that was warm and soft and full of little brass things gleaming in the lights of a Christmas tree. It was my second Christmas without the one I was so used to. I couldn't get over how I didn't miss one bit the Christmas at home. I missed Michael.

On New Year's Eve, we went to the same disco where we'd spent Christmas Eve because it was so much fun. Halfway through the revels, Jo disappeared. I went rushing back to the hotel in a taxi and there she was, lying on the bed, all teary-eyed.

"What the hell's the matter with you?" I was half drunk and wanted to get back.

"I heard someone say to someone else that Walt Disney died this week. And it's true." She pointed to an American newspaper she'd gotten at the coffee-shop newsstand. She blew her nose.

When, like Jo, you have no family, you never get to have any relatives die or to go to any funerals. Walt Disney was just as tough on her as it would have been for me if one of my uncles died. I said the wrong thing.

"Jo, don't forget Walt didn't let Khrushchev into Disneyland." She sat up on the edge of the bed and looked at me. "I mean, it's not like Mickey Mouse died. Or Bambi. Or Tinker—"

"Shut up."

"C'mon, Jo. Why are you feeling sorry for yourself? Feeling guilty about having a good time? Why is it you only want to have fun for so long, and then you decide you're supposed to be suffering?"

"Go back, Mattie. I just want to be by myself."

I looked at my watch. Twelve-ten. "Well it's too goddamn late. My attaché or whatever he was has no doubt hooked up with that French girl who was scouting him. The hell with it." I pulled off my shoes and headed toward the bathroom.

"I'm sorry, Mattie, but you really should have stayed there."

"I was worried about you."

She stood up, tall and beautiful, in her Damascus glitter, eyes like ice. "As of this very minute, you are never to worry about me again. Ever."

"What's that supposed to mean?"

"It means that I am going to do things with my life that will worry you and I can't let my regard for you get in my way. So don't let me get in yours, OK?"

"This was a test?"

"What?"

"You ruined a good party to give me a test, Jo. You did. You should have told me about this new slate you've come up with. You're really being selfish."

She started to cry. I went over and sat next to her on the bed. "Face it, Jo. What is there to do except go home to a terrific school, marry someone also terrific, and—"

"And live happily ever after?"

"Yes. Why not?"

"Mattie, I can't just live my life going from one compartment to the next, leaving everything behind me. That's your agenda and there's nothing wrong with it. I respect what you want to do. But I can't leave civil rights behind. How can you just turn that stuff off and leave it? What about those people in Philadelphia?"

"It's over. Philadelphia is over. I'm almost twenty-four. Time to grow up. Time for you, too."

"What has commitment to social causes have to do with growing up?"

"My motives were never the same as yours. I think you've never been able to face that. You want me to be idealistic and altruistic and all that, just like you are. Well, I'm not.

No one is. Except maybe Albert Schweitzer. I'm going to go home and marry someone with enough money to support me in this kind of style," I swung my arms madly about, gesturing around the four-star hotel room, "while I write my silly little stories."

"Your stories aren't little or silly."

"Yes they are."

She started to relax. Immediately, I knew she was thinking how charming to be a struggling, starving writer. She didn't hear the part about the rich husband. She took my hand. "Your father doesn't know everything."

"What's that supposed to mean?"

"I love your father. You know it. But he's the one who's convinced you that you write silly little stories."

"He's an expert, Jo. It's his job to know that kind of stuff. Every letter I get from him, he asks me what I'm working on, and to send him things. He's very encouraging and supportive and I'm lucky to have his criticism. And how did we get on this particular issue anyway?"

Jo looked at her feet.

"Now what?"

"I want to stay on this issue, Mattie. I've always wanted to say this, but it's been too tough. I think your father . . . unconsciously . . . sets you up so that he can pat you on the back after giving you a C minus. He doesn't take your writing seriously and never will because he enjoys his role as big strong father to his helpless little girl. I'm sorry."

I ripped my hand out of hers and walked out the door. What was my father supposed to do? Tell his boss at *The New Yorker* to publish an amateurish short story as a favor to his daughter? I turned around in the hallway and went back in and said those things to Jo. And I demanded that she apologize to me.

"How can you insult my father, Jo? If it wasn't for him you'd still be in that tenement with all the rats."

As soon as I said it I wanted to take it back but I couldn't do that. I sat down on the bed next to her to do the apologizing. "I didn't mean it, Jo."

"It's OK." She smiled. But her eyes were filmed over.

"What do I know about father-daughter relationships? Zero, but I do know about tenements. I think it's where I belong."

"Of course it isn't." Here we go again.

"And I don't mind if you stay mad at me. We've always been honest with each other about everything. I really do feel your father has a bias against you. It must come with the territory. I'm assuming that from what I've seen of you guys. The next time you finish something, send it to the *Michigan Quarterly* instead of your father. And I do love your father. You know I do. I'm not being insulting. Try to understand."

I'd stopped paying attention. "Listen, why don't we just forget both things for a while. My father and your tenement. OK? Let's just have some fun now. We'll be back eating yams in a couple of days."

"OK," she agreed, lying. "But . . ."

I went and fumbled in a drawer for pajamas. She wanted to talk to me, but I didn't want to hear. I wanted things to stay the same. I still even had hopes for Paul. I got in my bed with Durrell. But as I began *Mountolive,* Jo lay there planning. I was afraid to let her open up, spoiled shit that I was. And by the time I realized Jo had to open up to someone or do something crazy, she found someone else to talk to and she did something crazy.

CHAPTER
SIXTEEN

On New Year's Day a scenic bus tour of the city and "environs" was planned for the pilgrims. It was a holiday, so everything was closed down. Our whole group boarded a bus, new cameras strung around the majority of necks. The new Nikons and Minoltas were bought from sidewalk black-market vendors with American dollars, the world's favorite currency. I stuck with my Instamatic because fiddling with light meters was not my idea of enjoying the sights. Jo didn't have a camera. In fact, I'd never known Jo to take a photograph.

The day was sunny and clear, about sixty-five degrees, which is warm for Beirut at that time of year. We rode up into the hills behind the city, stopping at all the overlooks. The scene below reminded me a little of pictures of Rio. Instead of a statue of Christ, though, Beirut has a statue of Mary looking down on the city like the rest of us—Our Lady of the Bay or the Water, or something like that. The bus wound its way through olive groves and suburban villages, and I noticed how small the distances were; one minute we were stopping at a *souk* for one last souvenir plus a sip of *arak,* and the next down a Beirut avenue lined with brass-trimmed glass doors lettered in gold—Balenciaga, Christian Dior.

The end of the trip was down the boulevard skirting the

sea, and it appeared more breathtaking than it did the last time we'd driven around its wide sweep. We passed the American University and I told Jo we should maybe spend a year there before going to real graduate school. She sighed at me. Today, I hear that sigh, which was her sigh of indecision just before she made her decision.

The bus headed back toward the direction of the hotel, when suddenly the driver, who was also our guide, began gesturing dramatically for us to look out the right side of the bus at the picturesque fellow squeezing fresh fruit juice at a little kiosk. Everyone hopped up to take their shots, but the glance Jo and I got wasn't especially appealing. The guy stood there, sort of bored. He had no customers. His pile of fruit was small and in disorder, and the grassy plot behind him was scrubby with a littered path running across it.

Jo looked out her window instead and gasped, grabbing my wrist. I looked past her and saw a mammoth hole in the ground about four feet deep, stretched out to the length of a football field, including the stands. The hole was full of tarpaulin tents, cracked zinc roofs, and filthy open sewers. The whole place was teeming with people, mostly half-naked kids. It was worse than the streets of Lagos, where people marked off a section of sidewalk, set up an empty carton, and called it home. Here, there were so many. Jo and I were sitting right behind the driver, as far away from the pilgrims as possible.

"Yusef, what is that slum?"

"Where?"

"Right there!"

"Oh. Yes. That is just the refugee camp. But look to your right—we are approaching the old Armenian quarter where . . ."

Jo, still gaping out the window, interrupted. "Refugees from where?"

"They are from Palestine. They are nothing." He grimaced. His last comment obviously represented his own political point of view.

I said, "But there isn't a Palestine. There hasn't been a Palestine for twenty years." There hadn't been an actual Palestine for centuries, as far as I knew. Not one run by Palestinians, anyway.

"That's true."

"Then where are they from?"

"Uh . . . Israel. And what is now Jordan." He whispered "Israel" out of the corner of his mouth. "They've been there since 1948." Yusef drove with one hand. The other hand was really working over the worry beads now. "Ah look," he said, "the mosque of the blah-blah-blah . . ." All the pilgrims began snapping again.

I stopped craning my neck. Jo sat looking at her hands in her lap. "That was incredible, wasn't it?" I said to her. "Those people living like that all this time." She didn't hear me. She asked the driver, "What was that place called?"

"Which place?" Yusef inquired politely, enthralled by the silver head of hair leaning toward him.

"Where the Palestinian refugees were."

"Ah. The camp. That one is called Shatila."

Her eyes opened wider. "You mean there are others?"

"Many others."

"Where?"

"Several around Beirut. Many in Gaza. Most in Jordan —around Jericho."

"Are they all like that?"

"Yes." His face in the mirror above his head had an expression of surprise that Jo would expect a refugee camp to be any different.

"Oh." Then she said, "Thank you," without knowing it.

Jo went through the motions of getting through the afternoon, just like when John Kennedy was killed. I was grateful that we'd be going back to Cameroon the day after next. I figured she wouldn't have time to stay upset over the hole in the ground once we were back in Africa. If only I hadn't run out of pages in my passport. To this day I keep telling myself that if I hadn't left her alone to go to the embassy to get pages for my passport, or if only I hadn't dawdled through the seaside park, I'd have gotten back in time to prevent the whole thing from ever happening. If only I'd done it as soon as we got back from the bus trip, but I was sure the embassy would be closed. American embassies, of course, don't close. They're not grocery stores.

On January 2, I left Jo still asleep, and walked through downtown Beirut. If only I'd taken a taxi. But I like to walk. I came to the irresistible boulevard. The sea was wintry-looking but still beautiful. I just loved the sea. I mused how I could never be happy if I had to live far away from one. Musing made me walk even more slowly. I strolled up the drive to the embassy, which was bordered with hardy flowering plants in December. It was a grand building—so impossible to imagine a truck full of TNT driving up where I walked, straight to the glass doors, and the driver pressing a button that ripped the whole front of it away. Someone did do that, but that day I couldn't have dreamed such a thing, even in a nightmare.

The glass doors parted silently for me and I stepped into the cold white-marble lobby under a soaring ceiling so high and far away that I didn't notice it. In the center of the lobby, behind a small podium, stood a beautiful marine. His uniform was molded, uncreased, to his perfect body. His eyes flickered.

"May I help you?" his lips asked.

When a marine addresses a woman and doesn't call her "ma'am," it's because he has deduced that she is under eighteen, the cut-off point for marines to call women "ma'am." I knew that from Will. It was in his *How to Be a Marine* guidebook. The rules on how to be a killer are unwritten.

I smiled, but it was no good. I was wearing a skirt and loafers, and an old sweater. My hair was a little dirty, pulled back with a rubber band. I was tired of putting on eyeliner. In fact, I really was ready to go back to Cameroon. "You can help me. Who do I see about getting extra pages for my passport. I . . ."

He began to speak into the air. He must have pushed a button of his own somewhere. "Mistuh Sutton, suh, ah've got a kid heah needs a passport insert."

"Be right down," came a voice from the little podium.

"Mistuh Sutton'll be right down. He's the only gentleman heah today," he condescended to explain. "Y'all's lucky someone's around ta take care uh y'all." His straight nose twitched as if I smelled.

He was so obnoxious that as Mr. Sutton appeared, his heels tap, tap, tapping down the marble steps beyond the podium, I said "fuck" for the first time in my life out loud. I stared into the eyes of the marine, who was looking over my head. "Fuck you, you twerpy little soldier," I said to him. Then I smiled at Mr. Sutton while the marine's gorgeous, chiseled jaw fell down to his stiff, stand-up collar.

"Sorry about this, Sutton," I said in a very authoritative voice, assuming he was a nobody since the place was officially not operating. I stuck out my hand. "Mattie Price. State Department. I have to get to Nigeria tomorrow. Urgent business. I hope the British Embassy is a little more efficient than here."

"Sorry, Miss Price. It's just that yesterday was New Year's—a holiday—and today being Monday—well, we decided an extra day off would—"

"I'm in a hurry."

"Oh. Sorry. I don't know if the British Embassy will have someone to help you. You'll be wanting a tourist visa?"

"Tourist visa?" I laughed mirthlessly. "State business, as I said. You've heard of Dean Rusk, haven't you?"

"Oh. I see." He took out a small accordion of passport pages from a folder he was carrying and somehow sealed them into my passport.

"Thank you," I said. I gave him a nice smile. I was feeling a little ashamed about being so nasty to the man just to impress that creep of a marine. I turned and walked toward the doors. The glass parted once again, and Sutton was obviously out of earshot because the marine called out:

"Hey, sugah, if y'all git ridduh them knee socks, ah'll

show you a real good time, soon's ah git off."

I turned. He was grinning from ear to ear. Absolutely gorgeous. I just gave a little wave and kept walking, and twenty years after that I felt guilty about not giving him a smile, too—a forgiving smile, because his replacement to follow many times over was blown into fragments so small that only the sea gulls found the pieces.

When I finally got back to the hotel, Jo, along with all her stuff, was gone. There was a note for me.

Dear Mattie,

I've written my mother at her last address and Jones in Yaoundé, too, so you don't have to worry about any of that. I'm not going home. I am home. I've found it. I've gone to that camp we saw from the bus. If they give me a place to live I will teach school, or I will take health-care classes at the American University and help these people. They haven't anywhere to go and neither do I. You're my friend, Mattie, but I need a family. And it all makes so much more sense than teaching the crème de la crème of Cameroon youth about the birds of Great Britain.

I love you. When Jones comes around, make up a good story for me. Write it first, and he'll believe anything you tell him.

I'm sorry.

Jo

Four years at Bryn Mawr, *magna cum laude*, and Jo decides to be a nurse's aide. I was furious. I went back out of the hotel and got a cab. I'd forgotten the name of the camp and, like all guesses, the driver's was wrong. At the wrong camp, he tried to talk me out of going to any more of them, but I insisted.

When we finally arrived at Shatila, someone was waiting for me—a boy about thirteen years old. He was handsome and bone thin. His English was impeccably British. He told me Jo was with his sisters, teaching children to read. She would live in his mother's quarters. Tents are called "quarters," not "houses," especially for Palestinians, whose houses are in Israel, being lived in by Israelis.

Jo hadn't wasted any time.

"I want to see her."

"She doesn't wish to see you. She says for you to write to her instead. Here is the address." He handed me a piece of paper.

"Why are you people letting her do this?" I asked him, as if he were the pretender to some throne.

"We will take any help."

"But she'll never stay here. She'll change her mind. She did this impulsively, like she does everything else in her life."

"Whatever time the American woman spends with us will be time for us to gain any useful knowledge she has to bring us."

"Then what?"

"That will be up to her."

"You'll let her change her mind?"

"Of course. We don't imprison anyone."

I was thinking of harems. "Why don't you people move into Beirut?"

"The Lebanese will not allow it."

"Do you work?"

"The Lebanese do not allow us to work except at menial tasks."

"Can't you go to Jordan? Someplace like that? Syria?"

"Hussein does not want us. He is a Bedouin, not a Palestinian. Syria . . ." His voice drifted off.

"Where do you get food?"

"The PLO."

"The what?"

"The Palestine Liberation Organization. They are freedom fighters. And they take care of us."

I let that sink in. "Did your family come from Israel?"

He clenched his bony little fists. "My family came from Palestine, which is now occupied."

His little-boy head reached my shoulders. "Please," I begged him, "can I just talk to my friend?"

"No. She has told us to refuse you. She will send you word through the post."

I looked past him. Staring at me were a mass of women

and children, and spaced symmetrically among them were men with checkered Arab headdress. "How many people are in these camps?"

"In the camps in Lebanon?"

"Yes."

"Four hundred thousand."

"What?"

"Four hundred thousand."

"And in those other places?"

"Millions."

"A Diaspora." Michael's face registered behind my eyes. "What's that?"

"Ask Jo."

"I will."

"And tell her I will be back in June."

I turned away from him. The cab was not there. The boy touched my shoulder, and said, "Hang about." He may have had a strong voice, but his touch was as if a butterfly had alighted upon me and then flown away. The boy ran off, the crowd opened up a place for him, and he was right back, driving a Jeep with a red cross painted on its side. "I will bring you home." I hadn't any idea how he could possibly see over the steering wheel. His eyes were level with the horn.

I got in. "This whole thing is nothing but politics, isn't it?"

"Yes. And revolution."

"What is the Israeli point of view about you people?"

He grimaced. "There is no such point of view."

"Why are you being unrealistic?"

"You are as simple as your friend."

"You're the one who sounds simple." I felt like I was in a class at college.

"You have no idea what is going on."

"Neither does Jo. That's my friend who's moved in with your mother. She'll ask the same questions. Why are you really letting her stay with you?"

"Because Allah has sent her. She is exactly the person we have been praying for."

When people start backing up their arguments with God—Allah or whichever—it's useless to keep at it. The boy left me off in front of the hotel and I went in, intending to call Michael. But as I'd just been told, there was no Israel. The Lebanese felt the same way about that as their guests in the holes did. Hopefully, the Shatila people, the PLO or whatever it was, would realize that Jo would make a pretty crummy spy. I thought they just might kick her out.

I sat down and wrote Jo a long letter, telling her that if she wanted to leave, or if they kicked her out, she should go directly to the embassy. I would always be around to help her and if she wanted to go back home I would come through in June to take her. That's when our two years with the Peace Corps would be up. At least mine would be up. Hers was already up. And the next June, it wasn't so easy getting back to Jo. The day I left Cameroon for good, intending to stop in Casablanca because I couldn't resist the opportunity, I couldn't go to Casablanca. It was June 5, the start of the Six-Day War.

CHAPTER SEVENTEEN

When I got home to Buea, there was a message to go to the hotel, room nine, immediately. It's only in fiction, unfortunately, that those messages end up under carpets. I went over, knocked on the door to room nine, and the director opened it.

"You again!" He was in disarray—frantic. He ranted and raved about "this nonsense" and I tried to recall all I'd written in my made-up story. I'd written it over the Sahara on the plane ride home instead of looking out the window, but he would have none of it. This was a serious glitch in his road to the diplomatic corps or mayor of Sheboygan or whatever it was he was after. He yabbered about Michael, and about our going off to countries other than those on the continent—I decided not to go into my geological theories—and now this Jo friend of mine not coming home because she had important things to do.

"Important things to do," Jones repeated. He was waving her letter at me. "Ha! I have important things to do, too."

So I made up a worse story right off the top of my head.

"She's CIA."

"Don't be ridiculous! If the CIA ever got their hands on Peace Corps volunteers, God knows what international crises could develop."

"Oh. Well, I made that up."

"You made that up? Well for God's sake won't you just tell me the truth so I can get a handle on this?"

But what was I doing defending Jo? Didn't I want someone to go and get her? Forcibly, if necessary? No, I thought, I don't.

"Listen, Mr. Jones, how about we go to the bar for a drink. Face it. You're going to have to make something up, too. We'll just relax over a drink, and have a calm chat about what's really happening here. C'mon." I wrapped myself around his sweating arm. He wasn't the type you flirted with and he wasn't used to it. He turned beet red because my breast was leaning on his upper arm.

"Well . . . well . . ." he said.

"Well?" I said.

He coughed and disengaged himself from me. "Perhaps that would be a good idea. My God, this week has been an absolute hell."

He loved to talk about his problems. I sipped my drink and, smiling up at him, licked my upper lip. He blushed again and I casually took the letter from Jo, still clenched in his fist. Then I took a bigger sip. Straight bourbon. When I take a lot of alcohol on an empty stomach I become drunk immediately. In five seconds the back of my neck felt like rubber, which was probably why I began to laugh uncontrollably as I read Jo's letter to him. Jo can't write fiction since she hasn't a shred of imagination, but she sure knew how to appeal to Jones's feeling of authority and superiority. And she successfully focused in on phrases that appealed directly to his sixth-grade mentality. Basically, she knew he'd understand that she couldn't resist staying on in Beirut, since she'd found the real Peace Corps there. How could she continue teaching Cameroonian students about bluebirds when there were refugees in Beirut who were hungry and cold? "I know, Mr. Jones, how well you understand such social commitment."

Social commitment again. Shit. When I drink too fast, after I have my laugh attack, I end up crying. Why I always forget this series of events until it happens I'll never know.

Here this stupid man was all upset about Jo and he didn't give a hoot about Jo and I did. Jo was all I cared about and God only knew what would happen to her with those dispossessed, maniac Arabs. Now the Peace Corps director found himself with a hysterical drunken woman on his hands besides all his other difficulties, and he didn't know what to do. He handed me the soggy cocktail napkin from under his drink and told me, "Now, now . . . dry those tears, won't you?" while his head swiveled in all directions, waiting for help or to be arrested.

And out from somewhere came the adorable, miserable, fat Danish hotel manager, ever-wondering what he was doing in Buea, West Cameroon, at a hotel that had no access to automatic washers and dryers. This was covert operations? Danes have booming voices, especially this one, whom I suspected of being a manic-depressive.

"Hoho!" he shouted. "Drunk again!" Generally, he either ignored me or was crazy about me. The only time he didn't play his wacky role was when Michael left in the helicopter. The man would spot me and stare at me vacantly, or he would ask me to marry him—he'd give me anything I wanted if I would just ask. However, I tended to be shy around men who weighed three hundred and fifty pounds. He had a cup of coffee in his hand.

"Now, you drink this up and get sober, and I will finish your drink and get drunk, and then we marry, OK?" To the fragmented Peace Corps director, he said, "You are an official of the American government, yes? You can perform the ceremony. Start." The Dane enveloped my hand in his. His was warm and wet. I don't know what mine was like, but I started chuckling again before I knew I was. Jones was in a panic. How would he slither out of this one? I said, smirking, but at least not laughing:

"Listen, Jones, just send a message to Washington that Jo Parsons has quit her job as a volunteer, and your problems are over because she's gone to live in another country, which is their problem. It would only be your problem if she was staying in Cameroon. You're immediately off the hook. See?" He'd finished his drink and was a bit buzzy himself, and since he had no wits about him whatsoever, he grabbed at my solution at first. But he got in his gripes, too.

"This will ruin my chances for a foreign-service appointment. I know it. Here I've got just six months to go paying my dues with this preposterous organization. I'm the only director, I'm sure, to lose two volunteers. No other director has so much as lost one. When we had our meeting in Washington, it was a good joke about that Michael, but I doubt anyone will be laughing a second time."

"What about that volunteer in Afghanistan who wandered into Russia?"

"Well, yes . . . of course that was catastrophic, but they *found* him. And when the Russkies let him out he was still insisting that according to his map he wasn't in Russia. But they *found* him! My God, this is absolutely untenable!"

"What's this 'untenable'?" asked Hans. Hans was the Dane. I preferred to think of him as a Dane, not an Israeli, although maybe he actually still was a Dane—weren't they famous for helping Jews during the Holocaust? There was no feeling in my hand. I was sure Hans had dissolved it.

"Be quiet, Hans. Listen, Jones, I have a better idea. Don't tell Washington anything. No one will ever know. Jo has no family. Who will report that she never came back? Just throw away her plane ticket home."

He considered that for a minute, then frowned. "No. Can't do that. There's more red tape to this job, young lady, then just throwing away plane tickets. But I'll handle it." I knew immediately how he intended to handle it— ignore the whole thing. It was what he always did, according to that doctor. The records showed Jo's family situation. He'd realized I was right—no one would know.

"Now, I will say good night to you, Miss . . . uh . . ."

"Mattie."

"Yes. And you, sir." He stuck out his hand to Hans, who crushed it.

Jones left, rubbing his fingers, but turned and said in

what he thought was his fatherly fashion, "And don't go getting into any more trouble."

"I won't."

"Good."

Actually, I looked down at where my hand should have been—encased in the mass of Hans's flesh. Talk about trouble.

Six months later I almost did get in more trouble, but try as I could, I wasn't able to get an entrance visa into either Morocco or Lebanon. I spent two weeks trying; even when the Six-Day War was over, Arab countries were still considered unsafe. So I decided to try Michael in Israel. He'd written to me and invited me to visit him. He was an official immigrant. Again. I didn't intend to do that because I wanted to rid my system of him, but he was the only chance I had to get to Jo. I flew to Tel Aviv, where there was still dancing in the streets. So was Michael dancing in the streets, but I wasn't in the mood. He wanted to kill me for spoiling the fun that he was taking part in, but he loved me. And he couldn't believe what Jo had done.

"Neither can I, Michael, that's why I have to go get her."

"But why would she do it? An American woman living with Arabs . . . I mean, it's crazy."

"She did it because she felt sorry for all those people living in holes. Have you seen them?"

"No."

"You will, though, because now Israel owns the places where a couple of those holes are. Why isn't there a country for them, Michael? You can't imagine how those people have been living for the last twenty years."

"Mattie, there always has been a Palestine for them. Only Winston Churchill took out his pen one day, signed a piece of paper, and named it Jordan. It's the Bedouins who took most of the Palestinians' land away."

"And Israel the rest. Jo wrote to me that that's what happened."

"Ben-Gurion allowed the Palestinians to stay."

"Jo says after they left—hundreds of thousands of them—Ben-Gurion put a quota on the number who could return."

"The Arab League took care of that anyway, by threatening to kill any who came back."

"Michael, those people want to come home."

"Their home is gone."

"That's not fair."

"Mattie, should we give Texas back to the Apaches?"

I said, "Two wrongs don't make a right." Michael managed to ignore that gem.

"What do you think would have happened to Israel if the Arabs had won this little war? They'd have massacred all of us. We massacre no one. The Arabs in the land we won in this war can stay."

"As second-class citizens."

"What do you think they were before? Do you think they had the vote? They had nothing. And women, Mattie, are treated like breed cows. No. Not as kindly as cows are treated."

"Jo won't allow that to happen to her and she's there probably to try to change things for Arab women. Set an example, or something."

"Jo is not an example. She's a curiosity. They'll use her. Mattie, all the Arabs who live in Israel will one day have all the rights of Jewish citizens. I know it. This country was not created by victims in order to victimize others."

"Could have fooled me. Go see the refugee camps, Michael. Promise me you will."

He wanted to argue some more, but didn't. "OK."

"Now get me to Beirut."

Michael insisted he couldn't do it. We'd been in this little café and I told him that if he didn't help me, I'd hitchhike a camel ride with a Bedouin. He knew I meant it. He arranged this roundabout route for me down into Gaza and then onto some kind of freighter going to Lebanon. At one point he looked over my head and explained that it was the very route that the refugees took to get to Beirut.

"To the holes?"

"Yes."

"Hey, Michael, I know that you didn't put them there. And I'm not blaming this country either. I can understand survival. But it's going to have to get straightened out."

"The problem is not as big as it seems to you. I'm sure it was a very emotional thing, seeing the camp, but—"

"Michael, you go see those camps and then we'll talk about how big the problem is."

"All right." His eyes were very sad, I thought.

"Catch any more Nazis?"

Now the twinkle came back. "No, Mattie, I haven't. That's for people like this father of mine."

"Liar."

"Guess what?"

"What?"

"I have two little half sisters." Great big enormous wonderful grin. From Michael! I reached out to him, happy as anything. He drew back, so I knew exactly what he would say next. "Mattie, I . . . I sort of met this girl here."

"Yeah?"

"I mean, she was born here."

Maybe he thought I'd understand better than if she was another immigrant like him—rather than an old girlfriend from Scarsdale or something. "Michael, I knew that when you stayed in the lobby instead of coming up to my room to get me. I still love you anyway. But I'm glad you stayed in the lobby. I'm pretty weak."

"Ha!"

"I mean sexually."

"Ha!"

"No, no . . . I don't mean that either. I—"

"I know what you mean. You're still not saying it right." Now he reached across the table for me. I drew back.

"Ah . . . Mattie?"

"Yes?"

"She's waiting for me now. I think she thinks I won't come back from you."

"Bye, Michael."

"You've got everything?"

"I'll be fine."

"Let me know how Jo is. Tell her I'm concerned about her.

"I will. I know she's concerned about you."

He stood up and so did I and we leaned over the table to kiss each other, but then I shut my eyes and turned away and when I opened my eyes they had tears in them and Michael's had the same. He cuffed my chin and he left.

CHAPTER EIGHTEEN

Jo's face shot off beams of contentment that you'd see only in people like Mother Teresa in another twenty years. Of course, Jo didn't have the wrinkles and her veil was black, not white with a designer stripe. Even though she had on her clothes from college, when I saw that *chador* over her head I figured she'd snapped for sure. But Jo explained that it prevented the children from continually touching her silver hair. The littlest ones still tried to put their fingers in her glacier eyes, so most of the time she wore sunglasses. She didn't have the sunglasses on now because she was in her quarters. She didn't say "quarters," she said "house," but it was a tent. Perfect, I thought, smiling all the time—a woman in a Villager skirt with a coordinated blouse, Bonnie Doon knee socks, penny loafers, black *chador,* and shades. She'd snapped a little.

After the initial hugging and crying, I asked, "So how come you only wrote one letter?" while looking around the tent with awfully nice furniture in it.

"I'm really sorry, Mattie. These last six months were so extraordinary there were no words I could find that explained them. Even if I could have called you, I wouldn't have found the words. It's something only you could have done justice to. Besides, I knew if I didn't write you'd get mad and not write to me so often, which you didn't. I had

a hard time at first with those long letters of discourage-
ment, so I didn't write."

Here I was all set to start discouraging her, too. A man
walked in without knocking, but then I thought, How do
you knock on a tent? It was stifling hot. Sweat was dripping
down my sides from my armpits. Nice furniture, but no
electricity. Jo's face was as dry and smooth as marble. The
man said, "Excuse me."

"It's all right." Jo smiled at him and held out her hand.
He came over and took her hand in his. He was more
handsome than Mario, the Italian fake sculptor. And he
was very dusky-colored, which made him give off that authentic Arabian Nights kind of aura. "Mattie," Jo said, "this
is Ahmad, my husband." A spontaneous, horrible laugh
jumped out of my mouth. She said quickly, "Really, Mattie,
it's true."

Jo looked up at Ahmad and gave a laugh, too, only her
laugh was like jingle bells. Then this pitiful voice came out
into the room/tent and it was me talking while Jo's Arab
husband was shaking my hand and welcoming me to his
tent/house. "But we were supposed to be each other's maid
of honor," was what I was saying.

"What is this?" Jo's Arab husband asked her, thinking a
maid of honor was something deadly, since my face was
starting to break up. He still had my hand and Jo put both
her hands over the two of ours while she made me stare
into her eyes. She explained *maid of honor* to Ahmad while
holding my gaze. Then she said to me, "Mattie, the custom
is different here. Witnesses are family."

"I thought I was your family."

Jo said something to her husband in what I had to guess
was Arabic. He said, "Please excuse me," and left.

Jo made me sit down on a pretty French chair with a
needlepoint cushion. "Mattie, Ahmad didn't know you'd
arrived. He feels very bad. He knew how important it was
to me that I break this to you a little more slowly. I'm sorry
it didn't work out that way."

"Feels bad?" I stood up again and the little chair toppled

over backward, soundlessly, on the soft mat cushioned by the dirt directly beneath it.

Jo picked it up. "Don't go crazy, Mattie, just don't go crazy. You'll have to face this all at once. You just will. I have so much to tell you. Sit down. We'll have tea."

Jo went about getting tea things. She was right. I shouldn't go crazy. I had to sort out what it all meant. I was hoping she'd be the same Jo as before, but that one was gone. If that Jo was gone, what good would it do to sort things out? Did I want this new one? She was married. She lived in this place. She wouldn't be leaving. I watched her make tea. The zipper on the side of her little A-line skirt was half down. The waistband wasn't big enough to go around her. Her breasts stuck out roundly against the soft, worn fabric of her pink paisley roll-up-sleeve blouse. Where did those matronly breasts come from? Jo's build was perfectly proportioned. In about one minute's time the closest human being to me in all the world tells me she's married and doesn't tell me she's pregnant. She kept making tea and I kept saying, *pregnant, pregnant,* to myself. Pregnancy was what happened to grown-up married women and pimply, miserable little teenagers. Jo had never been the latter and I wasn't ready to accept the fact that she was the former before I had even started out to be that.

I stood up and ran out of that horrid place. It was the first, last, and only time I ever deliberately physically escaped a crisis, a confrontation, a discussion, anything. I was never one to run away. I think I did it because I was so sure she would chase me. She didn't. When I stopped all I saw were those big-eyed children staring at me and their polite parents looking the other way. I walked back.

In the tent Jo was crying in her Arab husband's arms. His hand covered the entire back of her head, and in the short instant I had to take this scene in before he noticed me standing there under the tent flap, I became miserable that I'd done this to her. She hadn't chased me because she thought it was hopeless. It wasn't. She was still my friend. And now I knew that she had the one thing that I always tried to give her but never could, a real family who loved her. I was always so selfish, I thought. And I thought suddenly of what she'd said about my father here in Beirut at Christmas. She was growing up—expecting me to see things in a new light. She put on lights, and I turned them off.

Ahmad said, "You see, Jo? Mattie is here for her tea."

When he said that, I saw him through Jo's eyes. He was a compelling man. Very proud. He carried himself like a president. Jo had found her important man. Too bad his cause was a lost one. It didn't matter to me. All that mattered was that Jo had found what she was looking for.

"I'd love a cup of tea."

Jo threw her arms around me, very emotional for Jo, and we did sit down to tea, and the first thing I said to Ahmad was, "Jo is a brilliant woman." I wanted to tell him everything so he'd know.

"Yes. She is."

"She was raised in worse poverty than this."

Jo said, "Not really, Mattie."

"Yes, really. You've got to tell him."

"I've told him everything. He knows everything there is to know about me."

"About your mother living over a bar with a black man?"

Ahmad said, "I find that spirited and admirable."

I ignored that. "But it was worse than this . . . Ahmad." (Very difficult to say his name.) "At least you people have each other. Jo had no one."

"That of course is another sort of poverty. The kind that produces a strong, powerful human being. The Palestinian poverty that you see here produces only anger. In order to survive, we must learn from Jo."

Jo said, "The rats here, Mattie, are much bigger, actually." Her face had this proud, peachy glow.

"Being pregnant has made you even more beautiful, Jo. I hope you're going to have this baby in a hospital."

Jo started to say how did I know she was pregnant, but Ahmad grew angry. "All the women in this camp who

choose to have a baby in a hospital, do so. Palestinian refugee women are not stupid. They want their babies to live
. . . to live and to find their way out of here."

"Listen . . ." I tried to say his name again, but the name
Ahmad refused to fall trippingly from the tongue. "Listen,
Arabs are a couple of centuries behind the times. We knew
a lot of Moslems in Cameroon, didn't we, Jo? Moslems base
absolutely everything on religion, including health. The
Koran's version of health is primitive. And things like civil
rights for people, or any rights at all for women don't exist.
Religion has never had any place in Jo's life. And now she's
supposed to adopt one that tells her what to eat and when,
what to drink, when to pray, when to have sex. Religions
take away your brains and Jo knows it's all a bunch of shit."

Jo cringed. Ahmad was tense, but didn't give in.

"A right to one's culture is a civil right. You would deny
someone such a right?" His voice was very controlled and
I realized mine wasn't.

"I'm sorry, I'm being nasty. I can't help it. But your
whole culture is based on a religion that is unrealistic. If
you follow its tenets, you'll never get out of here."

"The Jews' religion is just as untenable, but they got out
of their ghettos and we will get out of ours."

"That's because most Jews aren't religious. Most of them
have separated their culture from those crappy rules in
the Old Testament."

"It is the same with Moslems, though we don't admit to
it publicly. If we have to give up religious principles to
establish a country, we will. But you see, now that the Jews
have done this, they are going back to their Orthodox
practices. They are becoming dangerously fundamentalist.
Some are referring to the West Bank which they have just
captured from Hussein as 'Samaria' and 'Judea.' They will
use the Old Testament if they find there the excuses needed
to suppress us. But we will not be suppressed."

Now Jo interrupted. "If the two of you want to go on
with this marathon discussion, fine. But I'm tired. Mattie,
when you leave, who knows when we'll see each other

again. Shouldn't we make the most of this? Ahmad?"

"OK," I said. She did look tired. Very. Ahmad nodded, regretfully. He was also brilliant. I wondered who in the world he had to talk to. Jo wasn't political. Not when it came to ideology as opposed to morality. She didn't want to take part in what Ahmad and I were saying. "But I have something I have to say to you . . . Ahmad."

Their heads turned toward me together, Jo dismayed because she thought things were resolved just enough to carry on with civility. "Don't worry, Jo, it's nothing earth-shattering. I just want to remind you that I intend to keep up my half of our adolescent pact. When I get married, Ahmad" (suddenly easier to say), "Jo must come to the United States to be my witness. I'll never forgive either of you if she doesn't."

Ahmad said, "I would want Jo to do that, but I am not a wealthy man."

"Don't worry. I will marry a wealthy man. You'll both come."

And Ahmad knew immediately the frivolity of my demand. In his eyes the chances were enormous that if Jo stayed with him forever, we'd write letters back and forth, and then fewer letters, until finally there would be no more to say to each other. So, with a nice smile, he agreed. Jo and I met each other's eyes. We knew that there was no such chance. Jo and I would be the closest of friends, forever. That's what our glance was saying. The maid-of-honor part was a code from me to Jo. Jo was taking a vow with me, the one she'd missed out on by marrying an Arab Moslem—till death do us part.

"I love you, Mattie," was what she said to me three days later. Instead of good-bye.

I started home, and in the ruins of Baalbek, which I'd decided to check out before I left those parts of the world I'd missed, I met another returning Peace Corps volunteer, on his way home from Sierra Leone. He was a wholesome, Jesuit-trained, principled virgin, whom the prostitutes of the Arab world were giving a hard time. And all men I came across wouldn't leave me alone. So the two of us, in order to take advantage of the mutual protection we had to offer, spent six weeks traveling together through the Middle East, across Turkey, and along the route of the then-defunct *Orient Express.*

It was a learning experience rather than a fun trip, because the guy didn't have the foggiest notion of how to have fun. And I wasn't in the mood for fun. All I knew was that I had to ease my way back into the States. The reason Vietnam vets suffered so when they came home was that one day they were in Saigon, and the next day they were in San Diego. Not like World War II, when soldiers came home on troop ships that took forever. When I'd returned from Italy after six months, I experienced culture shock, which is, to me, finding out that what you missed during the time away wasn't all that terrific. After two years of Cameroon, something told me that potato chips weren't going to taste like ambrosia from the gods. Just before I left Cameroon, Paul sent me the latest Beatles record and while I listened, disbelieving, as they sang about living in a yellow submarine, I knew things weren't going to be anything like they had been.

This Jesuit-type guy, Eddie, was just plain afraid to go back to the real world, which in his case was medical school at Tufts. How a twenty-four-year-old male virgin was going to handle learning to examine a naked woman was beyond me. I mentioned that to him. He said he would be able to separate the body from the individual and that most of the bodies would be ill and presumably not erotic.

"Oh," I said. I liked that. I told him he'd probably be a good doctor. I gave him my home address and told him to send me an announcement when he started his practice. If I needed a doctor I would be glad to be his first patient. He was so flattered, he thanked me a hundred times, and over the next few days, he told me how great it was to hear me say words like *patients* and *practice.* Now he knew he could do it. Be a doctor. Big deal, but he was precious, like a puppy.

Eddie and I were both strong and energetic people, and we did enjoy exploring ruins and hidden frescoes and geographical anomalies. He was kind of like a college roommate who is not exactly your kind of person, but who isn't offensive either. At the end of the six weeks, we were in London and that's where we said good-bye. I gave him a Pierre Cardin tie that he'd admired in Paris. I'd bought it when he wasn't looking. He was embarrassed that he didn't have something for me. I told him not to worry about it. He said, "Oh, I wasn't worried."

Really weird guy. He'd make a great doctor. Who but a weird person would want to saw through someone's ribs or drill holes in their heads? But he'd have a good bedside manner because he was such a gentle soul.

Several years later, Eddie set up a practice in Stamford. Just in time for my first obstetrical visit, too. He told me I was a fine specimen and would surely have a healthy baby. It is a lot easier to have your private parts exposed upside down to an androgynous robot than to a Mr. Adorable who sits on the edge of the table telling jokes, I think.

I flew home.

CHAPTER NINETEEN

Home was exactly as I'd left it, despite The Beatles' yellow submarine. The only difference I could see was in the kids in the last three rows of movie theaters. Instead of necking they were smoking pot. Being home again was exciting. Thrilling. Gave me goose bumps. The thrill lasted as long as the goose bumps. When I'd left the states, two years seemed like a long time. But I realized that leaving Cameroon was much worse, since, most likely, I wouldn't go back again. Ever.

I found a job for the rest of the summer until grad school as a substitute answering-service operator in Darien, the very posh town next to Norwalk. I quickly found that with all the customers on vacation, the businesses that used the answering service didn't get that many calls. Emergency calls to doctors were taken by the woman who owned the business. So, after two days of staring at the switchboard hoping the little red lights would start blinking, I brought stationery with me to write a letter to Jo and to a lot of other people I owed a zillion letters, too. But once I got the pen in my hand, I found myself writing a short story instead. I finished the short story in three hours. It seemed like three minutes. When I looked up, a lot of red lights were blinking, and for a second I didn't know where I was. The red lights were saying to me, over and over, "You're a writer, you're a writer."

I was. I was alone, isolated, everything was dead quiet, and I liked it. I kept thinking how nice it would be to be alone all day and do nothing but write. My trip with Eddie had let me see that fun wasn't everything. I was tired of fun. I was sick at the thought of school. I wanted to be alone so I could write about all that I'd done with my life. I pressed the switch over one of the red buttons.

"Hello," I called cheerily into the headpiece. I forgot to see whose switch it was and should have been saying, "Bill's Bumper Service, good morning." Here I was so excited about deciding to be a writer and some poor woman was telling me she'd backed into her own garage door, which she'd neglected to open, and could Bill fix her bumper before her husband got home.

I said, "But what about your garage door?"

"Oh, no! I didn't think of that."

She was so distraught that I wanted to go fix her garage door personally. I gave her the number of "Frank, Your Mr. Fix-it Friend," before I told her Bill was on a job and would call in in a few minutes. I couldn't wait to get home to tell my father about my story. It was a funny story about a virgin tourist beset by a prostitute in the ruins of Baalbek. And I couldn't wait to tell him I was going to be a full-time writer. I was sure he'd want to hear this. He would have so much empathy. I wasn't going to graduate school. I was going to get some kind of job like a security guard at a safe place where I could sit and write while nothing happened. My short story I'd written was so good.

That evening, my father replied to this babble with, "Maybe I could call John Gardner and get you into his program at Bennington."

I blinked nervously at him as he took out his little black book. Why was I feeling intimidated? Because this was how I always felt with him but didn't know until that moment that the feeling was intimidation.

"But, Dad, I don't want to study writing. I already know how to write. I want to write stories. All day, I had a ball today writing a great story. Wait till you see. You're going to love it."

"I'm sure I will, Mattie, but not enough to agree to let you just throw away the doctoral program you'll be starting."

Let you? What was this "let you"?

"Dad, Ernest Hemingway didn't have a doctorate."

"He had wars to fight."

"Me, too. I just finished fighting them. The Peace Corps wasn't Vietnam, but it wasn't Camp Lejeune either. Now I have to write about all that before it goes away."

"That's hopelessly romantic."

"That's what you said Jo was. She's not. I'm not. You're the one who's being romantic."

"Now don't get excited. All right. Let me think." He thought for one second. "Maybe, Mattie, I could get you a job in New York . . . as an editorial assistant. Fred Roberts at Simon and Schuster is always looking for good people. He—"

"Dad!"

"Yes, honey?"

He didn't get it. He didn't get it at all. "Dad, you don't think I'll ever be a serious writer, do you? You don't think I'll ever get published, do you?"

"Of course I do. You've shown a great deal of talent and potential. But writing is not a full-time job until you've established a substantial track record. You'll have to—"

"You sound like Yossarian, Dad." I loved Yossarian. My dad didn't. "And those agents that you hate. How can I establish a substantial track record if I don't try to write something and get it published?"

"I don't hate agents."

"Some, you do. And that's not what we're talking about here. Dad, I'm going to get a job where I don't have to think or move—something to just support myself—and I'm going to write."

"What kind of job did you have in mind?" God, he knew how to condescend.

"I told you. I could be a security guard, the kind that—"

"Security guards work at night."

"No kidding!"

"And have to learn how to handle a gun."

Gun. The name Michael started boinging around in my head. I had all those gaps to fill in my novel. Goody, goody. "Well, Dad, then I'll sweep floors in a factory. I'll sweep real fast so that I'll get done in half the time so I'll have four hours left to write."

He laughed. It was pretty funny, considering my plan twenty-four hours earlier to go to Ohio State and get a degree in African studies. I'd been all excited about learning all those languages, including Arabic. I said, "Dad, I don't want writing to be a hobby anymore. In Cameroon I wrote almost a whole novel. I have notebooks full of parts to a novel. I want to put them all together."

This revelation brought no response from him at all. The wheels in his brain were working and working. I think it was too much too soon for him, since every day since I'd come home he'd done nothing but worry about Jo and go over in his mind how we could get her back. With each idea he had for getting her back I'd tell him a little more about the camp, or Ahmad, and finally, about Jo's pregnancy. He told me he felt responsible for her and he'd never be able to handle it, but I told him he was actually in love with her like all men who knew Jo.

"Mattie," he said, "will you please stop saying exactly what you want to? This is America."

We both had a laugh. "I think I've always had that habit, Dad."

"True. But you're old enough to know better now."

Then we sat across the kitchen table from each other drinking coffee, both now thinking about Jo, and I knew as I watched his worried face that I had to be like my friend Jo—just go out and do whatever I wanted to do. Pleasing my father couldn't fit into my plans any longer. I couldn't work around that wrinkle anymore. I told him that. He said:

"All right. You do what you must. Be your version of a

writer. Get the sweeping job. At least you aren't going to
marry some Arab." Not very satisfying, but at least I was
able to leave the table. My father was getting old, I thought.

My first Saturday with nothing to do arrived and I'd
looked forward to sleeping late and writing all day at my
desk, eating potato chips. But I couldn't sleep, and at seven
o'clock I went down to the kitchen, got my potato chips,
and came back up to my room. There were no sounds of
Land-Rovers going by on bumpy roads, no children chattering in pidgin, no monkeys in trees. No smells of rain
and mangoes. No mountain outside my window. No wonder I couldn't sleep. The potato chips tasted like what they
were, grease and salt. I wiped my fingers on my bathrobe.
I dug through all my notebooks. They took up all the
drawer space in my little desk. One drawer was devoted
to my Michael novel. I leafed through it, and even though
it was all so far from being finished, I had no desire to
finish it. I was starting to get homesick for Cameroon. And
for Michael.

I put it all back. I opened a brand-new notebook. I had
an idea for a short story, but I didn't know where to start.
I thought, Try starting it in the middle; but there was
no voice in my pen. My pen had forgotten how to talk. I
put the new notebook away and took out my stationery.
Dear Jo . . . Dear Jo what? I heard noises in the kitchen.
Thank God.

I went downstairs and had oatmeal with my mother.
I was twenty-four years old. I didn't like potato chips
anymore. The oatmeal was delicious. I couldn't write because I didn't belong in my old skin. But where would I
go? I began to cry. My mother told me to spend the day
with her.

"You'll never guess what house I'm doing." She gave me
her napkin to dry my eyes. It was soggy. Memories of Jones
in the Buea Mountain Hotel. I cried harder. She kept
talking.

"Remember the old metal house at Randolph's Marsh?"
I remembered. "Someone bought it?"

"Yes."

"No!"

Randolph's Marsh was along the shore, not far from our island, a very woodsy and hidden kind of peninsula—out of the way. In the thirties a group of professional couples who were Communists bought the land, and each couple, none with children, built a house. A black doctor with a white wife was one of them. Of all the original Communists, there was one family left. They did have children, but the children were grown and gone and the woman taught languages at the high school. I never had her. People in Norwalk still referred to Randolph's Marsh as that place where the Commies lived.

Each house was a work of art, made of redwood and with saunas, which, of course, no one had ever heard of in the thirties. There was one house that was Art Nouveau outside and Art Deco inside. That was the one made of metal. I don't know what the metal was, but it never rusted. You couldn't see it from the road because it was in the middle of a pine grove. The owner planted white pines all around it and they grow fast. The heirs would come once in a while and use it as a hideaway. My mother was saying now that the last of the heirs had finally sold it.

I went with my mother and saw the house again, but not through a child's eyes. Though the metal was darkened now, I couldn't help but exclaim over the figures pressed into the metal, which were quite astounding. The house had a facade of flowers and cherubs and gargoyles and garlands, with great swirls surrounding the windows. I went in with my mother and immediately went hunting for the stairs that led up to the turret, which my mother referred to as a folly. I'd decided, in the last few days, that I was a folly. How could I be a full-time writer? What does a writer do all day when his pen loses its voice?

There wasn't any metal inside the house. There was teak and sandalwood and ebony, and the banister up to the turret was carved mahogany. I knew mahogany. Same grain as my card catalog. At the top of the stairs was the turret, about twelve feet in diameter, full of light pouring in from a circle of windows. I stared out at the Sound, which can look so beautiful on blue days. The sea was dotted with tiny islands. I imagined myself buying a new antique desk, getting four men to haul it up the winding stairs, and writing, inside the turret, forever. I came down the stairs, miserable that it wasn't me who'd bought the house. My mother was in the library—walls of empty shelves and a huge dirty fireplace—talking to the new owner. She introduced me to Lawrence Quayles, who was handsome in a mature kind of way like my father, but not old. I told myself to be like Jo.

"Mr. Quayles," I said as soon as I told him I was pleased to meet him, "I'm a writer and I've been looking for a quiet place to write, and I wonder if I could rent your turret, the folly, for a few hours a day."

My mother gaped at me and then began to apologize to the startled Mr. Quayles, trying to tell him while apologizing that her daughter had always been fascinated with the house and that I was a teeny bit on the impulsive side. But I just interrupted her, bowling them both over with a babbling explanation of how I wanted to be a writer and though it was quite a romantic notion, of course, I wanted to be able to rent his turret during the daytime while he was probably at work, anyway. I would be working at night as soon as I found a factory sweeping job and that he'd never even see me.

As I started to get into asking him how much he'd charge for rent, but that I would manage no matter what he charged, I thought, For all I know this guy might have a large family and needs the turret for a bedroom or something. He was smiling, though, and there was a flicker in his eyelids. I saw that he wasn't as mature as I'd assumed; whatever he worried over made him seem older and, when his eyelids flickered, his troubles left his irises and I saw that he was probably in his late thirties. And he was handsome. His clothes made him seem older, too—very tailored and conservative. And expensive. Shoes, too. I had on my same ripped loafers I'd worn for the last two years. He said:

"Actually, I was about to look into hiring a live-in house-keeper. How would you feel about dusting and polishing in addition to sweeping? Could you write before or after you cleaned, perhaps?" He turned to my flabbergasted mother. "That is . . . I mean I don't wish to offend—"

"No offense," I shouted. "Cleaning is good exercise for writers." My mother's eyebrows shot up. News to her.

"Now, Mattie," she said, "Mr. Quayles is talking about a professional—a live-in housekeeper. I don't know if—"

"Oh, I'll live in. No problem." I'd just run out and buy a sleeping bag tonight.

My mother said, "I don't believe this girl."

I felt my heart leaping inside my chest, though no one would comprehend such good luck but Jo. The first thing I would write would be that letter to Jo because now I'd have something to say.

Lawrence said, "Let me show you the third-floor rooms. There are two small rooms up there. They would be suitable for a bedroom and sitting room, and you would have some space for yourself in addition to the turret." Space? I couldn't believe I'd be working for someone who sounded like Betty Friedan. "I'm afraid the ceilings are just six feet, but . . ." His troubled look came back.

"No problem, Mr. Quayles. Six feet will give me several inches to spare." Lawrence Quayles wouldn't fit, though.

My mother's wheels began to spin, brought about by her maternal instincts. "Mattie, it would really have to be air-conditioned up there in the summer, and perhaps Mr. Quayles wouldn't want to—"

"I'll pay for the air conditioning," I shouted. "Besides, writers are supposed to suffer. Just a fan would be fine." Mr. Quayles was smiling again, ever so faintly.

"Then it is settled. Mrs. Price, if you would just take care of the air conditioning or whatever you think is necessary. The windows here all open to the sea, but you are right about the attic rooms. There isn't any cross ventilation up there."

"Actually, Mr. Quayles," I said, pulling myself together, "I've just come from two years in West Africa. Heat is no problem."

"West Africa?"

"I was in the Peace Corps."

"How extraordinary. What country were you in?"

"Cameroon." No one ever heard of Cameroon.

"Most of Cameroon is quite temperate, though. Were you in the east or west?"

"West." I couldn't believe this.

"Very beautiful, I understand. Mountains."

"Yes. Very beautiful. A wonderful mountain."

My mother said, "I think it's time to start looking at some samples." She glanced dramatically at her watch. "Mattie, I left some of my things in the car. Would you get them for me while Mr. Quayles and I get to work?"

"OK."

I heard him say, "Charming, Mrs. Price," and my mother thanked him. He was very debonair. I practically skipped through the pine trees to the car. The drive went around to the side of the house. I saw Lawrence Quayles's car. It was a red sports car—little, and very foreign. I brought the sample books back in, and the two of them had their heads together over my mother's plans. I casually made my way to the stairs and went up to the turret. My turret.

The round room was ringed with small windows all touching, so that the view was three hundred and sixty degrees. The windows were placed at the height of someone sitting at a desk and I was sure the Communist who had designed the house was a writer, too. Whoever he was, he was ahead of his time. What he wanted was no doubt Plexiglas. I thought of Mark Twain's house in Hartford, where Mark wanted to see snow fall over his hearth. So just above the mantle, his chimney split like an impressionistic maple tree and in between the two branches of brick, Mark put in a massive window. People shake their heads on the tour, just as they would at this ring of wood windows surrounding me at waist level. We writers, I thought; Mark Twain, me, and the guy who built this place all looked for that special view that was different from the way everyone else saw the world. Would that all of us could describe the view as well as Mark.

Below, I could see the other houses, all in little clearings, set back from the road, and the red sports car and my mother's Ford, but I barely noticed them because of the vast expanse of the Sound, with all the little Norwalk Islands scattered just out from the shore. I could make out the naked Greek statues on Billy Rose's island. Talk about a folly.

I wondered what would make Lawrence Quayles, the kind of man you would expect to be living in either Greenwich or the East Side of New York, buy this strange place full of rooms, either tiny or massive—cozy corners that opened up onto ballrooms. I put it aside. I'd ask him later. I wanted to just lose myself in the view.

I looked past the Sound, past Long Island, past the Atlantic, and across the Mediterranean to Jo. We were still in the same place—at ends of protrusions of sea into the land. I planned to tell her that whenever we needed to communicate with each other, she could sit on the seawall of Beirut and I could sit on Lawrence Quayles's fallen-down dock and talk. We were still connected.

Actually, my first letter to Jo was mostly the big question sitting at the back of my mind. How does one go about cleaning a house? My mother had a housekeeper who came twice a week. All I knew was making a bed and tossing the dirty clothes into a hamper.

I heard my mother call to me. I went to the head of the winding stairway. "Mattie, would you mind driving out to pick up some lunch?"

"Sure."

I drove as fast as I could to the nearest deli. I couldn't wait to get back. I still hadn't seen the two rooms in the attic. It was hot out, so I stopped for some cold beer. Sitting in the built-in breakfast nook, Lawrence said the beer was too perfect. Too perfect? No American refers to a cold

beer that hits the spot on a hot summer day as "too perfect."
And as I listened more carefully to Lawrence speaking to
my mother, I could hear the accent. A little bit of an accent.
He and my mother went back to work. I went up to my
two attic rooms. They were wonderful. I felt like the maid
in a Victorian attic in Edwardian England. The small windows in each room faced the sea. With the doors open to
the hall there actually was some ventilation. But I liked
closed doors, not open. I decided to push for the air conditioning. I think because I was beginning to feel a sense
of power. Me.

"Imagine," I said quietly, "power."

Jo sent a letter back to me right away. And it was mostly
about "How to Clean a House." She told me to list everything that had to be done each day: get rid of the breakfast
stuff, make the beds, clear out the previous evening's litter,
like newspapers, and then do one major thing—do laundry
or vacuum or dust.

Then there would be the once-a-week stuff, like mopping floors and really cleaning the bathrooms. Finally came
the once-a-month stuff—washing windows or walls, etc.
Then she told me the Palestinian women all said that once
you have children all that organized stuff goes out the
window because then your first and foremost job is to take
care of the children and play with them, and if you keep
to your prechildren schedule you will not have time to love
them.

Jo was just now being advised that her new schedule
would make caring for children a priority over caring for
a tent so that motherhood would be joy rather than just
another chore. That was when I remembered that Jo was
getting ready to have a baby. I was getting ready to be a
real writer. We were both starting out on a new adventure.
We'd both mothered and written before, respectively, but
not seriously. Now we intended to be pros. It was exciting.

I wrote back to Jo, thanking her, and said I was worried
about just one thing and that was making Mr. Quayles's

bed. It seemed a very personal thing, like shaving your legs. I told Jo that I planned to just rip the sheets off the bed and stuff them into the washing machine every morning right away. I'd only make his bed with clean sheets. Jo wrote back that she'd do anything for sheets, even the sheets Lawrence Quayles slept in. I sent her sheets, the new kind that have a print. And I told her that I discovered Lawrence made his own bed.

She thanked me for the sheets, but only slept in them one night before hanging them on the walls in the children's section of the Shatila clinic. She said the kids loved the pretty little flowers, but the one night she and Ahmad had slept on them, Ahmad woke up screaming, thinking insects were crawling all over him and Jo. Then Jo asked if I'd send her nursing bras. My mother got them from somewhere, and I sent her four nursing bras and plain white sheets. It was a long time before Jo told me that she'd ended up ripping the white sheets into bandages for the clinic. There were never enough bandages. At one point not too far down the road, all the bandages in the world wouldn't be enough.

CHAPTER TWENTY

Lawrence Quayles was not around much while my mother orchestrated the rebirth of his house. I moved in right away while nothing was ready except the bathroom, which was all I needed. My mother didn't like the idea; Lawrence didn't mind at all, but she told me she was worried about me being all alone in a big house. I didn't tell her that not six months ago Jo and I were all alone in a whorehouse in Nigeria. I kept my job with the answering service for that month because I needed the money. I didn't want to take money from my parents.

Each morning, I'd go for a walk to a diner in South Norwalk not far from Jo's old bar, and have breakfast with the black people, who all wondered how Jo was making out. I love big breakfasts and no lunch as long as I don't have to cook it and clean up the dried egg yolks. Then, I'd take the bus to work, living for the moment when evening came and I'd be walking up the drive to the metal house, and on up to my high round room, where I'd write stories about my childhood, watching the late sunset and eating junk food. I'd write until it got dark, which in August wasn't until around eight o'clock. I would be a writer who could only write in the daylight. Artificial light, for me, was not conducive to writing, but rather to reading. Jo told me I should look upon reading as part of my work as a writer. I hope all writers know they should do that so they won't feel so guilty.

It would be years before I could get to writing about Africa again. I found it impossible to fill in the big gaps in my story about Michael. I had to write about everything that happened to me in chronological order. I don't know why. So I was to spend several years writing about being a child.

When it was too dark to write, I'd sit watching the lighthouse beam, like Emily Dickinson in her garret, making plans to write forever. Nothing would stop me. I pictured myself with a sweet little family someday, leaving them every morning to go to my tower and be back for lunch, after which I would spend the afternoon and evening devoted to home and hearth. I'd dream about the husband who would go along with the idea. That idea and the one about springing for airline tickets for Jo every few years. I felt I was ready to be married.

Since I'd come home, I couldn't get into dating again. Dating is for children, not adults. After a few go-rounds with some fix-ups, I chose to spend my leisure time with my brother, Paul, instead—Paul and his beautiful, slow-witted pregnant wife. Her name was Lisa and she adored him. She would kill for him. In the evenings, Paul would read or do research work that he'd brought home from the corporation where he was the resident scientist, and Lisa would knit. Or embroider. Or watch TV with the sound turned off so as not to disturb Paul. They reminded me of Lassie and the kid who owned her. When I'd visit, Paul and I would talk for hours and she'd make goodies and bring them out to us. She was an excellent cook; all that was creative about her went into her cooking and the things she created with her knitting needles and crochet hook. Once I asked her to teach me to knit a sweater and I made such a mess of it, but she kept telling me all these encouraging, reassuring lies about how well I was doing. Paul's wife had no idea how to find fault with someone. What a wonderful mother she'd make.

So there were no men in my life and I was happy with that, though I guessed it wouldn't be for long. So even though I wasn't openly looking for a husband, I slowly came to realize that I'd already found one, and I ended up getting married just six weeks after Jo's baby was born. It would have been sooner, but I wanted Jo there no matter what, and six weeks was when she'd decided she would be able to manage it. I married Lawrence Quayles.

When Lawrence described his life, I realized that we had nothing in common and everything in common. The coincidence of coming across Lawrence was incredible, but he completed a circle. The Bakweri of West Cameroon had a name for it—*juju.* Since I'd only been a Bakweri for two years, I needed a concrete way to deal with the smallness of the world, so I sat down and wrote a character study of Lawrence Quayles.

A CHARACTER STUDY OF LAWRENCE QUAYLES

Lawrence Quayles is a "businessman." A "consultant." He consults with well-known politicians, judges, and lawyers. What they consult about is "business." Lawrence is six feet two inches and has hazel eyes. Aside from his eyes he is dark. He looks a bit Latin, which isn't surprising once he reveals that his mother, who died when he was a young boy, was Argentine. His father is an Argentine citizen who was born in the industrial city of Hamburg, Germany. He was one of the early members of the Nazi party and served an Obersterfurmarse during World War II. He was convicted "in absentia" at Nuremberg for especially repugnant war crimes. At the time, his name was Ernst Frodden, and besides a murderer, he was a deacon at his church. With the help of his bishop, he was hidden in Rome directly after the war and issued false papers by the Vatican. (Lawrence chooses not to reveal to me the name he goes by at present.) Lawrence has a stepmother and half brothers and sisters with whom he has severed contact. When things grew dangerous for his father, Lawrence gave him most of the money he inherited from his mother and told him to use it to find another place to hide. He told his father not to tell him where he'd gone or what his new name was. He warned his father that he would turn him in the instant he found out where he was hiding. The father is more careful about hiding from Lawrence than from the Israelis, who are hell-bent on finding him. Thus, Lawrence is assured of not being tormented by his father any longer, though in actuality, he knows exactly where his father is at all times. He just doesn't want his father to know that he knows. He says that if the man were anyone but his father, he would turn him in, but he cannot because the man is his father. The only thing he gave Lawrence was his life, and Lawrence feels he owes him the same. Lawrence doesn't really feel that way and until he admits that to himself, he will not be content. I determined that myself by using common sense. But would I be able to get him to see that, or as Yossarian put it, "She loved him so much, she couldn't wait to change him"?

I was within a triangle of men who didn't know each other, but who were more related historically than brothers are genetically. Lawrence, whom I was to marry, Michael whom I didn't marry, and Ahmad, who was married to my alter ego.

After I wrote the character study, I went immediately to sleep, not waking till noon the next day. My brain did everything it could think of to keep my body from waking up. I crept over to my notebook first thing, but it was still there. And the memory of the conversation between Lawrence and me the evening before came flooding back to me. The conversation itself had been flooded with cognac.

We sat sipping almost till dawn across the black-glass coffee table on the metal balcony above the inlet that crept behind the house. My mother had said, "What do you put on a glassed-in black-metal balcony but a black-glass coffee table?" And Bauhaus chairs, naturally. It was a good thing for the Bauhaus chairs. If it had been love seats I'd have gotten comfortable and all stretched out, and more stretched out with each sip of cognac, and thus become irresistible to Lawrence. No woman is irresistible in a Bauhaus chair even if she's stark naked. I was wearing cutoffs and a T-shirt. Lawrence was wearing his *Fortune* 500 suit, and two-hundred-and-fifty-dollar shoes. Although Bauhaus chairs don't allow for alluring positions, they sure are conducive to serious conversation.

This conversation took place a week after Lawrence moved in. He cooked his own dinners, and after the second one invited me to join him. He made *cannelloni con crema,* a famous Argentine dish because of all the Italians who live in Buenos Aires. The next night, I bought hot dogs and hamburgers, and lit up the barbecue pit by the edge of the inlet. Dogs and burgers were the only meal I knew how to cook. I said to him while I squirted lighter fluid on the coals, "I understand from my mother that you're widowed."

"Yes, that's right."

"What was your wife's name?"

"Charlie."

"I'm very sorry."

"Thank you. Her name wasn't Charlotte or whatever. Her name was Susan. But she called herself Charlie." He smiled into my blazing charcoal briquettes, saturated with half a can of lighter fluid. "She called me Lawrie. She said that was very Ivy League."

Stupid me said, "That's neat. Can I call you that?" My mind was wondering what happened to Charlie and how I was going to put out the fire. At first, he looked to the inlet water, and then he turned to me. "I think I would like to hear it again. Yes. And it is certainly a vast improvement over Mr. Quayles. And you?"

"I'm sorry?"

"Where is Mattie from? The name."

"Oh. Martha."

"And may I call you that?"

"No."

He laughed. His first. "All right. I think you'd better stand back, or you may ignite." In a very understated gesture, he took my elbow, and pulled me back closer to him.

"Damn. I hope the fire department doesn't come out. It wouldn't get going, you know? I just kept squirting this stuff on."

"Well, come sit down. It will calm. And it will keep the mosquitoes away while we have something to drink."

We went up into the balcony, which was actually a metal deck. The glass walls were jalousied and we opened them. My mother had put screens in, thank God. No fire, even my version of the fire that destroyed Chicago, can scare the mosquitoes in Randolph's Marsh. Together, we carried the ketchup and mustard and plates and food platter there. We had our burnt hamburgers and shriveled hot dogs, and we talked as the sun set and the moon rose. We talked while the mosquitoes and all the rest of Randolph's Marsh went to bed. Lawrie broke out the cognac. Courvoisier. You might as well drink charcoal lighter fluid as Courvoisier. The lighthouse out on the water blinked and muted foggy sounds carried through the air around us. Lawrie's conversation was interspersed with apologies for telling me all that he was telling me.

He was a lonesome man. He told me about his whole life. He missed Charlie very much. Before we finally left each other, we found ourselves holding hands across the glass table. When he noticed, he apologized for that, too. I let him leave first, and waited a few minutes before I went to bed to avoid climbing the stairs with him.

In the turret, in the dawn light, I watched a barge dragged across the Sound by a tugboat too small to see. I thought about being twenty-four and about love. I had fallen in love with one man, I decided—sweet Will, in Hawaii, and I'd hardly touched him. And I'd made love to four other men: my college boyfriend, though that was debatable and I'd felt nothing; the Italian bomber (and I'd felt everything); Michael, who had a mission that didn't allow room for me; and a one-night stand with either a mercenary, a CIA agent, or another damn Nazi hunter, whatever. I almost forgot the other one-night stand, with the Peace Corps doctor. I decided that was experience enough to decide what I really wanted in a man. I wanted a husband. What am I feeling toward Lawrence, I asked myself. Love? Of course not, but maybe someday. Excitement? No. I recognized arousal and it was missing. There really was no physical chemistry, so what was attracting me to him? I decided, warmth. Warmth was very close to love. So I let it happen. And so did he.

Lawrence Quayles could have had his pick of many successful, beautiful women who populated his high-scale business world, including Charlie's cousin, who called him frequently. After I'd taken her third or fourth call, she said, "Aha! Now I know why he can't make it to lunch anymore." And I explained that I was just the housekeeper, but that I kept forgetting to say, "Good morning, Quayles's residence," because I was new at the job.

She said, "And what's your name? Cinderella?" Then she hung up before I could retort.

I asked Lawrie, Why me? And he said, "I have a romantic notion about writers. They live forever."

I thought that was touching. Warm. It was true: Charlie had left him nothing. He tried to find her by buying the metal house, which she had had an insatiable desire to own. A few years later, he told me Charlie would have lasted six months in such a place because the inconvenience to the city would have been too much of a bother for her. She was a runway model. But now, he loved the house as much as I did. The only thing I had to adjust to was that although he didn't call me Martha, he didn't call me Mattie either. In a kind of German-Argentine-English combination he called me something that sounded like Marthe or Marta. But only when we were alone. Otherwise, Mattie. Some of me he wanted only for himself, but he was willing to share ninety-nine percent of me.

The greatest thing Lawrie and I had in common was that he realized, too, that what we were was not in love, but we both looked forward to it happening eventually. I never felt jealous of Charlie because I understood how he could have had one love in his life. I had. Just Will. Michael was a fantasy. And the more I learned about Charlie, the more grateful I felt toward her for giving him two years of peace. But once she died, he went back to his demon, his father, who took up his thoughts and his dreams. Since he was not overwhelmingly in love with me, as he was with Charlie, his father was always there with him; I could feel the man's presence, and Lawrie's suffering. His guilt. His trying to rationalize not living up to his responsibilities to see that justice came to his father's victims.

Charlie had died of a brain aneurysm. She was in the throes of a terrible headache one minute and was comatose the next. He told me how he watched her for three days, lying there, beautiful and with an exploded brain that didn't show. He pulled the plug. In those days, before lawyers saw the possible cash amounts involved, people and doctors just turned the machines off. Dead was dead. That was the second conversation I had with Lawrie, and we went up the stairs together.

CHAPTER TWENTY-ONE

I walked behind Jo, on my father's arm, down the aisle, under the baleful gaze of Blessed Tekakwitha and her buddies. Hi, Pocahontas, I said, almost inaudibly.

"What?" my dad whispered. He was a wreck.

"Nothing, Dad, just keep walking."

Michael winked at me. Up until that wink, I didn't even know if he'd be able to make it. I was glad he did. And the second I set eyes on Michael, I knew immediately that I could do for Lawrie what Charlie had been able to do for him. Tears came to my eyes. I began to look like a bride.

During the entire ceremony, I plotted. Michael would see to it that Lawrie's father would simply disappear. That would be my condition. No bringing Lawrie's father back to Israel for a trial. Michael would just have to kill him the way he did von Hiltz, if that's what he really did to von Hiltz. I didn't want to believe it. Michael was now a teacher—a high school teacher. Only I knew what he really did for a living, and I never told Jo what I knew. I don't remember saying, "I do." Not until I watched Lawrie sliding a gold ring on my finger did I arrive at my wedding.

Rather a unique wedding reception we had, considering the guest list. There was Jo, with her tiny baby girl, and Jo's husband, Ahmad, the Palestinian freedom fighter. And

Michael, a Holocaust survivor living in the land Ahmad was fighting over, and Lawrie, the son of an ex-Nazi, one of the many being stalked by Michael, now an official Nazi-hunter. There were all kinds of cross sympathies and cross empathies and during almost all of the wedding reception the five of us sat in the bar trying to make each other understand the other's point of view, Jo and I basically the moderators. We represented the confused, ignorant point of view. Emotions ran high, but we all remained civilized.

The bartender, a Yale graduate student in Middle Eastern studies, gaped at all of us, mouth hanging open, while he listened to his thesis unfold onto the bar. Soon, he was scribbling furiously on coasters and napkins, and at the same time trying to mix drinks. My gin and tonics were nine parts gin to one part tonic. One had a Maraschino cherry in it. Forget slicing limes. Everyone got cherries, then olives, then nothing. My great-aunt on my mother's side asked if he wouldn't mind making her a piña colada. I thought he would throttle her. She got pineapple juice, rum, and a little container of half-and-half that he told her to pour in. Jo, out of respect for Moslem tradition, wasn't drinking alcohol. I didn't ask her what Ahmad's excuse was.

Finally, Paul came and dragged Lawrie off for some kind of toast, and Jo and I went to check on the baby, who was asleep in a basket right next to the wedding cake. Several wedding experts were appalled. Jo had been so exhausted the day before, having just arrived, and I was running around like an imbecile because no one had ever thought to tell me to buy white shoes, that we'd never had a chance to talk. So for the rest of the reception we sat yakking at the head table. She told me a lot of things I wished she'd told me before, including the fact that Ahmad was a graduate of the University of Michigan and had a law degree from Harvard. It was a relief for me to know that Ahmad would, because of his education and time in the States, understand Jo better. I was even sure he'd brought her pickles and ice cream when she was pregnant, as American husbands do. I didn't pay too much attention when she told me about his work with the PLO. All I knew was that Ahmad would most definitely come to his senses soon, return to the States, or at least move to Paris, where his parents lived. That would be so good for Jo. And the baby. She was charming. She was the second baby I'd ever really known since Paul's first boy was born three weeks earlier. There was a lot of matchmaking talk the night before about the two babies and it was very silly. And nice.

Jo was no fool. How could I have thought that? The more I thought about it, the more sure I was that Jo would end up in Paris. And as for now, she was a queen, even if only queen of Squalorland. Ahmad adored her, and they would both kill for their baby. The baby's hair was so light it was transparent, but her eyes were black like Ahmad's. Her skin was somewhere in the middle between Jo's porcelain and Ahmad's tan-leather color. She had an Arab name but her middle name was Mattie and I liked her a little bit. I didn't know how anyone could get too crazy about an incomplete human being who had no control over its bodily functions and was incapable of doing anything but cry, eat, sleep, or just lie around.

I told Jo evolution really stunk. First, human brains got bigger and so did skulls to accommodate them, while whoever was in charge of all this thought it would be hilarious to do nothing about making the human cervix proportionately larger. And besides, just look at horses, I told Jo. When they're born, they stand up within two seconds, and with human babies you have to carry them around for a whole year. Jo shut me up by telling me that Arab women helped each other carry the babies around. American women were too busy to help each other. I had no retort, especially since I intended to hire someone when it came to all that.

Lawrie understood completely my putting off the honeymoon for three days while I spent time with Jo. We pushed the baby in a rented carriage all over Norwalk. Jo showed the baby to the guy her mother used to live with. He still owned the bar, but now owned several others and wasn't around too much. While all the bar customers and the waitress gushed over the baby, I saw Jo take her ex-common-law stepfather aside and I knew she asked if he knew where her mother was. And I could tell he didn't by her face. But he gave her the hug I wanted to give, and it was better that it was him rather than me, because Jo was hugging her entire past good-bye. Now she was totally Ahmad's. He was all she had. He was now the number-one person in her life, then the baby, then me. It was all right, though, because that was the way it should be.

We ended our walk on the front steps of St. Thomas's. Jo laid a blanket on the grass and plunked the little baby on it. The infant bobbed her head around and tried to see what the traffic noise was all about. She tried to focus on the dandelions at the edge of her blanket. She went cross-eyed. Jo and I laughed, though we were both thinking about when we were thirteen and did our junior-high homework together at this very spot. Jo began to cry so hard that it was obvious she was more than just melancholy like me. I held her in my arms and didn't know how I was supposed to comfort her. A mother of a new baby needs her mother. Women who don't have a mother, or have one who isn't too keen on becoming a grandparent, suffer.

She cried for quite a long time while I said nothing and then we dried her face with a diaper. I did give her comfort because she needed someone to listen to her, and even though that's all I thought I'd be able to offer her, I found things to say.

"I don't know why, Mattie. . . . I don't know why she didn't at least tell me where she was going." I think I knew why. "Not even a note once in a while to let me know how the boy was doing in school. How the baby was managing."

"I think, Jo, that what she's doing now was the same as what she did before, when she left the mountains with you. She saw that you were special. She escaped for you."

Jo reached over to the baby and cradled her. She lifted her blouse and nursed her. Jo was waiting for me to go on.

"So, I think she set you free of your family, the one you

barely remember. And then, when she saw that you were able to be on your own, before she could influence any decision you might make, before you committed yourself to making some kind of decent life for her and the children, she set you loose. She saved you from the obligations you would have if she'd stayed."

"My mother loved me," Jo said softly, more to the baby than to anyone else. Her face turned up toward mine, and I could see the baby's little hand kneading Jo's white breast.

"Your mother loved you selflessly. She did. She was willing to give you up so you could go and do whatever you wanted. Whatever you had to do."

I looked away from Jo. Her damned mother. By not letting Jo take care of them, she was making Jo take care of another dusky baby, and take care of a displaced nation surrounded by treachery. Treachery on all sides.

Ahmad, meanwhile, was in Michigan buying guns. Michael told me that when I drove him to Kennedy. He'd learned this from "sources." The reason he told me was so that I'd be able to warn Jo to be careful. He wasn't the least bit worried about a handful of ragged Palestinian refugees even if they did have a few guns. He said they wouldn't be able to perform even isolated attacks against Israel, since there was no getting past the Israeli air force. He forgot that terrorists aren't detected on radar. To get good at it, it would take another twenty years, the same length of time it had been since they'd been forced from their homes. Absence makes the heart grow fonder. How could Israelis not keep that in mind?

Michael and Ahmad parted friends, soul brothers sort of, each knowing that one had as much right to Jerusalem as the other, each knowing they couldn't ever share it, but wishing it were possible. Michael was willing to die to keep it, and Ahmad was willing to die to get it back. Michael told Ahmad that as long as there were people with little black numbers on the inside of their forearms, there could be no compromise. Ahmad told Michael that as long as there were people alive who remembered a little house, a farm, a shop in or around Jerusalem, there would be no choice but to try to go back. (That was when I thought of the Arab candymakers.)

"Maybe," Michael told Ahmad, "your baby's generation will have the answer."

"I doubt it. How can she grow up to be a rational person when she realizes that the rest of the world doesn't live in a hole in the ground?"

"Nor will my children be rational, Ahmad—and I hope they're as beautiful as your girl—nor will they ever stop asking where their grandmother, their aunts and uncles and cousins are. My children will never give up their refuge."

Jo and Paul's wife talked a lot about babies during the days Jo waited for Ahmad to finish his business. Jo said to me, "What does this Lisa do?"

"Before they got married, she was an exercise instructor."

"Wow." Now she sounded like when we were thirteen.

"That's what we all said. But they're very happy, Jo."

"What do your parents say?"

"My mother said to me, 'What on earth do they talk about?' And I told her that they're too busy screwing their brains out to talk. I mean, you should see her in a leotard."

"Then what did your mother say?" Jo was starting to laugh.

"She said she hoped I didn't talk like that in front of Lawrence." Then I said to Jo, "You know, I was so worried that Paul would be a wreck over seeing you again. And what you would feel like. There's nothing there, is there?"

"No, there isn't. Nothing. He's back to being your older brother—kind of my older brother. I think Lisa is wonderful for Paul. He talks about the cellular basis for memory all day with the other whizzes. Think how refreshing she must be."

"She is. And he is refreshing to her. He takes her completely seriously. She thrives on the respect he has for her.

And they're awfully good parents. Like you and Ahmad."

"Like you and Lawrie will be someday."

"Yeah."

My mother came in with the baby, who was ready to eat, and Jo nursed her as politely as possible. "We weren't encouraged to do that in the forties," my mother said. She felt she'd really missed something. As I observed Jo and her intimate relationship with her baby, I wondered what I would do when the time came. Probably the same as Jo, since I knew that humans were closer to animals than angels and I might as well roll with it.

It was hard for Jo and me to say good-bye this time. Harder than in Beirut, when we were both semiangry with each other. I went on my honeymoon, red-eyed.

On our trip to Niagara Falls, of all places, I wrote about the wedding. I meant it to be really political, the way it was, but the story just wouldn't take that direction. Sign of a fiction writer. Can't tell the truth, no matter what.

My Wedding

Our old cat's favorite sleeping spot was the bed in the guest room. My mother had an extra-squishy, enormous comforter on it and the cat would nest in its exact center. The cat was an old tom, docile unless his territory was infringed upon. Then he went in for the kill and was known to hang on to the neck of a curious Lab or golden retriever with his teeth even while the victim was tear-assing down the street.

The cat must have been out patrolling when my mother decided to spread my veil of hundreds of square yards of "French Silk Illusion" across the guest bed to get rid of any wrinkles, as if there is any such thing as wrinkled illusion. The cat didn't dislike the sudden presence of fine, netted billows; in fact he thought it was meant especially for him, but he did feel the necessity of giving forth his signature to make it more secure. Otis couldn't be sure that maybe some alien alley cat might not just wander into the house and, like Goldilocks, sack out on the coziest bed.

The cat ejaculated about the entire veil before making himself comfy. My mother was able to keep secret the fact that she'd found Otis lying on the veil, but when we all placed it over my head, the entire wedding party's noses wrinkled up.

"What the hell is that stench?" the Bryn Mawr bridesmaids asked each other, never dreaming it was the veil.

But my brother, Paul, recalling a pair of shoes he'd once dug out of the back of his closet said, "I know that smell."

"What, what?"

"Cat jizz!"

"Cat what?" said my mother.

"Sorry, Ma," Paul said, "I think Otis sprayed."

Now I realized that the little amber dots dancing in front of my eyes were not caused by the photographer's flashbulbs. I thought amber didn't quite seem right. I yanked the veil from my head and threw it out the back door onto the lawn. The bridal party thought I'd gone mad until they discovered that, with the veil gone, so was the odor. My mother said we should wash it, not throw it away.

And we learned a bridal laundry lesson—something that should go into "Heloïse" right after "The bride should spend ten minutes lying on her back with ice cubes on her eyelids, which will both relax her and leave her fresh-eyed." When you toss a French Illusion veil into the Maytag, even on the delicate cycle, the veil comes out in exquisite shredded ribbons.

My maid of honor and best friend, Jo, tried to tell my hysterical mother that I was not the veil type anyway. I'd never worn a veil in my life, never would again, so what was the difference? "Besides, Mrs. Price," she said, "this is the sixties!"

My mother calmed, her eyes became slits, and she said through her teeth, "Where is that goddamned cat?"

Smart Paul had already closed the cat into the garage.

Jo went out and picked a bag of sweet alyssum out of our neighbor's garden and pinned it in little bunches into my long hair, ironed straight. Then she misted the alyssum, forgetting that the moisture would bring back the natural curl. I said, "I could have been lying around with ice cubes on my eyes instead of cramping my neck down under the ironing board, guys."

My father came in and said, "Oh, good, a hippie wedding after all."

But he was followed by my godmother, who said, tears forming, "Doesn't Mattie look just like she did when she was a little girl? Remember when she'd go out to the woods and come back with daisies and buttercups in her curls?"

Sweet alyssum smells like heaven, actually.

I wasn't a dewy-eyed bride, though my mother was a dewy-eyed mother. The last thing she read in "Heloise" was, "Just before the bride leaves the house, spray her veil with her favorite perfume."

That was as far as I got on my wedding short story. I guess I wasn't ready for anything heavy. Lawrie read it and he laughed and laughed. He'd never read anything else I'd written. He's very polite. He told me he thought if I'd wanted him to read my stuff, I would have asked. He told me the wedding story was wonderful just like I was wonderful, and he told me he was honestly surprised. He said even though he was quite sure I was a talented writer he'd never dreamed I had the talent to create humor. "Humor is just about impossible."

"So what do you know?"

"I know that I never laugh at anything that's supposed to be funny. Except Peter De Vries."

"You've read Peter De Vries?"

"Yes."

"He inspires me."

"He makes me laugh."

I was beginning to like this Lawrie.

When we came home from the honeymoon, I showed the story to my father. I told him it was my Peter De Vries story. Peter De Vries worked for *The New Yorker*, too. My father ignored the reminder, which was only meant to set him up for the fact that I was making an attempt at humor. My father's reaction to the wedding thing was I had to think more about writing in the third person if I ever expected to be taken seriously. Did I tell him he worked in the same place as Peter De Vries, who wrote in the first person and who was taken quite seriously? No, I didn't. You have to be older than twenty-four to tell your father he's being a real asshole.

CHAPTER TWENTY-TWO

Lawrie and I made no demands on each other. What we needed from one another was what we were. He did what he did; I did what I did. Sometimes Lawrie would tell me he'd have to be out of town for a week. My mother asked me once where he was. I didn't know. All I knew was that even though I loved the presence of Lawrie in my life, it was nice to be alone a lot, and I didn't miss him till I would hear his car come up the driveway. I missed him for the two minutes it took him to get in the door. I was always so glad to see him again.

I never felt guilty about rifling through Lawrie's papers. I never felt guilty about all the money I spent on a detective to find out about Lawrie's background to see if there were any clues as to his father's whereabouts. Everything the detective told me, I already knew: the suburb of Buenos Aires where Lawrie grew up, the background of his mother's family, where he went to school. The detective said there was no more. But he also told me that Lawrie's consultant work was with companies that held special government classifications that precluded further investigation. The detective said it was his guess that Lawrie was an unofficial diplomat, the kind who gets things done while the Henry Kissingers are out partying. I read the report to Michael at a pay phone. Michael said thank you.

We went skiing a few months after our wedding and

came home to find the house broken into. The things that were missing were not unexpected. The TV, all our liquor bottles, and "stuff that kids would take," said the police. The safe was open. Lawrie told the police that it would take a professional to open the safe, but the police said, so what, since nothing was missing. Nothing was missing, but all the papers in the safe were very neat, as were the papers on his desk. They'd been tampered with, and they'd been put back in their little piles very carefully. I called Michael. He said he was sorry, but that it had to be done. He knew as well as I that Lawrie could not find out. Ever. His retribution would be fearful.

Before the first anniversary of our wedding, Martin Luther King and Bobby Kennedy were killed. When Dr. King was killed I went to a service with all the people from the bar where Jo used to live. The people sang and screamed their way into oblivion. I went to New York when Bobby Kennedy was killed and stood in the miles-long line for eight hours to pass his coffin in St. Patrick's. In the most dreadful sorrow—horribly quiet sorrow compared with Dr. King's service in Norwalk—white people and black people and people speaking Spanish inched along together on the hot sidewalk while bank presidents left their offices to pass out paper cups of water. Crisp old men gave us drinks and would mumble, "I'm sorry," to us, guilty that Bobby hadn't been their hero as he'd been ours.

For a while I walked with a woman who had cerebral palsy. She walked very slowly and kept urging me not to wait for her. I saw Stephen Smith walking down the length of the line and I told the woman that if I went and spoke to him he'd probably be able to get a car for her like the celebrities were in. She said, no, she wanted it to take forever because now she didn't believe it happened, and the longer it took her to get into the church, the longer she'd be able to tell herself that it hadn't happened.

There were no tears to cry in the line because of the heat and because there just wasn't enough water. I kept holding my hair up off my neck and a Puerto Rican lady surrounded by children took a yellow plastic barrette out of her hair and gave it to me. I said, *"Gracias,"* and we hugged each other. Her bigger children held the littler ones. I gave them my cups of water when it was available.

A limousine went by. I saw Pierre Salinger in it. He was crying.

St. Patrick's was so cool. Frank Gifford stood at one end of the coffin. Little Irish kids and big Irish kids looked up as the Puerto Rican children filed past their father's body. The Irish kids were kneeling and they gripped the pews in front of them with all their might. I touched the coffin and I looked at Bobby's children and his nieces and nephews and at the Puerto Rican kids, too, in their Sunday best though it was so hot, and decided that the only thing that could displace my misery, disgust, and disillusionment was motherhood.

When I got home, Lawrie put Epsom salts in a pan of hot water for me. We sat on the sofa and I soaked my blisters. I told him I didn't want to put off having children any longer and he was glad.

Our two little girls were born three years apart. We named the first Delia, after Lawrie's mother, and the second Jo. Lawrie was grateful we had girls instead of boys. He told me he didn't know how to be an American father to a son, but any kind of father is allowed to love a daughter with free emotions; nothing had to be held back. His second daughter taught him how foolish that was—she taught him how to be an American father.

Delia was a scholar and a musician. She was born with a gift to create music, as I had been born with a gift to create images and transfer them into language. Lawrie and Delia would sit at the two baby grands at opposite ends of the family room and play. Between the two pianos was a gymnastic bar, and hanging from that during all the concerts was Joey: little and squat, a pack of beautiful muscles. She'd flip around her bar to the music, her hair in her eyes, improvising routines to Mozart.

Joey never sat still unless forced by tradition. At meal-times she'd sit on the outer inch of her chair, set to escape at the first possible moment. She broke the Little League sex barrier when she was ten. She brought me back to my backyard-ball days and the two of us taught her father and older sister the wonders of baseball. For Christmas and birthdays she would ask only for tickets to Red Sox games. Four times a year, we'd all drive up to Boston to Fenway Park. Delia said, "When I leave Lansdowne Street and go through the gray walls of this stadium and then see that green, green grass through the portal, I feel the same as when I'm going down the aisle of Carnegie Hall while the orchestra is warming up." To Delia, the anticipation she felt while the players tuned their bats and the musicians their instruments was as thrilling as the performance itself.

We came to love the city so much that we'd end up squeezing the ball game in between the aquarium and the museums and rides in the swan boats. Jo would have adored Boston.

Delia loved school and was in a program for gifted children that was a godsend. Joey hated going to school and did the minimum amount of schoolwork, just short of embarrassing herself. Her kind second-grade teacher said, "She doesn't really dislike school, she just likes being home better, which of course is a compliment to you and Mr. Quayles."

When Joey was four and Delia seven, Jo had her fifth and last child, named Abdur, which meant "hope." Arab names mean things. It was 1976, the year the Syrians took up sides against the Christian forces in Beirut, intervened, and disintegrated the Lebanese army, protecting the Palestinians in the camps from sure destruction. Though the Syrian motives were not altruistic (they were more interested in getting rid of Lebanon's Christian army, using the Palestinians as an excuse to do so), they prevented a great deal of bloodshed, which would in turn bring about other bloodshed via the Israelis, who could not let the Syrians sit at the top of the Golan Heights showering heavy artillery down on school buses. Every day I read in the paper about car bombs and assassinations and kidnappings. I couldn't write. I was so worried about Jo and her babies that I told Lawrie I was going there. It was the first time Lawrie so much as paused before saying that would be fine. Paul and his wife took our girls, and I left for Beirut.

Unlike his brother and sisters, the new baby wasn't fair-haired and dark-eyed; he was the opposite. I saw him as he turned three days old, lying in a bassinet in the nursery of the Italian hospital. I stood with Ahmad, looking at him. It was nothing like standing with a beaming American father in wonder over a new son. Ahmad knew each and every danger subsequent to this new child.

"Can't you send Jo and the children with me until things cool down a little around here?" I asked him.

"She wouldn't go and things will not cool down." He smiled at me. "The camps are now under the eye of the world. We will be safe. The baby is special, isn't he?"

"I'm sure you said that about all your children, Ahmad, but yes, he is."

"He sees. He sees already. The others do not see, even now, thanks be to Allah. They are happy."

"C'mon, Ahmad, don't go firing all that Arab hokus-pokus on me. He's just a baby. A beautiful one. And I want to see Jo."

"She's suspicious. You didn't come when the others were born."

"She knows I'm worried for her safety. I've told her that in letters."

"She's tired of defending herself to you."

"Too bad."

All the children were in the room with Jo, sitting on the floor playing a game with pebbles. Until they looked up, they were a bunch of little American towheads, but when they did look up they had the stamp of their father across all their dark little faces. The pediatrician had finished examining the baby, and Ahmad carried him into the room.

He held him while Jo and I hugged and cried. Then the children hugged me, too, and the eldest, two years older than Delia, said, "I was at your wedding, Auntie."

"I know you were, sweetheart," and I hugged her and then the others.

In Arabic, there is no word for a woman's friend, so I was "Auntie." I'm not much of a kid-hugger, but I was hugging Jo when I hugged them. And Jo looked so blissful. I remembered how much she loved her little half brother and sister, though I didn't know how much at the time. Now I knew what those looks and pats all meant.

I showed everyone pictures of Delia and Joey and of course they were most interested in Joey, who was named after their mother.

And the nine-year-old said, "And I am your namesake." She was cute. All the things she'd been told were now real, so she kept saying things like that. Jo and Ahmad laughed at her and she put her head down.

The second child, a boy, said, "Someday, you will have sons, too."

"Perhaps," I said. The only other children I intended to create would be on paper. Jo handed me the baby.

He stared about. He moved his arms and legs. He wriggled. He tried to look up at me behind his own head, so I turned him around. I laid my cheek onto his sumptuous black hair. My babies walked before they grew hair. I handed him back to Jo to nurse, and it was a long time before he let his eyelids drop shut. He fought so hard that he managed to keep one eyelid open a few seconds later than the other. We laughed.

Ahmad said, "You see?"

Jo nodded.

I had nursed my own babies. Physically, it felt very good and I relished my only other chance at being physically intimate with another human being. But I weaned them early. It grew boring. Of course, most of the time, children are very boring. The only people they're not boring to are other children, and adults who'd rather be children. My sister-in-law was always down on her hands and knees, or sitting in their circles, playing their games. She would have loved to learn this Arab pebble game. Boring.

Jo was staying a full week at the hospital, at Ahmad's insistence. It seemed after the last delivery she'd hemorrhaged. It wasn't serious, but they'd had to pack her back to the clinic, and by the time she got there, she'd lost a great deal of blood. In fact, Ahmad even insisted upon the hospital rather than the clinic. I told him to get a cot for me and I'd stay with Jo and the baby the rest of the time and keep her company.

Jo and Ahmad eyed each other, and his eyebrow rose slightly, which was his way of asking her if that was what she wanted. Jo said, "I can't think of anything I'd rather do than spend the next few days with Mattie and Abdur."

So Ahmad said, "Then I am very grateful to you, Mattie. It is difficult for me to be here very much and the children are missing their schooling."

In most places in the world, children go where their parents go. I'd forgotten.

"It'll be just like the dorm at college, Jo."

It was. The nurses adored me because I changed and bathed the baby and walked him in the hall when his milk wouldn't digest easily. I always put nondescript crying into terms of cause so I could stand it. He cried because that's what babies do. My philosophy has always been that it's better to cry in people's arms than in a cold crib. That's what Lisa told my mother when she accused Lisa of spoiling Paul's boys. Knowing Paul's boys, my mother was dead wrong. Walking crying babies is boring and tiring but they appreciate it, though they don't show their appreciation for weeks to come, when they smile at you in adoration.

The Palestinian nurses' aides were happy to know Jo was getting special care. They'd come and visit her before going back to the camp. They were young girls whose job was mostly to empty bed pans. The Italian nuns, who were the nurses, treated them with respect.

I unpacked nightgowns and a robe and slippers I'd

brought for Jo. She looped out on the smell of the sizing. The sizing, she said, smelled like Bloomingdale's and Lord & Taylor's. She got to giggling. The sizing might have been cocaine.

Old women from the camp brought food three times a day. I love Middle Eastern food. I gained five pounds during the week I spent in Beirut, four of them in the hospital alone. The baby watched our every move. He recognized his father the minute Ahmad would arrive in the room each night.

"You see?" Ahmad would say to us. Jo would nod and I'd shrug.

So Jo got a lot of rest and never hemorrhaged. I became attached to the baby. When I finally had to leave I felt like I was dying. I didn't stop shaking till I was in the Kennedy terminal with Lawrie and the girls. I felt as though I'd left another planet full of aliens, except for Jo and her children, who should have been with me.

In the limo, while the girls opened their presents and exclaimed over my dozens of Polaroid pictures, Lawrie said, "Beirut has changed then?"

"Not when you first see it. It's still the most gorgeous setting for any city in all the world. But then you start noticing all the soldiers with guns, and the young men who aren't soldiers who have guns, and of course the fire-damaged buildings. But it's not that. It's the people. They're always in a hurry to get where they're going. They don't do things any differently, just faster. Before the next explosion has a chance to go off. They used to just stroll and browse, all day and most of the night. There's no one out at night now. And in the camp, the people are very optimistic. The camps are cleaner now, but still a place of transiency. The Palestinians think that with all the fighting going on between the Moslems and the Christians, no one will pay attention while they begin making their way home. But, Lawrie, the route home is terrorism. They think that's the only way. As if they could intimidate the Israelis. They're fools."

"Then Jo is not safe?"

"Oh, yes. Very safe. Ahmad wouldn't let anyone harm a hair on her head. There are weapons hidden everywhere."

"That doesn't sound safe."

"Ahmad will take care of his family. He is one of the leaders. He has a patrol outside his tent door."

"The Palestinians, though, are expendable."

"I didn't mean for you to worry, too, Lawrie. Ahmad will send Jo to us if things get really dangerous. He loves them so much."

"I hope he will send them. But I wonder. People do not accept danger until it is too late. Usually. Ask Michael. He will tell you that."

CHAPTER
TWENTY-THREE

I called Michael as the situation in Beirut became almost unbearable for me to read about. I told him the Israelis had to stop bombing civilian villages just because they suspected terrorists were there. I told him that innocent people were being killed. He said that if the PLO wanted to hide under women's skirts and babies' cribs, then it was their responsibility when those women and children died. And he reminded me of Israeli schoolchildren who'd died. And I reminded him of Palestinian children who hadn't even had the opportunity to be schoolchildren, and it was Israel's millstone that they hadn't.

"And why is it our millstone?" Michael demanded. "Why the double standard? Do you really think Israel is supposed to have higher morals than the rest of the world?"

"Of course."

"Why?"

"Because you're Jews, dummy! God CHOSE you, remember? If you guys don't set the standard, who will?"

"Oh, Mattie!"

We fought on and on, but only to ease the burden of knowing that we were both half right and half wrong, and in the end Michael told me what I wanted to hear—he assured me that the camps were safe. The line was drawn there. Even though the leadership of the PLO lived in the camps, the huge numbers of people prevented any action. The Israelis, he told me, made this decision in spite of the fact that the Lebanese army wanted them to act.

"By 'act,' you mean nuke the places, right?"

"We are not barbarians, Mattie. Jo is safe."

But the emergence of Yasir Arafat was a source for more barbarism against the Jews than they had ever dreamed possible. The Israeli air force could not prevent the murders of the Olympians. Arafat, the first Palestinian leader who was a Palestinian himself, could have been a great man. Could have found the thread that might have connected him to the rational democrats of Israel. But he was a buffoon. And he wanted a homeland at the expense of the lives of the people who lived there and those who he said should have the land, too. His own people. Arafat, like all the other Palestinian leaders who had been Syrians or Bedouins or Egyptians, wanted to conquer Israel. He did not want a homeland via the avenues that were sane. He simply wanted to wipe out the Jews.

"Michael, you are not a barbarian, I know, but there are some. In Israel. And you know that."

"They are under control."

"I hope so."

"Jo is safe."

In the end, I bought open airline tickets for all of them and sent them to Jo. I asked her to promise me that they would all jump ship, even if on a moment's notice. She admonished me for my extravagance and sent the tickets back.

But things didn't get worse. They got no better, but there were no major catastrophes that might have led to an out-and-out attack by the Israelis. I relaxed.

My children were in school all day and I found myself writing more and more. Finally, I grew impatient with my father's advice that I wasn't ready to submit my stories for publication. And mostly, I grew tired of writing for the praise that never came. Finally, a few pats for effort were no longer enough. Lawrie told me he was worried that I would give up if I didn't send my stories somewhere. It didn't have to be *The New Yorker*.

"You deserve some acknowledgment for your incredible effort."

So I began to study. I studied present-day, slick fiction. I had stacks of women's magazines all over my room in the turret. I analyzed what kind of fiction *Redbook* and *Glamour* and *Ladies' Home Journal* were printing. Then I called the agent for several famous writers who published fiction in *The New Yorker*. He was also a family friend. I told him who I was and lied that my father said I should show him a story I'd worked on. It was my wedding story, only I'd expanded it and taken out some of the sexual language. I had Otis "spray" rather than "ejaculate." If I wanted to publish in *Redbook* I couldn't offend those *Redbook* readers. The agent was very nice, asked how my father was, and explained that normally he only sent out short stories for his clients who'd published novels.

"But since your dad said you should send something to me . . . well, I'll have a look. See what you've got."

"I am working on a novel, too, but I have a ways to go." I sure did, considering I hadn't looked at my Michael stuff for ten years.

"Good for you. Send the story right in, Mattie, and I'll keep an eye peeled for it."

He kept it a month. Every time the phone rang, my stomach would knot. I'd watch for the mailman as if I were a shut-in, the mail my only contact to the outside world. Every time my father called and said, "Hi, Mattie," I'd quake, thinking he'd run into the agent, who would say to him, "How could you think your daughter's story was any good? It's dreadful!"

The agent called. He apologized for taking so long. He told me that I'd written the quintessential, tried-and-true contemporary short story—no depth, but a lot of heart.

"And very tight, which is remarkable for a beginner. I was sure I'd get a stream-of-conciousness, no-plot affair. What a pleasant surprise. I'm sending it to Helen Brown." He left out the Gurley so I didn't know who he was talking about for days. "She'll love the hilarious sexual tension. How's the book coming?"

"I'm sorry?"

"The book you're working on?"

"Oh. I haven't looked at it in a while. I'm just now going to go back to it."

"Great technique. Put it on the back burner for a while and when you go back to it, all the problems leap out at you."

"Mr. Harding?"

"Russ. You're all grown up and my client besides. What is it?"

His client. I choked instead of spoke.

"Mattie?"

"I really want to thank you, but I lied to you."

"No book?"

"There's a book all right, but my father never gave me the go-ahead on that story. He wouldn't have liked it."

"Mattie, he wouldn't have liked it no matter what. Your father is the kind of man who has expected only perfection from his children. From himself, for that matter. I saw him last week and I asked him how your writing was going. He told me you hadn't gotten past the promising stage yet. He was wrong. I didn't tell him you gave me the story. If we get it published, we'll put our heads together and figure out a nice way to break the news to him. OK?"

Helen Gurley Brown called me. She told me everyone had read the story and they were still all laughing about it. Sexual tension represented by a jealous tom cat was just too too much. She told me she wanted first crack at serial rights to my novel. "What's it about?"

"It's a thriller . . . set in Africa."

"Yuck," she said.

Lawrie threw a publication party for me. Naturally, my parents came, although my father had been totally close-mouthed about the whole thing. He just said he was disappointed I hadn't shown it to him.

"Oh, Dad, you wouldn't enjoy a *Cosmo* story."

"I'm surprised you'd see anything redeeming about writing a *Cosmo* story."

"Redeeming? Dad, my name is going to be in the table of contents of a big magazine. Isn't that incredible?"

He said I was lucky there existed a market for trite stories when so many talented writers were starving. My mother cut into that conversation, and started talking about their new wall unit. Lawrie pulled me away, telling me that my father was just being emotional, but I was hurt.

Lawrie and I had invited the agent to the party. Kind of a surprise for my father, but he became furious when he realized who had sold the story for me. Now he dragged me into the kitchen by my elbow. I couldn't be in the room of my choice at my own damn party.

"You took advantage of my friendship with Russ Harding. Why didn't you come to me first? If I'd known you were willing to publish in rags, I'd have passed it on to him."

"No you wouldn't have. It's not your kind of story."

"And what may I ask is 'my kind of story'?"

"One I can't write."

"It's simply a matter of maturity."

"You and your goddamned maturity. I've been writing for years and years. Dad, it's time."

"All right, then. It's time. But it will never be time for any writing of consequence. You will never have the depth."

"Depth. I never tried for depth. My novel will have depth."

"C'mon, Mattie, what novel?"

The kitchen was pulsing. My mother was suddenly there. Russ Harding was, too. My father had never even listened to me when I'd talked about my Michael book. "Dad, why aren't you happy for me? You should be happy. You should be pounding me on the back, bringing me champagne. All this time Lawrie has been upset with me about getting nowhere. I couldn't understand why he wouldn't support me. But he was doing exactly that! And what were you doing? Stringing me along so you could pat me on the head like a big powerful successful man, and say, 'Nice effort, honey.' Dad, you helped me a lot with so much of your criticism, but—"

"Don't you dare give me credit for some drivel you managed to worm into *Glamour* magazine through Russ." His voice was cracked and ugly.

"*Cosmopolitan.*"

He walked out my back door and slammed the glass storm. One panel cracked. It was shocking.

My mother said, very quietly, "He's jealous, Mattie."

"He's jealous?" I made her words a question because I was unable to speak on my own.

"Yes."

"But why? He's the best editor at *The New Yorker*. Everyone knows it."

Russ said, "But before he became a great editor he had to face up to the fact that he was a lousy writer."

I leaned against Lawrie's chest when I found that his arm was around my shoulders. "I just wanted to make him happy."

My mother said, "This is corny, but in time, he will be happy. He'll be proud, sweetheart. Now, think instead of how happy you've made Lawrie. The only other times I've seen him so ecstatic were when Delia and Joey were born. And more important, you've made yourself happy. Just try to be patient with your father."

"Try, Mattie," Russ said, "because he's about to be quite miserable with guilt."

At that point, I exploded. It had taken ten years. "Well he's a goddamn fucking shit!"

"Mattie!"

"He really is one, Ma."

"I know. He is. But Russ and I will talk to him. And when we're finished with him, he'll know exactly how much of a shit he is. Will that make you happy?"

"Yes."

My mother and father had a three-day fight. They'd never had a fight that went longer than three minutes. Russ met my father for lunch. They had a fight, too, but that night my father made three calls and apologized to him, then to my mother, and then to me. After apologizing, he congratulated me.

I called my mother and said, "What happened?" I knew that a lot must have happened during those three days because my father kept referring to my mother by her first name instead of "your mother," which he always had done.

She said, "I told him I was sick of listening to him brag to people about what a cute little enterprise I had—redecorating little suburban houses. I told him I intended to go into the city and get a job at Bloomingdale's, which is what I've always wanted to do. I intend to be going on week-long jaunts to places like the Hamptons to decorate for all those Bloomingdale customers."

"Oh God. What did he say?"

"At first, nothing. He walked out on me just like he did to you. Then I left. I taped a note to the fridge, telling him how swell it would be commuting into the city together and that when I had to stay in the city overnight, perhaps he'd like to join me." My father has made a point to never stay overnight in Manhattan for reasons relating to the magazine. "I spent three days with my friend Sarah—she wants a new kitchen, anyway—and when I came back, your father was ready to change his ways." Then she laughed.

"What's so funny?"

"He'd spent one night at Paul's. Paul is away at Stanford for a convention of brains. Twenty-four hours with Lisa was all he could take. They made brownies together, he played two hours of Chutes and Ladders with the little one, and Lisa kept telling him that he should be exercising regularly."

I laughed, too.

The week my story appeared in *Cosmo*, Israel invaded Lebanon.

CHAPTER
TWENTY-FOUR

It was the week the Israeli ambassador in London had been shot. Damn idiots, I thought, afraid of what the retaliation would be. An eye for an eye—the way to survive when there is one million enemy for every one of you. Michael called me. I knew about Israel's invasion of Lebanon before *The New York Times*. Michael told me that no one was safe anymore. No one.

"Michael, you don't invade another country because your ambassador is shot."

"You do when you've tried everything else."

"You're going to destroy the whole country because the PLO is headquartered in Beirut?"

"Not destroy, Mattie. Keep any other incident from happening."

"But the guys that shot the ambassador are no doubt still in London. Why don't you invade England?"

He told me I didn't understand. I told him that he didn't either.

Ahmad called me, too. He said that everyone was all right, and that the PLO would protect the Palestinians from being killed by the Israelis. He told me he took his job very seriously.

"Your job."

"That's right."

"How involved are you, Ahmad?"

"I cannot say anything to you. Jo and I just wanted you to know that we have the situation under control."

"You are working with people who shot the Israeli ambassador?"

He didn't respond.

"Ahmad, please send Jo home."

"She is home."

"No she isn't."

He sighed. Arabs can really sigh dramatically. "You are right. She isn't. She won't be home until I am living in my grandfather's house outside of Jaffa."

"You'll all die before that happens."

"No, not my family. I might die. Then I will be a martyr. In my children's eyes there can be no greater honor."

"What kind of shit is that?" God, I wanted to kill him.

"What Allah wills, will be."

"Fuck Allah. What is all this crap you're into? It's crap. The point is to live. What does it matter where? If my children were threatened I would go anywhere."

"Where can we go?"

"Here."

"I'm talking about all of us. Ask Michael where we're supposed to go. Tell him to ask his father why he didn't go anywhere when the Nazis threatened his family. Ask Michael."

"Ahmad, listen. You are a human being. The hell with your grandfather's house. You must—"

"I am a human being, yes, but first I AM A PALESTINIAN!"

I'd never heard Ahmad thunder before. I thundered back: "You're an asshole!"

Jo managed to rip the phone from his hand. I could hear her muffled voice. I didn't give her a chance to speak. "Jo! Ahmad and his gang of religious fanatics are out killing Israeli children and now the Israelis are going to kill Palestinian children. Jo, Israeli guns are so much bigger."

"You don't understand, Mattie."

"Yes, I do. It's very simple. Come back home. All of you. Why do you want your lives to be so goddamned complicated?"

"You want us to all come and buy a little split-level in Norwalk and live happily ever after?"

"Yes I do. Why not?"

"It's . . . it's a matter of destiny."

"For Christ's sake, Jo, I can't stand this."

"I love you, Mattie. I have to go. Write to me at the American Embassy. There is no mail here. Stop crying."

I heard something strange. "What's that?"

"Jets."

We were cut off. I was sure the jets had blown them up. Reaching Michael again was as easy as calling the house next door. "The camps will not be touched, Mattie. Not unless there's an accident. There have been no accidents."

Lawrence held me in his arms all night on the living-room sofa. He told me that he was following the situation very carefully. He said he would use the company's Lear to get Jo and her children out if it became necessary. He reassured me and reassured me until I believed him. Then he said, "Go write now. Write your book so that you won't go mad with worry."

Michael had faith in Ahmad's humanity. He had faith in Ahmad even though he knew Ahmad was involved with the PLO. Michael thought of him as a rock of rationality and sanity amid barbarians. Michael hung on to two threads that he thought to be unbreakable. The one thread was his belief that the Israelis were the civilized ones, that they would not stoop to making victims of innocents. They had been there too recently to do that. The other thread led to Ahmad: that Ahmad represented the civilized, elite Palestinians, and that in the end, they would be the ones to survive and become the leaders, once the Israelis had killed off Arafat and his gang of murderers. Michael thought the two threads were steel, but they weren't. They were spun glass, and they were both breaking.

Lawrence told me that, yes, a stray bomb could fall on the camps, but the odds were no different from getting hit by a runaway cab on Fifth Avenue.

The Lebanese Christian militia, under their president-elect, Bashir Gemayel, fought alongside the Israelis, and between them, drove the Syrian troops from Beirut. It was time for the Israelis to withdraw, but they didn't. Instead, they said the PLO had to leave Beirut first. The incentive the Israelis used was to cut off the water to Beirut. It was summer. Summers in the Middle East are very very hot and dry. I was able to imagine how miserable the people in the camp must have been without water—how hot, how smelly, how sick.

But Jo kept writing that spending their days walking the miles back and forth to the wells was good for everyone. It kept everyone focused on just one thing: staying alive. Life became more and more precious. I couldn't bear it. So, I kept writing my novel about Africa, and the man hiding on the mountain, and the young, innocent Peace Corps volunteer trying to find him. And I kept selling stories to magazines, romantic stories about cracked china teapots or falling in love with the UPS man.

It was the summer of 1982, and the girls were old enough to run off to the beach by themselves. Instead of thinking about my girls swimming and Jo's children trekking for water so as not to die of thirst, I spent the long, hot days finishing my book. I loved writing barefoot, wearing shorts and a loose top and no bra.

Russ sold my book to Doubleday. The Doubleday editor called me right after Russ. Even though I was a little disappointed that it wasn't Mrs. Onassis, I was so excited that the saliva dried up in my mouth and I couldn't talk. The absolutely lovely young woman who was my editor told me that was OK because her saliva had dried up, too—she was that excited about my book. Lawrie and Delia were very proud of me. Joey asked me to ask Nelson Doubleday about tickets to a couple of Mets games. I mentioned it to Russ and he said, "Let's worry about foreign rights for now."

I sent copies of the manuscript to Michael and to Jo.

A few days after that, I was looking for rubber bands in Lawrie's desk. In the top drawer there was an article from a Chilean newspaper. It was in Spanish, and I knew enough Spanish to understand it. Three prominent men with German names had been reported missing by their families. They had last been seen skiing at a mountain resort. At that resort people hunted, killed, and ate boar just like in the good old days. One of the three then turned up dead. There were suspicions that the other two had possibly been mistakenly kidnapped by Israeli Nazi-hunters since there was some rumor about their war records. The dead man's name was the name I'd found out to be Lawrie's father's.

Lawrie called me from New York right while I was there with the article in my hand. He told me he'd be away for a while, maybe longer than usual. His voice was a monotone, no melodic rise and fall left over from his first language. I was sure he was going to find out.

"I love you, Lawrie," was all I said, instead of my usual cheery "have a good trip." He was too detached to notice.

The receiver of the phone had a gloss to it after I replaced it. I wiped my hands on my shorts. I hadn't an idea as to what to do and there was no one I could go to find out. Except Jo. I picked up the phone and called the Lebanese attaché's office in New York. Yes, the airport was open today, the woman announced happily. I called Pan Am and got a flight. I sent ten mailgrams to Jo via every place and person I could think of: in care of our embassy, to American Express, to the clinic outside the camp. I even sent one to Yasir Arafat. But if Jo wasn't at the airport, it wouldn't be too terrible. I knew where to find her.

I called Paul and asked him to take the girls for a while. He told me to call Lisa to arrange things. Lisa was so happy. She told me she couldn't wait to braid hair and teach manicures and have tea parties for the girls' dolls. I packed for myself and my girls and on the way to the airport stopped at Delia and Joey's school. On the way I bought a doll for Joey. A doll that came with a wardrobe. I told them I had to go to Beirut to Jo because there was an emergency and that Lisa would pick them up, and they'd stay with her. I warned Joey to go along with Lisa on the doll business. Joey said she'd play dolls only at night. Paul's boys played baseball from right after school till they lost the ball in the dark.

Delia said, "I hope she comes back with you, Mom, and all the kids, too." Delia never stopped longing for another baby sister or brother. I didn't tell them that the emergency, this time, was mine, not Jo's. I cried when I left Joey. She wanted to come with me. I thought, Please, Lawrie, don't take them away from me.

Jo was at the airport. She said first thing, "I loved the book, Mattie, I just absolutely loved it."

I began to shake and Jo held me for what seemed an endless time. I'd forgotten about the book. She got us into a cab and told the driver to take us to the Hilton. People in the streets were wailing. I hadn't read the papers yesterday. Gemayel had been assassinated.

"They blame us," Jo said. Then, she looked at her watch. Curfew was approaching. She was dressed up. Not just Western clothes, which she always wore, but a suit and a white blouse. Stockings. I thought she dressed that way because she was going to have dinner with me at the hotel, but she said no, she was going to a meeting.

"With who?"

"With a general," she said and smiled at me. "I'll tell you about it tomorrow. And you can tell me what's wrong."

"Everything is wrong, Jo."

"You're scared, aren't you?"

"Yes."

"I can't stay with you tonight. But we'll have the whole day together tomorrow."

"The whole day?"

"Yes. And we'll work it out, Mattie. We will."

She didn't know how wrong she was, but just to be able to tell her would start me on the track to being brave, which I'd have to be, and to fight, which I would have to do.

"Can you stay over with me in the hotel tomorrow night?"

"I can't. I have to be home by dark for the children."

"When can I see them?"

"Well, I could bring them tomorrow, but I thought—"

"The next day."

"Yes. The day after tomorrow we'll go on a picnic with them. They're dying to see you, even the baby."

"How old is he?"

"Six."

"Jo, it's been six years!"

"I know."

"Let's never go that long again, OK?"

"OK. It's so good to see you even under the circumstances."

The circumstances were horrendous. Jo was pretty tense and it was a bad time for me to be needing her so much. I apologized for that and she told me not to be ridiculous. I got out of the cab and the doorman took away my luggage.

"I have to run. I have to, OK, Mattie?"

"OK."

"See you for breakfast."

"Great."

A few steps from the car, I heard her say to the driver, "Israeli army headquarters."

I got a chill. I was afraid she was going there to blow it up. But she wasn't. She was going there because she had an appointment to see Ariel Sharon. But the general had canceled his appointment, and he didn't see her. He had other appointments to keep.

The hotel looked, smelled, and tasted American. If Jo spent a whole day there with me, she'd remember home. I began plotting. It was as if I had white paper in front of me, blank paper waiting to be mauled with words—a story for Jo, and for me, to keep me from going mad with anxiety. My room looked out over the Mediterranean. The sun slipped into the sea just the way it did in Hawaii and in Cameroon, but not at home.

* * *

She came at nine, and we had a long breakfast. She ordered croissants and coffee and I reordered her breakfast. "A huge breakfast is what we want, Jo, followed by a long liquid lunch and a great big late dinner."

"No late dinner, Mattie. I—"

"Don't you dare take charge. We are going to spend the day by the pool basking."

"I haven't owned a bathing suit in years. So, . . ."

I whipped a minuscule bikini out of my bag and waved it under her nose. "You do now. We'll be lounge lizards like in Hawaii, and I'll tell the waiter to make the piña coladas light on the rum." She began to frown. "Just for this one day, Jo. I need you to be my old Jo so I can talk to you."

"All right, Mattie."

I'd rented a cabana. I knew if we went directly up to my room to change, I'd start talking and we'd never get out of the room. I would be more cohesive by the pool, less likely to cry in front of all the other guests.

We had eggs and sausage and potatoes and toast for breakfast. We ordered everything and ate it all. Any luxury you could name was still available in Beirut as long as you were willing to pay for it. Jo pushed the sausage away with a spare spoon but devoured the rest. And when we were done she caught me looking at the three congealing, cold sausages lined up neatly at the side of her plate.

"It's not that I'm officially a Moslem. I just really try to live as much like my family as I can . . . in order to have empathy."

"I'm making you make excuses. I'm sorry, Jo. Don't. I make such demands on you. Have some more coffee. Then we'll sit at the edge of the pool with our feet in and you can tell me what to do about Lawrie, who is going to worse than kill me when he finds out what I've done to him."

"Lawrie wouldn't get angry at you in a million years. He adores you."

"He doesn't now." I could tell, with all her problems,

that she thought I was being dramatic about some silly quarrel we'd had. "Jo, he is probably very angry right now. And it will get worse '

She stood up. "Come. And tell me everything."

Jo marched out of her cabana, across the pool deck, a bank of flowers behind her and the blue Mediterranean behind the flowers, wearing the black bikini. The metallic threads running through the fabric glimmered like her long hair blowing behind her in the breeze. I thought, You can't keep a Bryn Mawr girl down no matter what. Even if she's a Palestinian wife with a million stretch marks living in a refugee camp. The men at the poolside bar stared. So did I. The pool had arced steps leading down into the water and we sat on them, just our feet under the water. Jo sat and she absorbed me. Her own vast problems were stuffed into a closet in the back of her brain. And I told her what I'd been doing to Lawrie since our very wedding. And she understood perfectly. Too perfectly.

"You have betrayed Lawrie. But you have betrayed him for the sake of justice. Because he is the man that he is, I know he will forgive you." She put her hand on my forearm. "But it will take him a long time." Her eyes met mine.

"He has such power."

"I know. But he also has great love. He cannot deny his children their mother forever. He loves them too much. Don't cry."

"How long will it be?"

"I don't know. But you will have to manage it, won't you? You will have to wait. I promise, though, that it will end."

"But the side that he's hidden from me, from all of us . . . it's a side that's so dreadful that maybe it will overtake him."

"The side that he inherited from his father?"

"Yes."

"The Nazi side."

And then we both stared straight ahead, Jo thinking, me desperate to hold on to my emotions. I couldn't. "Jo, if he

leaves me . . . if he takes those girls . . ." She gripped my
wrist and snapped her fingers for the barman. He hurried
over.

"Two . . . two . . . what are they, Mattie?"

I whispered, "Piña coladas."

She smiled her dazzling smile at the waiter and when he
turned, she pushed me into the water. I swallowed a gallon
of it and it was exactly what I needed. We became two
porpoises. Jo would see me through. As always. We swam
until we were exhausted and then mounted two floating
chairs with drink holders.

"What's in this thing?" Jo held her drink up, a glass of
creamy sunshine.

"Everything in it is wonderful, Jo. An adult milk shake."

She took a sip and licked the smooth bubbles from her
upper lip. She turned to me. "Can I ask you things?"

"Are we going to make a plan?"

She laughed and then she didn't. "There probably is no
plan we could make. And I know you know that. But are
you absolutely sure he'll know it was you? How will he be
able to tell where the information came from?"

"Because his brain and his wall safe are all that contain
the information. And no one's broken into our house lately.
I figured I could swing that just the one time."

"Maybe Michael will be able to hide the evidence."

"Michael will. But it won't do any good. Even with no
evidence, Lawrie will figure it out."

"Mattie, did you ever think about what you'd do if this
happened?"

"Since I met him, Jo, my imagination has been in my
notebooks. I haven't wasted any."

We drank and floated. Jo was trying to use her non-
existent imagination, I could tell. Her eyes were sharp and
unseeing. But there was no answer, even in her brilliant
head, I was sure.

"It's so quiet, Jo."

"Yes. It's Friday."

Three Israeli army officers came in, and they sat at the

poolside bar and ordered gin and tonics. They watched us.

I begged Jo to stay overnight. She couldn't. There were explosions at night, she said, and the children got frightened. She would be back in the morning with them. We would have an early dinner.

"Wait a minute. I'll get them rooms here. All of you can stay with me. Just for tonight, Jo."

"I'm sorry, Mattie. I will bring them in the morning. We will have our picnic."

I couldn't change her mind. "How is Ahmad?"

"He is in hiding." Jo whispered this. "Some of the PLO stayed. A handful. Everything is so dangerous now. Since Gemayel was killed. They think we did it. I think they did it themselves. Ahmad's sisters are watching the children today."

"Are you afraid of Gemayel's people?"

"We are afraid of everyone now. We have lost our usefulness as pawns. The Syrians and Jordanians no longer need us as an excuse to war with the Israelis over our land. They all have AWACS now. They will get it back without having to use us." Now Jo looked even farther away, somewhere into the blank sky. "Not without all of us, but with the few of us who are terrorists—insane people who are being used by them. A few terrorists are shedding so much blood." She looked at me. "Not Ahmad. Not anymore. Those terrorists protected by the Syrians, and by the Libyan who thinks he is God—they do not represent the Palestinians. They do not represent my family!"

She was chewing on a fingernail. There was nothing left to chew on the other fingers. "We just want peace. Just peace and a homeland. Everyone wants that."

"Jo, some—many Israelis understand that."

"Well all I know is that if things stay on this course, the Syrians and the Jordanians combined will take Lebanon and Syria. No Palestine, no Lebanon, and then, no Israel. If a way isn't realized—a way to share the great holy city and have it watched over by rational people instead of religious fanatics, it's over."

"Michael told me it was other Arabs, not Israelis, who drove Palestinians out of their land. King Abdullah—"

"Mattie, that was forty years ago. It doesn't matter who owned what when . . . who did what to who. What matters is *now*. Now. I just don't want my children to suffer anymore."

Now she was crying. It was the piña colada. There was no need for me to harp on it. She knew she should come back with me so that her children could stop suffering. But she would not betray her husband, no matter what the sacrifice.

I wished Michael, and all the Michaels, knew what the hell was really going on. None of them did.

CHAPTER
TWENTY-FIVE

There was a puff of smoke over the city that evening. A fire put out the day before had started itself up again. The new fire was put out, too. I sat on the patio, alone under the stars, trying to relax. I couldn't. I was terrified, still, though the terror was now calmed. I knew I would thrash around my bed all night, even though I was exhausted. But tomorrow was to be a nice day—a day with Jo's children, a day for all of us to share each other. I would see to it that those children would have a glorious day and if I was tired and grumpy, it would be no good. I went up to my room and took two sleeping pills.

Sometime between midnight and dawn, the noise began. Not Israeli bombs, sirens. The sirens were part of my drugged, bizarre dreams and in my sleep they pounded right through me, and their intensity didn't wake me until long after they'd awakened the rest of the hotel's guests as well as the entire city of Beirut. I made my way to the bathroom through the ceaseless racket and then down to the dining room, where all the miserable guests sat, all of them saying things like, "You'd think they'd have shut the things down by now."

It was six-thirty. I spotted an American couple. God knows what they were doing there, but they hadn't a clue as to what the sirens were about. They offered me some of their pot of coffee so I wouldn't have to wait. It was delicious. I was afraid that whatever was going on would ruin the day. I asked the waiter what was happening. He said he didn't know, but he did. All the waiters did. I could tell. They kept buzzing among themselves and glancing out the plate glass at every opportunity.

I went out to the lobby after I placed my order for breakfast, and asked the clerk why the sirens kept up.

"It's nothing to concern yourself with, madam."

"I'd like to speak to the manager." I didn't like the tremor in his voice and the coffee in my stomach began to bubble.

"The manager arrives at nine. But it is nothing. Some sort of shooting went on last night. It is the Red Cross sirens transporting the . . . injured."

"But the sirens have been wailing for hours and hours."

"There were many injured, I believe."

"Who did the shooting?"

"No one is quite sure yet."

"Who was shot?" He didn't answer. "You know, don't you?"

"Really, madam, I—"

"Where did the shooting take place? Tell me!"

He sighed. "In one of the refugee camps."

The coffee rose up in my throat, perking with more force. "Which one?"

"Sabra . . ."

Thank God. I swallowed and sweat popped out all over me.

". . . and some say perhaps the Shatila camp as well. At least the rumors which I have . . ."

I mouthed the word, "No," and the coffee emptied out of my lips and splashed across the counter. I turned and ran out to the street. The doorman grabbed my arm.

"The curfew remains in effect through this day, madam. There are no taxis."

I wrenched away from him and ran, in my sundress and sandals, into the chilly morning. The sea was flat, no chop at all, and the rising sun behind me turned the center of the sea blood-red. Everything else was still, too, flattened, but for the wailing sirens. I ran toward them, toward Shatila, toward Jo, praying to God and at the same time cursing Michael and his immoral Israelis.

Soldiers were everywhere—Israeli soldiers, all in a panic, all trying to keep Red Cross vehicles moving into the area and the reporters out. The Christian militia was nowhere and an Italian from the U.N. peacekeeping force was trying to understand what was happening, but he could speak only Italian. I asked him in Italian how many people were killed and he asked me who did it.

There was no sign of anyone connected with the Lebanese army or government anywhere. As I came closer and listened to the newsmen shouting back and forth to each other, I found out who did it. The same Christian militia that was now missing. All those Arabs turned Presbyterian because they thought they'd have a better chance of getting green cards if they were.

I stopped in the middle of the growing chaos. I couldn't see where I was and I couldn't breathe. People were hysterical, screaming to be let by to find their families. It had been a Crystal Night for Arabs. And then I saw the old wood fence and realized I had arrived. The tents were ripped, the zinc roofs full of holes. Not exactly a Crystal Night, because the Palestinians had no money for windows. I thought, At least when she lived over the bar, Jo had windows. Jo.

In between hospital vehicles I got a glimpse of the narrow winding strip of dirt that was the road leading through the fence into the heart of Shatila. All over it were splotches and puddles of red paint. The vehicles were leaving tracks of red paint as they drove past me. The crazy Christian Arabs didn't break windows so they spilled paint. Jo was fine. By tomorrow she'd be out there with all the women in their black dresses mopping the red paint into the open sewers.

All the while I pushed closer until I could smell the odor of the paint and I kept saying to myself, *It's paint, it's paint.*

Other people were pushing through with me, and I was the only one not screaming. They were pounding on the Israeli khaki-green chests, demanding to be allowed into the camp. I remembered the hole in the fence that Jo's kids showed me once—a shortcut to the stream where they washed clothes. Where they went for water when the Israelis cut it off. The hole was covered by a flap of tarp, the same muddy color of the fence. I fought against the crowd, trying to get around them. When I found the tarp there were two Israeli soldiers guarding it. They were very young. One was down on his haunches crying and the other was trying to comfort him.

I squatted down, eyeball-to-eyeball with the one crying. "Where were you? Where were you when this happened?"

"Sleeping," he sobbed.

"Sleeping?" I shook his shoulders. "Sleeping? You promised you'd watch them, you dirty bastard. Sleeping!" I kept screaming the word at him over and over.

His friend pulled me away, and I had to wrench myself from his grip. I lifted the tent flap and went through, and in the camp, with its rutted paths and squashed-together shacks, it was as still as a cemetery—a great contrast to what was going on outside. The silence was horrifying. Only Red Cross workers were in there with wheelbarrows. They'd used up all their stretchers and they went from one pile of bodies to another, trying to determine if there was anything left alive. The wall of a stone house that stood behind the clump of bodies nearest me was splattered with more red paint and blue brains and was full of neat black holes. Most of the pile at the foot of the wall were men. Not all. But the two women did not have silver hair.

I ran, leaping over a foot-wide gutter. The gutter's thin trickle of filthy water was mixed with red paint, congealing at the edges. Blood with water. For the first time of all the times I had been in Shatila, I didn't have to swat flies from my sweating face. The flies were in an orgy of feasting and egg-laying and didn't have to fight living people. Jo's house was suddenly there in front of me, and I ran through the empty front room where everything was knocked over and scattered, but no red paint. Please, please, let there be none of it in the bedroom.

But there was. All over the sheet covering Ahmad and the littlest boy. The boy blinked at me with his clear silver-blue eyes and then I was aware of the half-dozen men around the bed; all big, stern, and enraged men, too small a group to have done anything about the slaughter. Ahmad's head was swathed in bandages and his one eye that was exposed was closed.

"Where is she?" I screamed. Arms went around me. "Where, where, where?"

The arms kept me from strangling Ahmad. A voice close to my ear said to me, "His legs were shot out from under him trying to get to her. And then he was shot in the head. He is dying."

"Ahmad! Where is she?"

He moved and his eye opened a slit, too swollen to open more. "Mattie." His voice came out from the bandages. "You must help her."

"I will. I will. Tell me where she is."

His fingers moved toward the little boy cradled in his arm. His black hair was plastered to his chalk face. "She is here. He is all that's left of her."

I strained against the steel arms, toward his soft, dry words until my muscles just collapsed in grief. I turned toward the chest of the man holding me and sobbed and sobbed until crying became an involuntary condition of my body and there was no way of stopping it.

The man's voice was soft, too. "You must take the boy. He will go with you. He understands. He sees. He and his father have already said good-bye. There will be no one to care for him if you don't. You must save this boy."

I tried to get air into me through the crying that I had no control over. And when I could at least breathe in and out, I said, "Let me speak to Ahmad." The man let go of me. I went to the bed and knelt beside it. "How did the baby live? Was he with you?"

Ahmad's hand moved and I took it. He choked. Then he said, "He was found under Jo's body. Take him away. Take him, Mattie."

I laid my face in Ahmad's hand until I finished crying. Then I stood. Ahmad's head turned, just barely, toward the boy. He spoke softly to him in Arabic and the child slid out from under his father's arm and out of the covers. His forearm was wrapped in white gauze stained with red paint. He stood next to me and Lord knows I made every effort to form some kind of smile on my face for this poor baby. He smiled, though. And clearly, in perfect English, he said, "My father said I am to call you, not Auntie, but what your children call you." He couldn't say it, though. His father's hanging arm swung slowly toward him and Ahmad's hand touched his back.

"Mom."

The quiet little word came at me like a tornado, whirling the room around. But I held. Mom—the most innocent-sounding word in American English, and it dealt him such a blow to say it, and to me, hearing it. But that child had had all he could take. Enough. He needed me. But before I swept him out of there I kissed Ahmad's bandages. He seemed asleep. I stood and looked at the circle of men as I picked Abdur up into my arms. "I'm sorry," I told them.

One said, "Take the boy. But he can walk. He is a big boy."

"I need to carry him," was the last thing I said to them. I told Jo's child to put his head on my shoulder and make believe he was asleep. In the doorway, I looked back at his father once more. Ahmad was motionless. Abdur lifted his head and looked at him, too, but I pushed his head back and whispered, "Close your eyes." Again, his grimy black hair touched my cheek.

Before I got to the tarpaulin flap in the fence he was sound asleep. The bodies at the base of the stone house were gone. Like Jo was gone. And her eldest girl, named after me. All of them.

At the fence there were two new Israeli soldiers. I walked

past them. They were so young, so unprepared. With all their training, they'd never been taught how to stop, prepare for, or clean up after a massacre. They just stood, stiff as stone.

Even with Abdur in my arms, I walked quickly so that my mind wouldn't derail. I had to get him out of this nightmare and then I would try to imagine how I'd ever get myself out of it. I walked all the way back to my hotel and I laid Abdur on the huge bed. I covered him and then I waited for him to wake up. I sat in the chair for four hours and never took my eyes off him. As soon as he moved, I got up and ordered food from room service, telling them to leave it outside the door. I dragged a table over to the bed and set everything out for him. But he just lay on the bed on his back, staring at the ceiling. I sat next to him and pulled him up. I explained to him that I had to go out alone to find a way to get him to the United States with me. I told him that he had to stay in the hotel room until I got back and that the people in the hotel would guard him. I put a can of Coke in his hand. He drank it—a long, long swig.

On the night table was a packet of hotel stationery and a pen. He finally spoke. He said to me, "While you are gone I will practice my letters."

I stared at him. He would practice his letters. I hugged him to me. "Yes. You practice your letters." Oh, Jo, what a wonderful kid you have.

I stood up. "You eat, Abdur, and then practice your letters. And then rest. I will put up a sign outside the door which says that no one is to disturb you. If someone knocks at the door they have made a mistake. Ignore it. Do you understand?"

"Yes."

"It might take me a long time."

"Many days?"

He was prepared for many days. "No, darling. But maybe many hours. Come to the door now. There is a lock that you must close when I leave. When I come back I will use

a special knock so you will know it is me." I knocked "Shave
and a Haircut," on the table.

He walked with me to the door. I hugged him and repeated everything into his ear. "Promise me you'll go back
to sleep if you feel tired."

"I promise." I stood up. "Mom?"

I lost my breath. "What is it, Abdur?"

"No one shoots people in a hotel."

"That's right."

"See you later."

"See you later."

I stood in the hallway and listened to the bolt slide across
the door. At the front desk I said with the authority of a
king, "See that no one disturbs the child in my room."

"Yes, madam."

I did my best at the American Embassy. This time, the
marine didn't even register. I just asked to see someone
about a lost passport. An attaché led me to his office. I
acted like a frazzled dummy and there could be no question
that I certainly looked the part without any special effort.
The attaché wasn't buying. Things had tightened up, and
today, the underlying official emotion was horror.

"You lost your son's passport. Where is he?"

"He's at our hotel. He's only six. I didn't want to bring
him out."

"He's all by himself."

"No. The hotel supplied a nanny for me "

"You'll have to bring him here. Absolute policy."

"My plane leaves tonight. I don't want him out on the
streets today. It would scare him. All these ambulances and
soldiers running around."

"It's policy."

"All right. How long will it take?"

"To issue him a passport?"

What else, you idiot, I thought. I smiled and nodded,
dodo-like.

"Depends."

"Depends?"

"Yes. On various circumstances. May I see your passport?"

"Certainly." I took it out of my bag. He flipped through it.

"Tourist visa? Not a place to bring a child for a vacation. Alone."

"We're not alone. We're together."

"I meant without your husband."

"Well, my husband left yesterday while I finished up some business. I have a feeling he has . . . Paul's passport."

"A passport is the one document that must be guarded carefully and kept on your person at all times. At all times."

I wanted to smash his face but I let him go on scolding me. Then he said, "Finish up some business, did you say?"

I'd made a mistake. So I pretended that I had my pen in my hand and my notebook in front of me. "That's right. I've been assigned to do a feature for the Cleveland *Plain Dealer*."

"What sort of feature . . ." he glanced down at my passport ". . . Martha?"

"A feature on the Miss Lebanon contest."

He stared at me. I stared back. He finally asked, "Do people in Cleveland care about the Miss Universe contest?"

"The people in Cleveland care about everything."

"You don't even live in Cleveland."

"I'm a free-lance writer. The wire services often pick up pieces in the *Plain Dealer*. That's what I'm hoping for." I wondered if that was true. He was staring again. "It'll be a human-interest kind of thing. I've already got an interview with Miss Israel. I'm hoping to have it out right in time for the Miss Universe contest."

"So you're a journalist?" He was searching through the passport.

"No, a writer."

"There's a difference?"

"Yes." I reached over and showed him the first page, where it said OCCUPATION: WRITER.

He closed it and handed it back to me. "You'll have to

bring your son here, Mrs. Quayles. I'm sorry. There's nothing I can do. But there won't be any problem as long as you bring him with you."

I walked along the seaside boulevard. I couldn't do it. They'd probably ask him to recite the pledge of allegiance. Or sing "My Country 'Tis of Thee." I couldn't teach him enough in such a short time. I was so afraid they'd take him away. I thought of Lawrie. Taking my girls away.

I got in a taxi and asked for the Israeli military headquarters.

The soldiers were very calm, but all of them were chain-smoking. And the churning in their stomachs showed in their maddened eyes and flushed faces. I said I needed to speak to a man named Michael Graham who was a Nazi-hunter and lived in Tel Aviv.

The soldier at the desk took me to an office. I told the new, older soldier that my friend, an American married to a Palestinian, was killed along with her family, with the exception of her youngest child, in Shatila. I told him I had the boy and I had to get him to the United States with me. I asked him to please help me, and if he couldn't, Michael Graham would and could he reach him for me. The whole time I spoke, his telephone rang ceaselessly, but someone else in his outer office was answering it. When I finished, he said:

"The woman who was killed, your friend, was married to a terrorist who shouldn't have even been in Lebanon. But I'm sorry."

I took a Kleenex out of my bag and hung on to it. "How do you know her?"

"Her presence in the camp has been known. She is married to . . . she was married to a killer. That's what we told her. She was here two nights ago."

"She came to see Ariel Sharon."

"Yes, but he couldn't see her."

I pulled the Kleenex in half. "He was busy."

"Yes."

"My friend's husband was maybe a killer. But Ariel Sharon is a killer, isn't he?"

He looked over my head. He said, "Yes."

"And you?"

"I am a soldier."

"Who takes orders?"

He slammed his fist so hard onto the desk, I thought it would chop in half like in a karate trick. His deep loud voice bellowed, "NO!" And then he took his fist and cradled it in his other hand. The office door opened and I felt someone standing there.

I said to them, "Help me save this little boy."

He stood up. "Follow me."

He gave orders as he walked, asking for a car and a call to Michael. He took me outside and a closed Jeep pulled up. He spoke Hebrew to the driver. The driver kept nodding his head. A man with a war weapon came over to us. The officer told me to get in the backseat, that I and the boy would be driven to Israel, where someone would meet us and where the boy would be issued appropriate papers. Then we would go to the United States from there.

He turned away from me. I was looking at his back, still so straight. I called to him. "Please. The boy has a wound on his arm."

He did not turn, but he answered. "I will see to a doctor."

"Thank you."

He was gone. I only wished he would assassinate his general.

The man with the gun got in the front seat and the driver started the engine. The man with the gun turned around to me, touched his hat, and said, "I'm terribly sorry, you know."

They were all sorry. But the two important ones weren't. The general and the prime minister. Had they forgotten they were Jews? Had they forgotten grevious injustice so fast? I leaned back and closed my eyes. I was getting angrier and angrier. I tried to relax, because in a few minutes I had to help Abdur get through this. Not Abdur. Paul. I'd tell him that, first off. That his name would be Paul.

At the hotel drive the soldier with his gun told me he would accompany me to my room while I packed. I said no—told him to wait outside, but he insisted. Following orders. My fury broke out. It wouldn't be stopped. I told him that his Lebanese friends had just butchered the child's parents and his brother and sisters. I pushed his gun aside with the back of my hand. "You wait here for me! Here!" He did.

The elevator took forever, up and up and up. I did my knock on the door and called his name. He opened the door and he was shaking harder than I was. I picked him up and cradled him. Beyond his body in my arms the television was on. No sound. Just red paint everywhere, and the same crazed people I'd fought my way through that morning. It seemed a long time ago now, but not a déjà vu. Vaguely, you think you've experienced a scene before with déjà vu. I remembered every detail, and I could match the screen with the sounds I'd heard. All the sounds came rushing back, but I'd coated myself with steel; Abdur had no such protection. I walked across the room and turned it off. I hugged him and hugged him and it was like hugging a vibrating spring. I walked to the window, my back to it, and over my shoulder Abdur stared out at the sea that I knew his mother loved. He calmed.

I said, "Help me pack. We are going now."

"To America?"

"Yes."

"And I will begin to call you Mom now?"

"Yes. And I will call you Paul. That's my brother's name. He was a good friend of your mother's when we were young. In America, you will be named after my brother, Paul, and since he is my brother he will be your uncle."

"I understand." He pulled back from my shoulder. He smiled. "Here in Lebanon I am named after my father's brother. My Uncle Abdur who lives in Paris."

He was pleased. "Will you help me pack?" I said.

"Oh yes."

He scrambled down out of my arms and I gave him my carry-on bag. He arranged all my little bottles of shampoo and cosmetics and deodorant and aspirin up and down the bottom of the case in neat rows. He was careful and methodical. He was packing ammunition. I hurried through the closet and drawers. When we were ready, I knelt in front of him so he'd know I expected him to pay especially close attention.

"Abdur . . . Paul, two Israelis will drive us out of Lebanon. One has a gun. He will not hurt us. He is here to protect us."

"He lies," came the small dark voice.

"Not to me."

His wide crystal eyes stared into mine. "You speak like my Ummum. You are as brave."

"No, sweetheart, I'm not. I could never be as brave as your mother. I don't know anyone who could."

His eyes filled. "I think Ummum was too brave. If people are too brave what happens is the same as not being brave at all."

I couldn't believe his words. In the United States, a boy so smart would know his multiplication tables. In Beirut, he knew the finest points of survival.

He walked by my side, straight and tall, his skinny shoulders thrown back and his head high. Abdur looked at the soldiers with open contempt. During the long hot ride south, he never once was a little boy. He was his father and the mother he had that I didn't know as well as I thought I did. He was the side of Jo that evolved when she left the Peace Corps to stay in Shatila.

We approached the border crossing. I could see a civilian standing with the soldiers. Michael.

"Abdur—"

"You are forgetting to call me Paul."

"Paul. Did your parents talk about Michael Graham?"

"The Jew?"

The two men in the front seats flinched. "Yes."

"The last thing we talked about . . . my father and me . . . was about him. His mother died, too, and his new mother saved him from the Nazis."

"Yes."

Michael hugged Abdur. He told Abdur that he loved
Ahmad and Jo. That he was so sorry. Michael had a baseball cap for him. He told me it was all he could think of
to do. The cap was a ridiculous Pirates hat, black-and-gold
stripes, and when Abdur's jet hair disappeared under it,
he could have been any American's son. We went to another Jeep. I sat in the front, Abdur in my lap. With the
soldiers gone, he was asleep in minutes.

Michael told me that Lawrie was on his way to Israel but
that he had several stops before getting here. I would have
to get on the first flight possible, so he would meet Lawrie
and turn him back around. He was sorry but people would
soon begin looking for whoever it was that had been cutting
up red tape and absconding with false papers. I hardly
heard him.

"Michael, Lawrie knows?"

"He knows."

"What did you say to him?"

"It wasn't necessary to say anything. He was afraid you
were dead. So was I."

In Tel Aviv, I kissed Michael good-bye. He held Abdur
and me in his arms and we all three wept. It wasn't Michael's fault.

At an airport motel the Israelis took care of us. Everything became legal: our border crossing and the proof that
I had a son—six years old, black hair, blue eyes, three feet
ten inches tall, name: Paul A. Quayles.

A doctor was there. An old man. He cleaned Paul's wound.
He gave me penicillin for him and told me that it was not
a serious wound—a graze. The heat of the bullet had sterilized the crease it made.

"There will be a small scar."

The old doctor had a scar in the same place on his own
forearm. A row of faded black numbers. He cradled Paul's
head gently before he left the room.

I filled up the bathtub for Paul and made the Israelis
wait. Then they waited for me while we had a meal. Paul
was starving, but he hesitated.

"What's wrong?"

"Is this pork?"

"No, it's beef."

"We do not eat pork."

"Neither do they."

"Who?"

"The Jews. It is a rule, a religious rule."

He was surprised. I wanted to go into the long list of things that Jews and Arabs had in common, beginning with the animosity of the rest of the world. Some other time. I ate with him.

When the trays were taken away, a man in a business suit came in with a camera. He told me he would take Paul's picture for his passport. I told the man to let me have a chance to comb his hair. He said, "One or two minutes."

While I combed his hair, I explained to Paul why the man wanted to take his picture. Then I told him that I had only two little girls and that I'd never combed a boy's hair before, but that I would give him an American hairdo.

He sighed. He was an old man. I parted his hair on the side and combed it over his forehead. His face, when it wasn't framed with shaggy hair, was Jo's. Those great North Italian eyes blinked. I looked away, but told myself I'd have to stop doing that. The man came back with his camera and Paul looked at him. I was crying again and I didn't know I'd started. I put my hands to my face and pushed my cheeks smooth and breathed deeply.

The man sat Paul down on the sofa and gently lifted his chin. He told him not to move and to look into the camera. He took three pictures. A few minutes later, officially I had a son. Paul and I looked at the picture together. Neither of us commented. His black hair was already falling back into his eyes. The picture in the passport was Jo's son. The little boy with the ragged dark hair was mine.

The man who had taken the picture asked me for the number of someone who could meet me at the airport. I gave him my brother's name and then thought to ask if I could call him myself.

"Yes. That would be better. Explain to your brother that

upon seeing you, he must immediately hug the child and
pick him up into his arms. A happy reunion, a speedy trip
out of the airport."

"What time will we arrive?"

"Three-forty P.M., New York time. Refuel stop in Paris."

"Can I wait until I'm in Paris to call my brother? He'll
be sleeping now."

"We would prefer if all arrangements could be made
now."

But I didn't wake Paul. He and Lisa were sitting with
my mother at their kitchen table drinking coffee. They
hadn't slept the whole night. My father was at my house,
alone, keeping vigil by the phone. My mother answered
the phone at Paul's. I didn't expect to hear her voice, but
when I did, I was a little girl again, and I began to cry.

All I could say at first was, "Mom," but then I said, "Jo's
dead." That was all I could get out. Jo's little boy hung on
to me for dear life while the man took the phone from me
and talked to my mother. He told her I was perfectly safe.
She must have been crying, too, for the man's voice had
become soft and soothing.

The doctor came back in and gave me a shot of whiskey.
He had another Coke for Paul. Paul watched me swallow
the whiskey. He gave me such a Moslem look of disap-
proval. He was very precious. I took the phone.

"Mom, I'm OK. I have to talk with Paul."

And my mother said, "Couldn't you have called before
this?"

Paul took the phone. "Are you OK, Mattie?"

"Yes. Jo died."

"Mother told us. I'm sorry. I can't believe such a thing."

"Listen, Paul. Jo's husband was very badly injured. When
I saw him, he was dying. I don't think he could possibly
be alive anymore." My son, Paul, next to me on the sofa,
was almost in my lap. He was clutching my clothes. "Jo's
littlest boy survived. The others didn't. I've got him and
I'm bringing him home. He has . . ." I looked at the three
men around me. One nodded. "He has an American passport. You must meet us at the airport."

I gave him instructions. Paul told me he was writing everything down. I could hear Lisa sobbing. Then Paul said, "Everything will go very smoothly, Mattie, I promise. You just get home. With Jo's boy."

"My girls, Paul, they're—"

"They're very worried."

"Tell them I'll see them soon. Tell them they have a brother."

"I'll tell them. Mattie . . . Mattie, what about Lawrie?"

"I don't know. Michael says he's on his way here. Michael will turn him around."

"Mattie, the man is beside himself. We couldn't stop him from trying to get to Lebanon. Mattie?"

"Yes?"

"He came to see me two days ago. He told me he was divorcing you. I went over to your house to try and figure out what was going on. He said you'd done something unspeakable and that you'd run away. He wanted me to try to reach you to tell you there was nothing to be afraid of. That the cut would be clean. That the girls would be with him, but you could see them whenever you wanted to.

"I thought he'd gone crazy. He wouldn't say anything else. Then, yesterday, when he heard about Shatila, he called me again. I went back over there. He was in a frenzy. And his lawyer called about this divorce business and he screamed at the lawyer to get off the phone. He was waiting for a call from Washington.

"He was a maniac. I keep saying that, Mattie, but whoever could think Lawrie would ever behave like that? I told him to try to reach Michael. As soon as I said Michael's name he fell to pieces. I thought maybe you'd left him for Michael. But that wasn't it. Something's wrong with him . . . something's happened, and I—"

"Yes. Something happened. But he called Michael?"

"It took him a long time to get control of himself. Then it was hours before he finally reached Michael and he had to spend such a long time trying to calm Michael down once he'd told him you were with Jo."

The three men in the room began pacing and looking at their watches. "Paul, I have to get off. I'll see you at the airport, OK?"

"What will I tell Lawrie? I know Ma has made him promise to check in with us."

"Tell him I love him. Tell him I need him very badly and that I'm sorry."

CHAPTER TWENTY-SIX

It was not necessary for Paul to meet us at the airport. In Paris, when the last of the departing passengers left the plane, there was Lawrie, breathless, standing over me. Although I had tried to convince myself that Lawrie would forgive me, I knew that even if he did, our lives would be so completely turned around that we would not be able to stay what we had been. So, when I looked up into his face, a pain shot up my spine and I was shivering. Lawrie picked me up to him and held me for a small moment to make sure I was alive, I could tell. Then he guided me back down into my seat. He could tell that I wouldn't have been able to do it alone. He leaned over me toward Paul and held out his hand. He said, "I am your friend, your Aunt Mattie's husband."

Paul shook his hand, unsure, not knowing what he should say. I said, "Paul, this is Lawrie." After that, Paul was to call Lawrie by his name, not "Dad."

Lawrie sat with us and told me Michael had reached him in Paris and that he'd called the girls and my mother. He told me all the little details he'd thought of and gotten organized, and he went through the list in a tone of voice I didn't recognize ever having heard before. I knew he wasn't looking at me when he spoke and I didn't dare look at him while I listened or I would have started shivering again. When we were in the air once more, Paul fell asleep across three seats, his head on my lap, his feet in Lawrie's, and the rest of him in the seat that lay between Lawrie and me like a no-man's-land. Lawrie's hands rested on Paul's baby ankles, cradled them, patted them, stroked his small calves. And Lawrie talked at me again in the same list-making voice, although it wasn't a list he was giving me.

"I have spoken to your brother. He says that you told him to tell me that you are sorry. You must not apologize to me because I am unable to forgive you. Over and over, Mattie, I asked myself why you had done it. What was in it for you? What kind of hidden perversion had you been concealing inside yourself where I couldn't see? Were you creating an adventure—the kidnapping or murder of my father in order to have something for your writing? My questions and doubts and confusion kept me functioning while I planned what I would do to you for this.

"I told your brother that it would be a sharp ending, hoping he'd tell you that. But it wouldn't have been. And then, later, when I feared that you had died with Jo—only then did I realize what has held the two of you together for so long and through so much—and so I knew why you did it.

"You were totally and completely willing to sacrifice everything—your children, your home, your contentment—to draw this scourge from me. But it wasn't your business. It was my business."

I tried to break into this speech. I'd never heard Lawrie give speeches to anyone. When he reprimanded the children, it was just the reprimand—no reasoning, no explanations. He spoke right over the beginnings of my protests, on top of my words, so harshly that I couldn't stop him.

"Jo knew from the time she was a child that her life was meant to be sacrificed for something. She was a martyr. Not a neurotic person who loves to originate a crisis in order to suffer, but an authentic martyr. A real one. And in you she saw someone who would have done such a thing

270

in a minute, if you loved someone enough. Men think of women as needing to belong, as having a built-in sense of duty to their families. It is a mistake to think that such a need and such a sense of duty is so limited. It is all part of the human desire to leave our children in peace. You and Jo would both risk everything—"

"Shut up," I shouted. Paul's arm moved up across his chest. His brow wrinkled. Lawrie just went on, but his voice was softer.

"I am a powerful man. You never ask me questions. You see them come to our house. You see all these men whose pictures are in the paper every day. The men who run this country. And they come to me, the *consigliere* of their legal mafia. You risked exactly what happened to my father. I could have done it."

"I will not listen, Lawrie."

"You will. You need to know the shame I feel as well as my anger. I am ashamed that it took Jo's death, and the thought that you had died, too, to make me stop thinking like a madman. I know what you did for me, but I am not grateful. I am enraged at what you have been doing all these years. Enraged at myself for not knowing. Enraged at the secrets you could hide so easily. And I am enraged that I had to learn under such horrible circumstances how much I love you. Such anger doesn't just go away. And neither does such love. I need you to accept both."

Paul woke up. Lawrie picked him up into his lap. He whispered into that little boy's ears wonderful words about Jo that I had forgotten to say to him. How much she loved her family. How much she loved us. He talked to Jo's boy about his oldest sister at our wedding when she was just a baby. He told Paul his sisters and his brother all lived in a little place in his heart, and he told Paul that his own mother died when he was ten years old and that he still visits her in his heart, where she will always be, and that they talk and comfort each other every single day. The two were actually clinging together, and I saw how much

Mary-Ann Tirone Smith

of Lawrie there was that he'd denied me and all I'd denied him to give to Jo instead.

In the limo, on the way back to Connecticut, Paul slept again, and Lawrie said to me, "I love this boy." Lawrie's voice was finally back to normal.

272

LEE COUNTY LIBRARY
107 HAWKINS AVE.
SANFORD, N. C. 27330

EPILOGUE

Not long after we read about Ahmad in *The New York Times,* he came for Paul.

In the six years that we had Paul, Joey taught him, and her father, too, how to play baseball. Paul got very good, and he would have been an all-star on the Norwalk Little League team—terrific shortstop.

Delia taught him to play the piano and he was good at that, too. He began to pick out songs that were from his roots as well as "Rockabye Baby," which he must have heard his mother sing. In a year's time, he was composing beautiful melodies, which, each day, grew more and more complex. And very quickly, more quickly than we ever dreamed possible, everything about Paul became American, except for his music.

Lawrence and I talked on the phone to Ahmad and to Michael, who both lived on the West Bank in a town that would be a test. A town where the Israelis and the Arabs had the same rights. Hussein was beginning to hint that the part of Jordan that touched the West Bank would begin a quota system, whereby small numbers of Palestinians from the Jericho camp would be allowed to filter back. The River Jordan, Ahmad said, would perhaps become a cradle again, impregnated with the fragile embryo of a new country. The U.N. peacekeeping force was suddenly very busy.

But it was happening. And if there exist two people more
tenacious than Ahmad ibn-Burash and Michael Graham,
I haven't met them.

Ahmad apologized to me. He said he didn't know if he
would live or die after the massacre, though he was sure
he would die, since he wanted to so badly. But in case he
lived—came back from the pull of death—he couldn't be
sure of his son's survival. If he were to live, before he could
go about trying to find a way for his people to survive, he
first had to be sure that his son would. He was sorry.

We tried to explain to Ahmad how difficult this would
be for Paul, but he assured us it would not. I believe he
must have told Paul that he would come back for him again.

And so, one day, while Paul was out under the birch
tree, tossing the baseball high in the air and catching it
and throwing it again, I heard him shriek. He shrieked
something like, *"Abababab,"* so loudly that I stopped halfway up the stairs of the turret for one second and then I
ran to the top in time to see, through my round of windows,
Paul, hurtling across the green grass toward the road. Paul
was screaming the Arabic word for "Papa," over and over.
Jo's husband had a very small limp. One eye was glass.

When they had gone and it was night, I left Lawrie lying
in our bed with Delia and Joey in there with him, and went
outside. I walked in the moonlight out to the dock. The
sea no longer held any comfort. I came back up the walk
of the big, metal house, and then I went and stood under
the birch tree. At my feet was Abdur's mitt. I picked it up
and could just barely make out the name, Paul Quayles,
printed in black Magic Marker across the leather, almost
completely worn off because he was such a good little ball-
player. He hustled after everything, his coach told us. He'd
go for a line drive that Luis Aparicio couldn't have reached.

"He's all heart, that boy, all heart."

We get a lot of letters from him. He is in a school, half
Israeli–half Palestinian. But he makes sure to let us know
that the Palestinian kids are from Jordan. He would like

to meet some Palestinian kids from Lebanon, he says. He writes a letter every day to one of us—Grandma or Grandpa, Delia or Joey, his cousins. He misses us as much as we miss him, but if only we could be as strong as Paul. As Abdur.

Ahmad writes, too. He says Abdur really doesn't remember the attack on Shatila, only watching it on TV right after it happened in the hotel room while I was gone. Ahmad feels guilty that the burden of doing something about the drastic mess of the Middle East should fall to children. He says it frustrates him that leaders and presidents will not come to Jerusalem. The bravery of Sadat is not to be found. Not yet, he adds. Jo's kind of optimism. I told him children don't recognize burdens until they grow up and look back. People talk about how horrible it was for us fifties children to suffer through air-raid drills in school—flinging ourselves under our desks, wrapping our arms around our heads. We didn't suffer. We thought it was hilarious. A game was all. So maybe things should be left to children. Like school busing. It's always children.

Louisa called me from Honolulu after she got my letter about Paul. Abdur. She wanted to share the comfort that she found in contemplation at the foot of a Shinto shrine. She spoke of lotus blossoms and blue glazes, gossamer webs and precious solitude. Her soothing voice suffused me with warmth. With solace.

The birch tree is gone. I cut it down with a handsaw. Each limb took me about an hour. When Lawrie saw, he arranged to have the stumps removed and then he came upstairs. He stood in the doorway of my folly.

"Can I come in?" He'd never asked before.

"Yes, Lawrie."

"You won't mind?"

"I want you to."

He stepped over the threshold. It felt good to have him.

"Will you come with me next week? To Belgium? I will be busy, but we will find some time to go to Brugge. For a few nights. It's so beautiful there."

"I have just a few weeks to correct my galleys."

"Can't you bring them?"

"Yes."

Lawrie had two glasses and a bottle of wine in his hands. He walked over to my desk, pushed aside some papers a little, and put down the two glasses. The wine bottle had no label. The bottle was an old friend. My father was still getting Jo's Carema from Italy.

"Would you like to pour?"

"Yes," I said.

First, I sucked in my bottom lip. Then I took the bottle from Lawrie and poured the beautiful wine. My hand didn't shake because I'd willed it not to, but I had to wait a moment before I could drink the wine. Wait until I was able to stop biting my lip.

LEE COUNTY LIBRARY
107 HAWKINS AVE.
SANFORD, N. C. 27330